The Last Refuge of a Scoundrel

Book 4 of Lady Knights series

Cara Maxwell

DRAGONBLADE
PUBLISHING, INC.

ARE YOU SIGNED UP FOR DRAGONBLADE'S BLOG?

You'll get the latest news and information on exclusive giveaways, exclusive excerpts, coming releases, sales, free books, cover reveals and more.

Check out our complete list of authors, too!

No spam, no junk. That's a promise!

Sign Up Here

www.dragonbladepublishing.com

Dearest Reader;

Thank you for your support of a small press. At Dragonblade Publishing, we strive to bring you the highest quality Historical Romance from some of the best authors in the business. Without your support, there is no 'us', so we sincerely hope you adore these stories and find some new favorite authors along the way.

Happy Reading!

CEO, Dragonblade Publishing

Additional Dragonblade books by Author Cara Maxwell

The Lady Knights Series

In Bed with a Blackguard (Book 1)
Lost to Lady Scandal (Book 2)
A Spinster's Last Stand (Book 3)
The Last Refuge of a Scoundrel (Book 4)

CHAPTER ONE

March 1818
London, England

THANK GOODNESS HER brother was a rake.

Even luckier, her younger sister Josephine was an incomparable diamond of the first water.

It was a perfect combination, really. If someone managed to look past her brother's antics, promenading in primary colors with yet another beautiful woman on his arm, they would of course see Josephine. Rather, they would see Josephine's bevy of suitors. After entertaining a marquess for her entire first season—and turning him down—rumors abounded that the younger Miss Jacobson had set her sights on a duke.

Though no one would ever refer to the "younger Miss Jacobson."

For that would imply that the members of the *ton* realized there was an *elder* Miss Jacobson.

But whereas Josephine was all delicate giggles and elegant flourishes, Jane Jacobson was a wallflower, plain and simple. No one noticed a wallflower, especially when she grew in the shadows of a sunflower and a rose.

Which suited Jane perfectly.

At that very moment, the newly minted Duke of Dorwich was

escorting Josephine into the center of Viscount Remington's ballroom. Meanwhile, her brother Joseph held court with a woman on each arm. If it hadn't suited her purposes so well, Jane might have laughed.

Instead, she snuck out of the ballroom.

Neither her rakehell brother nor her flighty sister had any notion that the reason they'd secured an invitation to this particular event was because of *her*.

They'd all been surprised when the invitation arrived. Viscountess Remington and Jane's mother, Viscountess Bellbrook, were not on good terms. While her mother and sister were busy congratulating themselves, Jane had slipped out to find her maid and ensure her pale blue gown was ready for the occasion. It had the biggest pockets for sneaking out documents.

Her spectacles were tucked into one of those pockets. As she slipped through the side door she'd spied earlier in the evening, her hand fell to touch them reassuringly. If she found anything worth stealing, she'd need the spectacles to read it.

Jane closed the door softly behind her. It was cleverly decorated with plaster and gold paint to blend in with the wall of the ballroom. That meant it was most likely a servants' corridor. There was both risk and reward to using servants' corridors. There were no *ton* grand dames to look down their noses at her. But if she ran into a servant, she'd be quickly steered back to the ballroom.

The corridor was lit with lamps, but Jane closed her eyes and forced herself to listen. While her vision might often fail her, her hearing was impeccable. She found that closing her eyes helped hone her ability to hear minute details.

Two sounds, two different directions.

The hallway must split off. The louder sound came from the left but was getting softer. Those steps were retreating. To the right, the sound was constant. Not footsteps, but the clatter of porcelain and glass. Perhaps a butler's pantry in that direction, and one that was currently being manned by at least one servant. She must go to the left, then.

Without wasting another moment, Jane opened her eyes and hurried along the corridor. There was the split. She went left. A swinging door appeared. Hopefully, Viscount Remington's staff were attentive to oiling the hinges.

She paused long enough to listen for voices, then pushed noiselessly into the rear atrium of the viscount's townhouse.

Satisfaction surged through her. The Duchess of Guilford had only been able to provide a rough sketch of the main floor of the residence, which included none of the servants' passageways. But based on the layout she'd studied and her own excellent skills of deduction, Jane had suspected that a well-camouflaged door in the ballroom would lead her here.

Three rooms opened off the atrium, which also provided an exit to the gardens in the rear of the house. The heavily clouded sky above cast the gardens in shadow and provided additional cover for Jane as she snuck across the atrium. This part of the townhouse had been only sparsely lit for the evening; clearly it was not meant to be visited by guests. Most of the revelers would respect the unspoken boundary.

But Viscount Remington had given up any right to privacy when he conspired against his queen.

Jane did not allow the revulsion to creep up on her. She'd already allowed room for any emotional reactions to her quest. A week ago, she'd been tasked with this quest and briefed upon the details. That same night, she'd called for a bath, locked the door to her bedroom, and allowed her temper to rage while she scrubbed at her skin and hair. She could not begin to fathom how Queen Charlotte, once so beloved by all of England, had suddenly become so unpopular. Nor could she tolerate the threat to the very woman who had commissioned the Round Table and the lady knights who sat around it. So she'd scrubbed and scrubbed, until she glistened pink and new, ready for battle.

From then on, her approach had been calm and collected—precisely what was required for such important Lady Knights work.

Viscount Remington was a traitor to the Crown. He was plotting the death of his queen.

And he was not working alone.

Jane's slippered feet skipped across the tiled atrium with the grace of a dancer. She might not be a diamond of the first water like Josephine, but she'd had Dominique as her dance instructor. Her fellow lady knight's poise and grace was unmatched.

What Jane did not possess, however, was Dominique's skill at picking locks. She could only hope that Viscount Remington was cocky enough to leave his study unlocked. What cause would a loyal subject of the Crown have to lock their study, in any case?

Her fingers landed on the brass handle of the study, and in the same forward step, she applied pressure and slid the door open. A smile tugged at Jane's lips. It was exactly this sort of arrogance that led to most of her targets' downfalls.

The study was better lit than the atrium, and it took Jane's eyes a few blinks to adjust. Either the viscount had been in this room directly before the ball commenced and no one had come along to douse the gas lamps, or he meant to return at some point. The latter possibility meant she had to be quick and efficient with her search.

The Duchess of Guilford's sources had identified Viscount Remington's involvement in a scheme to assassinate the queen. But they'd also hinted that he did not act alone. Jane's charge was to identify his co-conspirators.

She started with the desk. Always.

Statistically, in her investigations, the desk was the most likely place for incriminating documents to be hidden. It was so obvious it made her eyes roll. With methodical efficiency, she extracted her spectacles from her pocket and began to search.

Top drawer—unlocked, no false bottom, estate paperwork.

The column of narrow drawers on the left was next. She always worked left to right, so that if she was interrupted while she searched she would be able to find her place again. Each drawer was stuffed with ephemera, including empty ink bottles and broken quills.

Egads, the viscount was a slob.

To the right, then. More estate paperwork. Jane's hand stilled over a sloppily written receipt for the purchase of flowers and bulbs. It was likely innocuous, though it seemed a peculiar thing to save. But if Viscount Remington's other drawers were any indication, it might just be leftover mess. Jane slipped it into her deep pocket nonetheless. She would look it over later to ensure there was no secret code embedded in the letters and numbers.

Hands landing on her hips, Jane let out a little *pfft* of frustration.

The desk was clear of any incriminating evidence. Perhaps she had underestimated Viscount Remington.

While she readjusted her opinions, she surveyed the other likely options for stowing away information that would lead to a lifetime in Newgate at best, a hanging at worst. There was a wall of bookshelves. Not quite a library, but enough tomes that it would take a considerable amount of time to search. It was the most likely place after the desk. It was so easy to slide a scrap of paper between the pages of a favorite book.

A favorite, she reminded herself. It would not be random; it never was. What sort of book would Viscount Remington favor? She wondered as she drifted closer to the wall of books, eyes flitting along the rows. Any book out of line with the others, any disturbance in the dust, might indicate—

Footsteps!

She took half a step for the desk then readjusted. That was a terrible plan. She could hide well enough if someone merely opened the door and looked around, but if they came into the room, she'd be discovered.

With a split second to make her decision, Jane grabbed the first book she saw, opened it at random, and dropped herself into the wingback chair across from the desk.

>>>><<<<

"BASTARD OUGHT TO serve something other than rataff—eyyy—uhhh," Roland Hawkridge slurred as he burst through the door of Viscount Remington's study.

He paused, one hand on the door to hold himself up while he lifted the flask in his hand and took a deep, noisy swig of the scotch whisky within.

"Ah, that's fine," he said, smacking his lips loudly before tucking the flask safely away in the inner pocket of his navy broadcloth tailcoat.

He kicked the door shut behind him with enough bravado that he stumbled forward into the study.

Well on my way to foxed.

He'd been nipping at that flask all night. The part must be played well, after all.

He caught himself on the back of a chair, expecting it to rock under his not insignificant weight.

Except it did not. Because it was occupied.

"Well, well," he tutted. "Hullo there, miss."

Two chocolate-brown, bespectacled eyes appeared over the top of the book, which she clutched so tight her knuckles were white.

She squeaked like a mouse with its tail caught in a trap, and sprang away just as quickly.

But the little mouse did not realize she'd met a hawk.

"Ah, ah, ah," he said, wagging a finger while simultaneously settling his elbows on the back of the now empty chair. An impressive feat, really, given the amount of whisky he'd imbibed in service of tonight's mission. "Running away so soon?"

"I... I am... I am not meant to be here," the little mouse mumbled, still holding that book tight against her.

The comparison was apt, Roland realized, as he took her in with a more discerning eye. She was a tiny thing. In her early twenties, he'd wager, though she was still dressed in the pastel palette of a debutante. If he stepped around the chair, he doubted her head would reach his shoulder. He was tall at nearly six and a half feet, and dwarfed most men and women alike. But the little mouse he'd caught in his trap was in a class all her own.

"Where are you meant to be?" he said casually, adopting the playful tone he'd often used with his friends' daughters. Bollocks, the woman was young enough to be his daughter.

Maybe he *was* getting too old for all of this.

"In the ballroom," she said, her chin rising an inch. "I am here with my family," she added.

Of course, he wanted to snort back. But something about the young woman was prickling at his instincts. She looked very much like a spinster wallflower who'd snuck off from the revelry to hide. He didn't recognize her, though he supposed that was not all that surprising. He'd spent so much of his last twenty years abroad on various missions, he hardly knew his own family members.

But there was something about the line of her chin—

"If you will excuse me, my lord, my family is—"

"Your Grace."

She swallowed audibly. "Your Grace," she corrected herself.

"Hawkridge," he said by way of explanation.

He watched the recognition dawn in her brown eyes, which behind her spectacles were set in a round, flat face above a small, pretty pink mouth. *Quietly pretty,* his mind supplied. His mind, which was surprisingly clear for someone who was pretending to be sotted.

Or was half sotted. It really didn't matter which.

Bollocks, he'd forgotten to slur his words.

"The Duke of Hawkridge hisssself, at your surface—service," he gabbled, bowing ridiculously low. Actually forgetting he was in front of a chair, he banged his head.

If he wanted to look like an idiot, he was making a convincing job of that, at least.

The woman's grip on the book loosened at the same time her pink lips drew together into a grimace. Not a look of horror, like a young wallflower might have upon discovering herself next thing to compromised by a duke just north of forty. In her eyes, those lovely brown eyes, Roland saw something else entirely—calculation.

A new thought occurred to him.

Roland was attending Viscount Remington's ball not because he enjoyed such things or because he had a family to supervise. He was here because his presence had been ordered by his superior, Lord John Cartwright.

His presence in the study, rather than the ballroom, was no mere accident—for all that he'd made sure he looked like nothing more than a drunk, bumbling fool. Was it possible that this young woman...?

No. It was absurd.

Grabbing the chair to hoist himself up from his unsteady bow, he brushed past the girl as if she was nothing. Which she most likely was, Roland reminded himself. He was meant to be a drunk duke in search of liquor, and he would best play that out. It was the surest way to get rid of the wallflower so he could get on to his actual mission—searching the study.

"Ah, there it is. I knew that tight-fisted bastard was hiding the quality," he said, making for the sideboard laden with three crystal decanters on the other side of the room.

Behind him, there was only silence.

Perfect. She'd think that he'd forgotten about her and try to slip out of the room. He gave her more time to do it, taking his time unstopping each bottle and taking a whiff. He even added a bawdy little tune to heighten the effect.

"... *in her web we'll tangle and twirl, embracing the scandal, a forbidden pearl...*"

"Begging your pardon, Your Grace."

Roland kept pouring the rum he'd chosen. But inside, those same instincts that had had him reconsidering the little mouse in the first place were screaming once again.

He didn't risk speaking again right away, slurred or not. He turned and looked at her from beneath a furrowed brow, letting the confusion show.

"Perhaps you ought to return to the party. I am certain Viscount Remington will be missing such an esteemed guest. I will not mention your... state... to anyone," she said earnestly.

The little mouse was trying to get rid of him. Roland's eyes slid to the book she'd been reading when he entered, now held loosely at her side.

A Gentleman's Guide to Animal Husbandry.

She hadn't been reading in the study, hiding from her family. His little mouse was something else entirely.

Hand curled around the glass of rum, Roland swaggered closer. The young woman showed no sign of trepidation. She was forgetting herself. A meek wallflower ought to be retreating from a sotted duke with a certain reputation. Another confirmation that there was more to her than she appeared.

"Aren't you the one who ought to be returning to your family?" He winked broadly. A bit much—which she confirmed with the wrinkling of her petite nose. Every single part of her was petite, he was noticing.

As if remembering the situation she'd found herself in, she blushed madly. Her cheeks colored, the coral pink spreading down her delicate neck toward her bosom.

"Yes, I shall," she squeaked. "But it will not do for us to leave together."

And clever to boot.

She was still trying to get him out.

There was still a possibility that she was nothing more than a bookish wallflower hiding from the revelry. Awkwardness could account for her strange behavior and the unlikely tome clutched in her hand. Maybe she'd grabbed it to avoid being seen reading something more inappropriate.

But Roland's instincts were all pointing elsewhere. And his instincts were rarely wrong.

It was the main reason he had lived to see his fortieth birthday.

It was those instincts that had him sauntering forward and swiping the book out of her hand before she could tighten her grip.

"Interesting choice in reading material," he said, pretending to read the title for the first time. He made a show of peering at it again, mouthing each word, then looking up at her with wide eyes.

"I find all reading interesting," she said. Behind her spectacles, Roland could feel her eyes raking over him. Was she making the same deductions as he? Did she see through his ruse of foxed, bumbling idiot?

Roland leaned past her and tossed the book onto the empty chair. "A young woman such as you would, by necessity," he said into his rum.

Her pert mouth tightened. "I do not take your meaning, Your Grace."

"I think we understand each other quite well." He took his time taking another sip. "We are both quite skilled in the arts of deduction."

"You may speak to your own skills, sir. But you know nothing of mine," she said. The ruse of wallflower was wearing away to nothing.

"Ah, but I think I do." He leaned in close, taking a gamble that would either confirm his suspicions about the high-browed chit, or would convince her he was truly sotted. "I am the Crown's most elite agent, madam."

"Miss."

The whisky in his gut burned. Had he made a mistake?

"How quaint," he choked out.

The woman did not retreat. Their faces were still mere inches apart, his head hovering near where it had been when he whispered those words that might damn him. If any other guests entered the room, the woman would be irrevocably compromised. But that was not Roland's primary concern at the moment. His ears strained to listen as she whispered back in falsely honeyed tones:

"You may be an agent of the Crown, but if you cannot detect the absence of a wedding band, you cannot be its most elite."

Her fist hit his stomach with startling speed. It surprised him, to be sure, but from the expression on her pretty face, Roland suspected it shocked her more. His abdomen was nothing but tight, lean muscle. She'd have to try harder than that to knock the air out of him.

The precision of her next movement confirmed his suspicions. He caught her arm a second before she reached his ear, where her sharp little fingers would have attempted to render him unconscious with a precise application of pressure.

"I can detect another agent when I encounter them well enough," he crooned, as if he spoke to a lover rather than an adversary.

She jerked her arm back as if he'd burned her through the pale blue satin gloves she wore. *Hardly more than a debutante,* he thought, shaking his head. Yet if he'd moved a second slower, she'd have had the upper hand.

Was he getting slower, or was she just that good?

Roland ignored the rising disappointment in his gut as he realized it was certainly the former.

"The Crown's most elite agent," she repeated, distaste dripping from every word, "is wrong again."

With precise, razor-sharp motions, she retrieved the book from the chair behind her and replaced it on the shelf. Then she turned back to him, snapping her spectacles closed and stowing them in her pocket in one fluid movement. Graceful, smart—a new agent, given her age, but adept for all that.

Roland could almost respect her, if it were not for the haughty tone.

The same one she used when she paused at the door, fixing him with a look cold enough to whither the early spring daffodils. "I am not an agent. I am a lady knight."

CHAPTER TWO

S COTCH WHISKY, RUM, brandy... It all served the same purpose. It dulled the pain of his reality.

Not a physical pain. Roland ought to be grateful for that. After twenty years in service to the Crown, he was lucky to sport nothing more than scars for his trouble. There was that twinge in his left knee from the mission he'd undertaken for the Duke of York personally. But that seemed a small price to have met and served one's monarch so directly.

The scar over his heart, the one he'd gained on behalf of dear Princess Charlotte... That felt like a physical pain these days as well. Four months had not been enough to wipe the pain from his own heart, nor from the hearts of his countrymen.

He took another long drink of brandy.

White's was busy, but then, when wasn't it these days? When he first gained membership, it had been a different establishment entirely. Sometimes, Roland considered seeking out a smaller club, a place where he might escape the young rakehells of the *ton*. He had little in common with them, even if one removed the difference in age from the tally sheet.

But habit was a powerful force.

So, there he sat, sipping his brandy in a corner and hoping no one would approach him.

Which, of course, was when the Earl of Lionsgate entered the room.

"If you do not want to be around other people, you could retreat to your ducal estate instead of glowering at every man who enters," Leo, also known as the Lion, said unhelpfully as he took the seat across from Roland.

Leo wasn't exactly a friend. Friends were a liability in the world of spies and secrets. As was family—another reason Roland had stayed far away from the Hawkridge family for the last twenty years. But Leo was a colleague, and a capable one at that.

"Brandy?" Roland said by way of greeting.

"Naturally," Leo agreed, accepting the bottle that had been poised beside Roland's half-drunk glass. He looked around the room for another glass, or someone to fetch one, found nothing, and lifted the bottle directly to his lips with a shrug.

A few younger men laughed over-loudly by the billiards table. Roland winced.

"Why do you come here if you dislike it so?" Leo asked. He took another swig then passed the bottle back.

Roland shrugged. "Rumor had it you were still in Africa."

It was Leo's turn to shrug, though his enigmatic amber eyes gleamed as he said, "You ought to know better than to believe every rumor you hear."

"I ought to know better." Roland sighed. "It's becoming something of a refrain of mine lately." Two brown, bespectacled eyes flashed in his mind.

"You're on the queen's detail," Leo said casually, staring out the window.

Statement, not question.

Interesting. Leo had either been briefed or he'd peeked into the files at Cartwright's office.

Was Cartwright about to pull Roland from the mission? Was that why Leo was here, to prepare him for the blow? Was Leo to take over?

As quickly as the thoughts came to his mind, Roland dismissed them. Cartwright had been nothing but loyal and forthright in the decade they'd worked together. He wouldn't hesitate to remove him from a mission if he mucked it up or if someone else might do it better. But he wouldn't tell Roland like this.

Which meant there must be another reason that Leo had been briefed. Roland decided not to delve into that for the moment, tucking that bit of information away for later. His instincts told him that was not the important part of this conversation. Leo had sought him out at White's and brought up the queen. That spoke clearly enough about his intentions.

"Not a detail, precisely," Roland corrected him.

His eyes darted around the room over his next sip of brandy, but he already knew what he'd find. They were out of earshot of any other patrons—the sound of their voices was prevented from carrying by the boisterous billiards game taking place. Of course, Leo would have surmised all of this before speaking about a confidential matter.

"I've been tasked with Remington," Roland said, eyes finally back on Leo.

The other man nodded, still gazing out the window. "Remington is a slippery one, to be sure. But not very clever."

"So I have heard," Roland said.

"I assume your search of his study was fruitful?"

Roland gritted his teeth. Beneath his fingers, he could still imagine the satin of her glove. "I am afraid not."

Those catlike amber eyes slid over to him, one eyebrow rising in something between surprise and amusement. "I had assumed him the type to leave some bit of evidence lying around in his desk or tucked into a book."

"I did not have a chance to conduct a thorough search," Roland admitted.

The second eyebrow joined the first.

"I was waylaid."

Leo reached for the bottle of brandy, but Roland got there first, pouring himself another few fingers before handing it over.

The Lion was grinning by the time his fingers closed around the bottle. "She must have been a pretty chit to have distracted a legend like you, Hawkridge."

"She was," Roland admitted before he could think better of it. "But it's not what you think. She's a *lady knight*."

Leo paused with his mouth full of brandy, but forced it down before asking, "What the hell is that?"

"I have no notion," Roland said. "But I expect I shall find out tomorrow. Cartwright has summoned me, and not to any of the usual places."

"Then I suppose my presence here was superfluous," Leo said, though it did not stop him from swigging more of Roland's brandy.

Prat.

"I was meant to review any potential conspirators and lend my expertise," Leo explained. "But it seems I have nothing to offer."

Roland rolled his eyes. "If you are waiting for me to moon over you and extol your value to the Crown, you've selected the wrong audience. I am too old for that nonsense."

"Same to you, old man." Leo winked. He was only ten years Roland's junior, but just then, it felt like a lifetime.

The Lion was new to his title, while Roland had been the Duke of Hawkridge for more than a decade. Not that he'd spent any time tending to his ducal duties. The way Roland figured it, he was more use to his country as a spy than as a foppish lord. However, it seemed that for once the Home and Foreign Offices were in agreement—with each other, not him. This was his last mission.

The estate agent who'd managed the dukedom since his father's death had retired. Roland still did not know if it was the man's choice or if Roland's own superiors had conspired to induce him to it—as a way of forcing him to finally face his ducal duties.

In the end, it did not matter.

What did was that he had one last mission, one last chance to matter before he was consigned to worrying about plantings and farms and a thousand other dull matters that threatened to make his eyes bleed.

And he had mucked it up by getting into a tête-à-tête with Miss Lady Knight.

That didn't fit her. "Little mouse" was better.

He did not even know her name.

Though Roland suspected that at noon tomorrow, he would.

On the other side of the room, silence fell. Then the crack of one ball hitting another, followed by a chorus of exclamations, positive and negative, filled the air around them.

Leo leaned forward, using the cacophony of sound to cover his low voice. "Tread carefully, Hawkridge. Remington is not the mind behind this plot to assassinate our queen. Whoever is... they are mad. Cunning, perhaps, but mad to think that they can manage this."

Roland itched to ask how Leo knew. Something about the glint in his amber eyes, the tilt of his head... He knew more than he was saying. But whether he withheld the information on Cartwright's orders, or for some reason of his own, Roland could not discern. His gut told him there was more Leo had to tell.

But the moment passed, and the other man was standing, straightening his coat.

"The silence," Roland said abruptly.

Leo lifted one eyebrow.

"The reason I come here, instead of wallowing at home," Roland said, staring into the empty bottom of his glass. "I cannot stand the silence."

He could feel Leo's gaze upon him, practically hear the machinations in the younger man's mind as he weighed his words.

"You would not be the first agent who struggled to transition back to civilian life," Leo finally said.

Roland sighed heavily, pushing to his feet as well. "Therein lies the problem. I do not want to transition back."

But this was not about what he wanted, not anymore.

CHAPTER THREE

J ANE HAD NEVER been so embarrassed in her entire life. That included what had happened... *No.* She would not think of that. She did not think of that. Certain events deserved to stay in the past and never again see the light of recollection.

But the note she'd received from the Duchess of Guilford, stuck under the flower pot in her mother's garden, would live in her memory forever.

Report to PH at the usual time. You have much explaining to do.

No salutation. No details.

As if any were needed.

She'd failed spectacularly, and managed to make a fool of herself and the Lady Knights in the process. Jane's only consolation, bare as it may be, was that Roland Hawkridge must be similarly stewing in his own shame.

The Crown's most elite agent, my foot.

She reached the Pendleton Hotel just as the first few tables were being seated in the dining room for luncheon. For anyone watching inside or out, they would notice only a well-dressed young woman meeting friends for a meal to socialize—if anyone deigned to notice her at all. They usually did not, but still Jane kept up all the proper precautions. Her analytical mind would allow nothing else.

But instead of approaching the maître d' and giving her name, Jane waited until a party of guests crossed the lobby and went through the door to the stairwell instead. The duchess kept a suite of rooms for her perpetual use on the fourth floor. It wasn't precisely a secret; Miranda was a frequent guest in the dining room below. But nor was it common knowledge among the *ton*.

Jane had been summoned here only once before. Most of her meetings were conducted at Miranda's home, under the guise of some social gathering or another, or at the Royal Academy, as they were both avid art lovers.

The last time Jane had been here at the Pendleton was when she'd been granted her first quest. She recalled the palpitations of her heart as she'd climbed each of those steps to the duchess's suite.

Today, her heart was pounding for an entirely different reason. When that reason materialized at the top of the stairwell, said organ nearly stopped functioning entirely.

The Duke of Hawkridge turned to smirk at her as her booted foot touched the landing.

"We meet again, little mouse," he crooned.

Like he was talking to an animal.

Her friend and fellow lady knight, Ethelreda, would have stomped on his foot. Jane prided herself on her restraint, but even she could see the merits of her friend's methods just then.

"Do not call me that," she said, imbuing her voice with authority. There was no need to pretend now to be anything other than what she was—a cunning and accomplished lady knight in the exclusive service of Her Majesty, Queen Charlotte.

Hawkridge opened the door to the corridor with an irritatingly oblique flourish. "But it fits you so well."

Jane felt her mouth tighten. She let it. He ought to see her displeasure, learn that she was no one to be trifled with. Not that she had ever expected to see him again. An uneasy feeling was beginning to take root in her stomach.

You have much explaining to do.

It seemed she was not the only one being called to account this afternoon.

"Miss Jane Jacobson, daughter of Viscount Bellbrook. You will call me Miss Jacobson, naturally." The glint in his eyes as she brushed past told her Hawkridge had seen her order cloaked in politeness easily enough.

His smirk lifted at one side as he opened that slash of a mouth to say, "Perhaps."

Jane decided to ignore him. He was infuriating, but she'd dealt with plenty of infuriating men. She was an unmarried, nobly bred young woman who lived a secret life as a spy for one of the country's reigning monarchs. Infuriating men were part and parcel of every part of her life.

Was he any different than her brother? Jane asked herself as she walked to the end of the hall, where the duchess's suite was situated. A corner suite meant more escape routes.

No, she decided. Fifteen years older, yes. But if her brother continued with his current pattern of behavior, he'd be an unmarried, irresponsible lord by the time he reached forty as well.

Not entirely irresponsible, her more rational side argued as she lifted her hand to knock delicately on the door. True, it was common knowledge among the *ton* that the Duke of Hawkridge had long neglected his title. But now Jane knew why.

Hawkridge waited behind her—she could sense him off her left shoulder. By the sound of his breathing, his back was against the opposite wall. Good; she'd prefer he kept his distance until they could part ways indefinitely.

But the door before her remained stubbornly closed.

"Would you like me to pick the lock?" His voice rumbled from behind her.

"I am perfectly capable of picking a simple lock," Jane bit back, without dipping her eyes to see what type it was and whether she truly could have picked it herself. "The duchess is expecting me—there is no reason to force entry."

She heard him push off the wall.

"The duchess?" he said, voice intentionally low.

"Who do you think we are meeting?" she replied, matching his whisper.

"I am not certain I should tell you," he said, but then added a second later, "Cartwright."

Lord John Cartwright? She'd met him dozens of times over the years. Egads, he was a friend of her father's. He could not possibly be—

Of course, in the next breath the door opened to reveal that, in fact, John Cartwright *could* be an agent of the Crown.

"Well timed," the rotund man said, stepping aside to allow them to enter.

Jane's mind was doing cartwheels as she crossed the threshold into the familiar room, which had hardly changed in the three years since she'd first visited. She attempted to fit everything she knew about Cartwright against an entirely new reality.

Had he been the one to initially bring her to the Duchess of Guilford's attention all those years ago, as a potential lady knight?

"A bit fancier than your usual abode, Cartwright," Hawkridge said behind her, followed by the sounds of the two men clapping each other on the back.

Jane ignored their masculine nonsense and walked directly to the table on the other side of the room. While it might have been intended as a dining table, the Duchess of Guilford had put it to use as a makeshift desk, neatly organized with thick stacks of paper and two gleaming engraved inkpots.

Invisible ink, Jane thought.

Cartwright must be very trusted, high up in the Crown's secret services. Miranda had never shown such casualness with Lady Knight's matters before.

"Good afternoon, Your Grace," Jane said, curtsying before taking her seat across the table just as Miranda motioned to it.

"Thank you for coming, Jane." Then the Duchess of Guilford stood and—to Jane's eternal surprise—bowed. "Hawkridge. It's an honor to meet you."

An honor. Jane resisted the urge to twist in her seat and see just what was so honorable about the infuriating man. It did not matter, in any case, because a second later he was waving his hand casually and taking the seat beside her.

"Please, Miranda. We've known one another for years," he said.

The duchess inclined her head gracefully as she too resumed her seat. "Socially, yes. But we've never met before as professionals."

Hawkridge winked. "I never knew we were in the same line of work. Though I oughtn't be surprised; you've always been a wily one."

Miranda blushed. The Duchess of Guilford, stern and fearless leader of the Lady Knights, blushed. Jane was here expecting a reprimand. What was really going on? Had her understanding of the situation been that far from correct? She'd need another bath tonight to scrub away her deficiencies and analyze where she'd gone amiss.

"We can all reminisce another time," Cartwright said as he rounded the table.

Instead of taking the chair on Hawkridge's other side, he took the one immediately next to Miranda. As if the two of them had been working in tandem and been interrupted by Jane and Hawkridge's arrival.

He was an equal, Jane realized. Not any other agent, but a colleague. The male counterpart to the Duchess of Guilford, perhaps. Jane tried very hard to keep the surprise off her face. But the flicker of amusement in Miranda's eyes as she leaned back in her seat and crossed her arms told Jane that to some extent, at least to someone who knew her well, she'd failed.

"You two failed spectacularly at Viscount Remington's ball," the duchess said, shifting into her professional persona in a breath.

Jane had been ready for it. Beside her, she felt the slight shifting of Hawkridge's body as he moved from relaxation to attention.

She sucked in a breath. "I did not know—"

"Someone ought to have—"

"—there would be another—"

"—there were two agents assigned to the ball," Hawkridge finished, cutting her a glare.

Jane returned it in force. She did not appreciate being interrupted. She may be an unmarried wallflower in the *ton*'s ballrooms, but here—

"You never know when other agents are in play," Cartwright said forcefully, fixing Hawkridge with a reproving look. "It is the height of arrogance to assume a matter as important as Her Majesty's safety was being entrusted to one office, let alone one individual agent. We also have a footman in Remington's household in our employ. Should I reveal him to you as well and risk his cover?"

A wave of shame rolled through Jane's stomach.

But Hawkridge was not so easily cowed. "If we were both being sent to target Remington's study, we should have been made aware of one another's presence. We spent so much damn time trying to get rid of the other, we had no opportunity to search."

"Do you think you would be better suited for my job, then?" Cartwright said, jowls wobbling as he leaned forward on an elbow. "You don't even want to manage an estate, Roland. A bevy of insolent agents is much worse."

"That is not what I meant," Hawkridge said tersely. But he didn't argue further.

The Duchess of Guilford cut a look to Cartwright, some sort of silent communication passing between them. Then her dark eyes slid back to Jane.

"Is there something you would like to add?" she asked directly. "I did say in my note I would give you the opportunity to explain yourself."

Jane was not going to apologize or try to mount a defense. She was not a petulant child, despite the moniker Hawkridge had tried to saddle her with. Better to state the facts and get on with it.

"I searched Remington's desk before I was interrupted. There was nothing of immediate note, though I did find this receipt," she said, slipping it from her reticule and placing it on the table between them. "I've gone over it with all the most common codes and found no hidden message. So it may very well be exactly as it appears to be."

All eyes went to the receipt.

From the corner of her vision, Jane could see Hawkridge flexing his fingers, itching to get a hold of the document and examine it for himself. She lifted her jaw an inch—there was nothing he would find that she had not.

Not that it mattered. The duchess added it to one of her neat piles and nodded. "Do you have anything more?"

Jane shook her head. "I did not have time to search the bookshelves."

Miranda sighed, exchanging another look with Cartwright. The man's thick, bushy mustache twitched.

"So you do not have much at all," the duchess said, disappointment evident in every syllable.

Three years ago, Jane might have melted under that disappointment. But now, she was strong and competent.

"I will find another way into Remington's study to conduct a more thorough search," she said. Her spine was already straight, but she met both the duchess and Cartwright's gazes as she spoke. "I am confident I can do so without being detected, nor compromising the cover of the footman you already have in place."

Hawkridge muttered something that sounded distinctly like *just like a little mouse.*

"I share your confidence," Miranda said coolly. "However, while your task has not changed, your methodology will."

Jane felt her mouth pucker, but she held her silence and waited for Miranda to continue.

"From now on, you will be collaborating with Hawkridge," she said.

Hawkridge shot out of his seat. "I work alone."

"Sit down, Roland," Cartwright said, eyes rolling above his round cheeks.

The Duchess of Guilford picked up a sheaf of paper, flicking to the second page. "On the contrary, Hawkridge—I have a list here of five instances where you have partnered with other agents." She held it out to him. "Would you like to verify my sources?" The challenge in her dark eyes was palpable.

Jane almost wanted him to do it, just for the entertainment. But his hands stayed where they were, gripping the arms of his chair.

"Five instances over the course of a twenty-year career," Hawkridge bit out.

"Yes, well. Jane has not had the benefit of twenty years of experience. Perhaps in your final outing as an agent of the Crown, you could impart some of your wisdom to her," Miranda said, eyes leveled at Hawkridge.

Jane knew it was not meant as a jab at her; Miranda was not underhanded like that. If she had a problem with how Jane conducted herself, she would have brought it directly to her. But still, the words stung. She may only be twenty-three, but she was the most capable of the lady knights. She knew it, and so did the duchess.

Jane stood then too, preparing her entreaty. "With all due respect, Your Grace, I do not need assistance on this quest—"

"Mission," Hawkridge said sharply.

This time, she did turn to him, let him see her furrowed brow and thin-lipped glare. "I am a lady knight. It is called a quest."

"Enough squabbling like children," Cartwright interrupted. "If I wanted to play schoolmaster, I'd spend my time at home."

That was exactly what this was like, Jane realized. She and Hawkridge were like two misbehaving children being called into the headmaster's office for admonition. And now, they were being punished.

Cartwright cleared his throat and said, "Roland, you will appear tomorrow before Miss Jacobson's father to submit your request to court her formally."

All the air emptied out of Jane's chest.

She would not swoon.

No one had ever gone to her father with such a request. No one had ever even looked at her in that way—

Except—

No! she screamed to herself.

Hawkridge was already arguing. "We'd be better off faking her parents' death and assigning her as my ward. It would be more believable—"

"I have an elder brother," she snapped. "I am not a child, Your Grace. This quest will not be successful if you cannot acknowledge that my skill matches your own—"

"Matches my own? You saucy little—"

"Ahem." Miranda's fake cough cut through the bickering. She pinned them each with a stare. "The weather is bracing. I suggest the two of you take a walk in the park across the street and work out your differences. We"—she glanced to Cartwright—"haven't the time to manage the particulars for two professionals such as yourselves."

More shame in Jane's gut. She'd never lost control of herself like that.

But there was something about the Duke of Hawkridge that made her want to scream. A week of successive baths would not be enough to scrub out her frustration at the infuriating gentleman.

Man, her mind amended. Duke he might be. But gentleman he was not.

"Seek out Jacquetta and Thane. They might have information to offer you," the duchess said, as if it were half an afterthought, eyes already on a sheet of paper she'd drawn from her stack.

Cartwright adopted Miranda's dismissive manner, walking past them to the door.

"Your charge remains the same," he said, hand on the doorknob. "Positively identify Remington's accomplices. We all know he is too dull to be at the heart of this."

Then Cartwright opened the door, effectively ending the conversation, and leaving Jane and Hawkridge no choice but to walk through it into an uncertain future.

CHAPTER FOUR

H E'D BEEN WRONG about everything.

For someone who prided himself upon the veracity of his instincts, it was particularly devastating. The elegant Miranda, Duchess of Guilford, was leader of the Lady Knights—an organization he could only surmise was commissioned by the Crown itself. Hell, he'd shared a kiss with her twenty years ago behind a garden hedge, before she'd been a widow or a duchess.

But Cartwright… Roland thought he'd known the man. He thought that despite his years neglecting his dukedom, he'd at least done his country proud through the dozens of missions he'd completed for king and country. He'd thought he had Cartwright's respect.

Yet the evidence of precisely the opposite was walking down the stairs in front of him, the high neck of her seafoam-green pelisse touching the nape of her rich chocolate-brown hair so that not even a fraction of an inch of creamy skin was revealed to his view.

He ought to go back up through that door, into the suite of rooms where the duchess and Cartwright looked so cozy, and tender his resignation, effective immediately. He'd put off his ducal duties long enough, clearly, if the world was determined to punish him so.

Roland was ready to do it. He even paused on the next landing, so that the little mouse scurried a whole flight ahead of him.

But even as his body began to turn, his feet planted themselves stubbornly.

This was a threat to the queen. To Princess Charlotte's own grandmother.

If he walked away from this, he'd never recover from the shame. He owed this not only to the lost princess, but to the woman who'd raised the sweet soul that had brought so much light into his life.

This was his last mission before retirement. While he might not like the circumstances, it would not be the first time he'd been placed against seemingly insurmountable odds. Roland could even agree that all the times he'd been forced to partner with a colleague, the results had been fortuitous. As the Duchess of Guilford had clearly known, holding her blasted list under his nose.

But as Miss Jacobson rounded the next corner, disappearing from sight with absolutely no care as to whether he was actually following behind her, Roland's stomach clenched in frustration.

He doubled his pace to catch up.

For being half his size, she was very quick. By the time he reached her, she had one hand on the door leading into the main artery of the hotel.

Roland used his height to hold the door closed above her, ignoring the irritated huff from below him. "We have much to discuss," he said.

"Not here." She tried to shove the door open.

Not happening. She might pretend to be his equal in the games of spy craft, but when it came to brute strength, Roland would always have the advantage.

"Let me pass," she bit out.

He dropped his voice to a conspiratorial whisper. "Where are your spectacles, little mouse?"

She moved so damnably quickly, he had no time to protect himself—or his balls.

He shrank backward, sucking in air and trying to still the spinning in his head. He could not allow the pain low in his gut to immobilize him.

"My name is Miss Jacobson. Jane, if you must," she said, her sigh long-suffering.

"Jane," Roland choked out. "You are a cruel thing."

"You ought to learn that I will not be managed," she countered, not a trace of sympathy lining her round, perfectly symmetrical face.

"Because you're damned intractable?" Roland managed. The sharp pain had subsided and his breath was back. But that dull throbbing in his gut would take minutes to fade, which she well knew.

Jane did not deign to respond to that allegation, instead turning back to the door, now unobstructed.

"Do not follow me," she ordered him sharply, then disappeared through it.

Roland counted to ten and then followed, despite her order. He could not let her depart without agreeing to some sort of plan. Otherwise, he'd be forced to appear on her doorstep with nothing more than a half-baked plan to ask for her father's permission to court her. If her father refused, this whole mission would be in jeopardy.

As it was, she was not as intractable as she tried to appear. She stood near the entrance of the hotel, talking with a young woman he did not recognize. Not that Roland recognized any of the current generation of debutantes. The woman, dressed in peach and laughing girlishly, was clearly just that.

He did not interrupt them, but did make a point of walking a bit more slowly than usual as he sauntered across the lobby and out onto the street. The wind whipped against his cheeks, making him wish he'd thought to don a greatcoat, but if he kept moving he'd be fine.

But until Jane appeared, he had nothing else to do but pretend to fiddle with his pocket watch.

A minute ticked by. Then another.

If she was purposely taking her time so that he would be forced to stand out here in the cold…

She tumbled forward into this shoulder, nearly knocking him into the street and directly into the path of a carriage. The driver swerved, and Roland's reflexes had him throwing them both back, grabbing Jane's hand to keep her from tumbling into danger.

Bollocks—was she going to be this much trouble the entire time?

But when he looked down at her, scanning for injury, he did not miss the twitch at the corner of her pink mouth.

"You—"

"Thank you, Your Grace. I do think you've saved my life!" she said quickly, her voice filled with breathless admiration. Roland nearly snorted. "How shall I ever repay you?"

It was a thin ruse. But then, there was no one within earshot other than the footmen stationed at the doors of the hotel. No one visible, at least. They had to remember that, always.

"I was about to take a bit of exercise in the park," Roland forced himself to say. "A young, bright thing such as yourself will make it a much more enjoyable experience."

Thin, but believable.

"Of course, I would be honored," Jane said, a light blush creeping onto her cheeks.

Impressive.

Impressive? He admonished himself instantly. She was hardly more than a debutante. Blushing was practically a requirement. It was not impressive.

But despite his thoughts, Roland held out a hand. "Shall we?"

She smiled, and Roland realized it was the first time he'd actually seen the expression now upon her face. It was pretty. She was pretty. But he found himself wondering what a true smile would look like, when it actually reached her eyes and lit those warm brown orbs? What about a laugh? Would it be small and shrill, matching her stature? He doubted he would ever hear it.

Despite his offer, she did not take his hand. She blushed again, glancing downward and clasping her hands demurely in front of her. That was fine with Roland.

They'd barely stepped into the street before her sharp whisper cut over to him. "I shall arrange a meeting with Lord and Lady Thane as soon as possible."

Roland's hand curled into a fist. "Why will you be the one to set up the meeting?"

"Because Lady Jacquetta Thane, née Lawson, is my longtime friend, as anyone with a finger on the pulse of London Society would know," she said, not looking at him.

"I have no time to take the pulse of London Society. I am an agent of the Foreign Office," he said, increasing his pace to keep up with her tiny but rapid steps.

"Bully for you," Jane said, not even looking back to see if he'd follow as she strode for the park through a gap in wheeled and hooved traffic. He was now in step with her. "You have no prior connection to Jacquetta or her new husband. Other than being irritatingly difficult, like Grayson," she muttered.

"Grayson? You are quite familiar with Thane, then." What was that feeling in his stomach? Anger? He had no reason to be angry—at least, not about her affiliation with Grayson Thane.

That name, at least, Roland knew. Thane had been in the Crown's sights for years. Until, mysteriously, they'd received word that he was no longer *persona non grata*. Roland had assumed the wayward son of a duke had made some sort of deal with the Crown. But now he wondered about Jane's involvement.

She cut him a look before starting down the path leading into the shaded grove of trees. "I shot and killed the leader of the criminal enterprise that enslaved him, spent months in Barbados helping the royal governor dismantle said enterprise with Grayson and Jacquetta's assistance, and stood witness at their wedding before going back to England on Thane's own ship. You could say we are acquainted."

Roland's step faltered. He was damned glad that Jane was facing the other direction so she did not see it. If all of that was true, he'd gravely underestimated her. Which she'd been telling him since their first meeting in Remington's study.

She must be exaggerating. The facts she'd stated *could* certainly all be true. But perhaps she was coloring her involvement with more importance than reality. That must be it, of course. He could no easier imagine the tiny Jane Jacobson, his little mouse, holding a pistol than he could see her tangling with a criminal as notorious as Grayson Thane.

Overestimating her abilities could be even more dangerous than underestimating them, his brain told him.

But Roland's gut clenched in warning as he strode to catch up with her once again. Hell, why was he always having to catch up with someone whose strides were half as long as his?

"You may set up the meeting with Lord and Lady Thane," he said as he joined her on the path.

He did not attempt to take her arm or steer her. He did watch her mouth tighten at the implied permission given by his statement, but she proved she had more self-restraint than he when she said, "My mother hews to decorum. Do not call until the appropriate hour. Do you recall when that is?"

He rolled his eyes. "I may be unaware of who is swiving who, but I am a duke."

"Yes, the Duke of Hawkridge, a profitable dukedom located in Northumberland and managed at a distance for the last decade since you assumed your title upon the passing of your father," she recited.

He chuckled. "What did you do, read my entry in *Debrett's?*"

"Yes." Jane nodded. "But I knew most of it already. As I said before, I keep up on all *ton* matters. It is extremely useful in my work."

"Pfft."

She sighed in exasperation and gave him a long look, as if speaking to a child and not a duke nearly twenty years her senior.

"I take it you did not recognize the young woman I spoke to inside the Pendleton?" she asked, lifting one delicately arched brow.

Roland could sense that he would not like what was coming next. But he shook his head because he could think of no other way to avoid it.

"A debutante?" he said just as she opened her perfectly formed mouth to speak.

"Indeed, a debutante. Lady Theresa St. James. She made her debut this season with my younger sister, which means we are acquainted, and I was obligated to stop and greet her," Jane said.

They'd nearly finished their circuit of the park. Whatever set-down was coming, she would have to deliver it quickly. Roland was quickly running out of time and interest.

"She told me that her uncle is taking her out to the Ascot Heath later this week to see the new racehorse he purchased, as she is quite fond of riding. She is going to invite my sister."

Roland sighed. "As interesting as this is, we shall have to speak more tomorrow when I call upon you. We cannot plausibly continue this interlude at present if we want to maintain the thin excuse you constructed."

The glint in those clever brown eyes ought to have been a warning.

"Lady Theresa's uncle is Viscount Remington. Thanks to my knowledge of *ton* connections, we now know precisely when his study will be available for further searching," she said.

And a second before she stepped into the street, Roland saw the first true smile upon her face. That was when he realized he'd truly been wrong about everything.

CHAPTER FIVE

B Y THE NEXT morning, the bright red skin she'd scrubbed for a
whole hour had faded to a pretty pink glow. Jane took particular
care as she dressed herself, choosing a striped lavender and white
gown that made her look less like a debutante and more like the
twenty-three-year-old woman she was. Not that she expected anyone
in her family to notice—at least, not until Hawkridge arrived.

Luncheon passed uneventfully. Her brother left to pay calls to his
round of lady loves, none of whom he actually intended to marry. Her
sister went off to join her embroidery group. Jane did occasionally go
along with her; debutantes were so prone to gossip, she could often
gather as much intelligence from one of those embroidery circles as
from lingering by the punchbowl at five balls.

Only her mother, father, and herself remained.

Fortuitous, really. If her brother had been there when Hawkridge
arrived, he would have puffed up his chest and done something stupid.
Her sister, who had not so secretly declared her intention to marry a
duke, would have been tripping over herself for an introduction. Jane
didn't have time for either of them. She needed this courtship
formalized quickly so she could move on with the rest of the quest and
be done with Hawkridge once and for all.

Unfortunately, that seemed a longer and more distant proposition
with each passing hour. Quite literally. The hours passed and Roland

Hawkridge still had not deigned to call.

Jane's plan was already forming in her head. She would beg off the evening's engagements, saying she felt ill, sneak out of the house, and stalk the truant to whatever den of iniquity he'd decided to haunt in favor of actually doing his duty to the Crown.

Then the knock sounded.

Jane's mother glanced up from her embroidery. Jane kept her eyes on her book, kept her seat on the sofa in the parlor, and tried to pretend that she took no interest in what was happening around her.

The butler entered, handing the calling card to her mother.

"The Duke of Hawkridge?" The viscountess sat up, confusion written all over her face.

"Shall I admit him, my lady?"

"Yes, of course—it's the Duke of Hawkridge," she said, coming to her feet and flattening her dress frantically. "Whatever could he want? I don't even recall speaking to the man except in passing. Fetch his lordship, perhaps. Jane? Have you any notion what this is about?"

Jane carefully closed her book, marking her place, letting her mother run out her line of haphazard thought.

"Mother, I—"

"Hawkridge? What a surprise," her father's voice echoed from beyond the parlor.

Her mother's eyebrows rose so rapidly they nearly disappeared into her hairline, but she had no time to question, and Jane had no time to offer an explanation before her father and the duke walked through the open doors of the parlor.

"I apologize for not sending a note before arriving," Hawkridge was saying congenially. "But it has all happened rather fast, and I must admit to being caught up in the emotion of it."

Jane wanted to roll her eyes. He was making a decent job of it. A skilled agent of the Crown, she could fairly admit. But so was she.

When he added the next sentence and all eyes landed upon her, she was already blushing prettily, just like she'd practiced in the mirror that morning.

"I have come to pay my respects to your daughter, Miss Jacobson," Hawkridge said.

Her parents stared at her in stunned silence. If her mother's rapid blinking was any indication, the woman was near to swooning. Her father was harder to read, as usual. He was eyeing her as if seeing her for the first time, like an apparition who hadn't been sitting at the supper table for the last twenty years.

Jane stood, carefully smoothing her skirts. She must be exact here. Her parents knew that while she presented a quiet persona to the rest of the world, she held very strong opinions. She'd decided last night, wrapped in her warmest, fluffiest dressing gown, that she would pretend to be besotted with Hawkridge. Anything else—pretending she was accepting his suit because she was out of options, or to needle her sister, or any other idea she'd analyzed—was bound to fall apart.

"Mother," she began again. "I meant to tell you before His Grace joined us."

"Tell me what, precisely?" Her mother looked between Jane and Hawkridge, as if she could not fit the images together.

"His Grace and I met the other evening at Viscount Remington's ball," Jane said, pushing a smile to her face and flicking her eyelashes in Hawkridge's direction.

"We were all in attendance that evening," her mother said, now staring at Hawkridge.

Jane tried to see him as her mother might. He was tall—very tall, actually, when compared to her own diminutive stature. Lean and muscled, which she'd felt when she punched him in the stomach and then again in the balls. Though her mother wouldn't be able to ascertain that much. His hair still had a shadow of the darkness of his youth, but it was mostly silver now, precisely trimmed. He was older, yes, but attractive still. And he was a duke. He was a more than decent prospect for a wallflower such as herself.

If only he weren't such an intemperate arse beneath that hand-some veneer, Jane thought just for herself.

"Indeed," Hawkridge said, bowing respectfully to her mother. "I apologize that we were not able to become better acquainted that evening. I was called away at the last moment. But I have come here now."

More blinking. Egads, her mother was not this daft.

Neither was her father, whose dark brown eyes had narrowed now. But Hawkridge wasted no more time.

"Viscount Bellbrook, Lady Bellbrook, I would like to formally request your permission to court your daughter, Miss Jacobson. I have been most impressed by her comportment and graceful demeanor and wish to explore a match between us." It was very formal, but it accomplished the job.

Jane bit her bottom lip, looking between her mother and father with what she hoped were pleading eyes. No one spoke for several agonizing breaths. She'd begun constructing some sort of response when her father, who had been watching the exchange in silence, stepped in to the void of awkwardness.

"If you will excuse us for a few moments, Your Grace, I would like to have a private word with my daughter. I will have tea brought up directly," he said with a snap of his fingers.

The butler, who'd been hovering just outside the parlor doors, hopped into motion.

"Of course, of course. I would not wish to intrude upon a family moment," Hawkridge said, waving effusively and already striding away, in case they meant to have that conversation right in the parlor.

But her father only inclined his head and then turned to stride from the room, expecting Jane and her mother to follow. Jane avoided her mother's gaze, casting a longing glance over her shoulder at Hawkridge as she left, making sure that her mother saw it. From the widening of her mother's eyes, she'd accomplished that task.

Her father led them into his study, only the next room over. He closed the door behind them and turned to Jane, without any preamble.

"Jane, are you in some sort of trouble?" he asked.

"Richard! Why would you say such a thing?" her mother cried.

"The Duke of Hawkridge is standing in our parlor, asking to court the daughter who has eschewed marriage since her debut five years ago," he said, though he patted his wife's arm comfortingly.

Her mother shook his hand away. "They are taken! Did you not see the way they looked at one another!"

"The duke does appear to be in earnest," he allowed. But his eyes landed on Jane.

I am prepared for this, she reminded herself. *I knew my father would be more difficult to convince.*

They weren't close, precisely. Rather, they were cut from the same mold. Quiet and observant, both Jane and her father sat and watched while the rest of their loud family flitted and swirled around them. But the affection between her mother and father was real; they were in love and had been for Jane's entire life. It was that emotion that she needed to prey upon now.

"This is a coup! It could be the coup of the Season! The Duke of Hawkridge! I never imagined such a thing for my Jane..." her mother jabbered.

But her father... he still watched her with those eyes, twins to her own. "Are you open to the duke's suit, Jane?"

No blushing now. She worried at her bottom lip a bit, then nodded solemnly. "It is true, I have not had much interest in marriage before this. But the way I see you and Mother..." A well-placed glance back in the direction of the parlor. "I would like to know the duke better, at least."

Not a big declaration of love; that would be out of character. Cautious, careful—that was much more her personality. Her mother was nodding rapidly, instead of blinking, her mind clearly swirling with the possibilities. After a long moment, her father nodded as well.

"Very well. If you are amenable, I will allow Hawkridge to court you," he said.

Her mother clapped her hands excitedly. "Let us not keep him waiting!" She was already halfway to the door.

Her father hung back, offering Jane his arm.

"You promise you are well?" he said quietly as he escorted her back to the parlor.

The tremor in his voice reached down and circled around Jane's heart.

She thought she'd kept it hidden, that disastrous mistake. She thought there were only two souls alive that knew of it. But the way her father's grip tightened on her arm... Perhaps he suspected more than he'd ever let on.

But Jane had no more time to think on it, because they were back in the parlor and faced with her pretend future.

⊱⟫⟩⟨⟨⊰

WOULD THEY SAY no? The thought had occurred to Roland as soon as Cartwright put forth the ridiculous idea.

But it wasn't so ridiculous, some irritating part of him reasoned.

Jane Jacobson was twenty-three and unmarried, a certified wallflower. She was less than a Season away from being declared a spinster. Though, Roland supposed, with one child a rakehell and the other a diamond of the first water, it would be easy enough for Jane's parents to forget about her.

How could anyone forget about her? He'd been thinking of the chit since the moment she stood there staring him down while clutching *The Gentleman's Guide to Animal Husbandry* and pretending it was perfectly normal for a young woman to take an interest in such things.

Even though he had been slow to assume his duties as the Duke of Hawkridge, Roland would now be expected to court a lady, take her to wife, and produce heirs. Jane was of noble birth, from a respectable family, and had many child-bearing years before her. Courtship between them was a reasonable proposition in the eyes of the *ton*.

No one needed to know that Roland actually had no plans to marry or produce heirs anytime soon.

He tried to sit on the sofa, but his long legs jumped uncomfortably. It was either stretch himself out or stand. Roland took up a post by the mantel, rather than appear unduly comfortable in the Jacobson home.

He'd finished reading the title of every book on the shelves that stood on either side of the hearth when the parlor doors opened and the trio returned.

Roland bowed by reflex, and Jane curtsied before taking the seat on the sofa he'd abandoned himself minutes before. He wondered if she could still feel the heat of his body through the thin layers of her gown.

"Ahem," Viscount Bellbrook said.

He'd been staring, Roland realized—at Jane.

He forced his sigh inside. At least he looked the part of the besotted suitor, even if he was ready to strangle the woman at every other turn.

"My daughter has decided to accept your suit, Hawkridge," Viscount Bellbrook said. "You may call on her tomorrow afternoon."

"We have been invited to tea tomorrow afternoon with Lord and Lady Grayson Thane," Jane said, still sitting on the sofa, prim and straight as a statuette of the Virgin Mary herself.

All three sets of eyes swung to her, mouths momentarily silenced.

"How lovely!" her mother said. "I shall accompany you—"

"That isn't necessary, dear," her father interceded, one eye on his daughter. "Lady Thane will be plenty chaperone."

"But—"

"Let the girls speak to one another without you looking over their shoulders," he admonished her.

Girls. Ha—even as he heard Viscount Bellbrook say it, Roland wondered if the man knew that his daughter and her friend were the farthest thing from it. Vixens. Sirens. Lady knights. But the long look that Bellbrook gave his daughter spoke loudly to Roland. He knew his daughter was up to *something*. But he was giving her the space to do it.

Interesting.

Whatever it was that Viscount Bellbrook suspected, Roland was certain that it could not be the truth. Women as spies—Roland had encountered that often enough. They were certainly as intelligent as men, often more self-possessed. But young wallflowers of the *ton*? Not even Mrs. Radcliffe could dream that up.

But he played the perfect gentleman as he bowed yet again, this time taking Lady Bellbrook's hand and bringing it to his lips suavely. "Thank you for your blessing, my lady."

The woman blushed, of course. From behind him, Roland thought he heard his little mouse squeak.

CHAPTER SIX

"IF YOU SCOOT any further away, you will fall out of the phaeton," Roland observed drolly, flicking the reins in time with a click of his tongue.

The matched pair of dapple grays sprang into step and they were away from the Jacobson house, though Roland had the distinct image of Jane's mother peering out the window pinned in his mind.

Lady Bellbrook had sorely wanted to accompany them. But he'd chosen the phaeton with purpose. It was only meant to carry two, though Jane was so far away from him on the seat that there was ample room for another person. Additionally, it was an open conveyance, which meant that their drive could essentially be unchaperoned, while also making a declaration to everyone of note in Mayfair and beyond about his and Jane's pseudo-courtship.

"This is meant to be a courtship," he reminded her as he steered the team of horses through the busy London streets.

"Yes, and in a respectable courtship, we would never touch except while dancing or promenading," Jane said. She did not move any closer.

"We are supposed to be falling in love." It was amusing. She was not afraid of him; she'd proven as much already. She was also committed to her mission—quest, as she insisted upon calling it. So why was his little mouse hiding from him now?

"I was considered quite a rakehell, once," Roland said, giving her a roguish grin for all of Mayfair to see. "Anyone old enough to remember will expect me to seduce you."

The challenge landed perfectly. Jane straightened, moving several inches closer to him. "You can try," she said.

This had not been his plan.

But he would enjoy seeing the perfectly composed lady knight unravel.

"Give me your hand," he instructed her, eyes still trained on the road.

"Why?"

"To begin my seduction, of course."

Jane scoffed. "What is the point of holding my hand? No one will be able to see your supposed seduction."

"What they will see is the two of us, heads tilted close in conversation. They will see your face as I do this." He yanked free the white kid-skin glove that buttoned at her wrist in one deft swipe. He was rewarded by a little moue of her lips.

"You are insufferable," she hissed. But she did not pull back her hand.

"If you are as committed to your quest as you insist, then we should make sure we do not fail this time." As he spoke, he dragged his thumb over the center of her palm, from the base of her center finger to the rapidly beating pulse in her wrist.

"We ought to use this privacy to discuss the villains who wish our queen ill," Jane gritted out. Her eyes were firmly fixed forward, even as she sucked in her bottom lip between her teeth.

"We shall discuss it at length with our hosts once we arrive," he said. And they would. This moment in the phaeton was not for discussing a strategy—it was for adding credibility to their ruse so they could conduct their mission successfully.

That was why he was stroking her hand, making love to her palm and tracing the letters of his name on her heart line. It was not because he found her attractive. That would be entirely unprofessional.

Her hands were so small. Everything about her was. He'd noticed it before, but with her palm curled inside of his, it was abundantly clear. But so strong. He could sense the strength in each finger as he laced them between his own and squeezed. She could not help but squeeze back, unable to leave a challenge unmet. He loved that about her already.

They reached a busy intersection, and he eased the team to a stop, taking the opportunity to lift her knuckles to his mouth and brush his lips over the top of her bare skin.

Her eyes flashed, the chocolate brown darkening. What would those eyes look like in the evening, with the genuine smile he'd seen just once on her clever face? What about in the early hours of the morning? Had anyone ever seen proper Miss Jane Jacobson in the throes of passion—

The horses stepped forward, the cart in front of them lurched into motion, and he had to tear his hand away to take control once more. He reached for her again, but Jane was already shoving her hand back into her glove.

"We have arrived," she said, nodding past his shoulder.

Roland tugged reflexively on the reins, bringing them to a crisp halt—leaving him wishing he had such control over himself.

Because nothing about the throbbing in his trousers was professional.

⋙⋘

SHE OUGHT TO have stayed on her own side of that phaeton.

She'd let him bait her, an intolerable occurrence she could never allow again. In doing so, she'd felt something she thought impossible—the first fluttering of attraction. Jane may be a wallflower teetering on the edge of spinsterhood, but she was not naïve.

As he handed her down from the open carriage in front of Jacquetta and Grayson's newly rented townhouse, she could not stop the shiver of awareness that snaked up her palm and right to her womanly core.

Attraction was an inconvenience at the best of times. Now, when she'd been saddled with a partner and was in danger of disappointing Miranda? It was downright unacceptable.

Not that she'd felt much attraction over the last several years. Flirting was Dominique and Jacquetta's area of expertise, not hers.

As the door swung open, Jane reminded herself of that fact. She was the composed one. She was the methodical one. She was not the one to fall head over heels in love with a man who inconveniently deposited himself in close proximity to her latest quest. Despite the fact that was precisely what the three other lady knights had done over the past year.

"Ay! Captain! It's the pretty wench with the pistols!"

Jane blinked, half tempted to lift her hands to her spectacles, wondering if they'd somehow turned magical and transported her back in time by several months. Standing in front of her, fully kitted out like a butler, was one of the seamen from aboard Grayson's ship.

"Who's the old bugger you've brought with you, Lady Jane?" the piratical butler said, sweeping a less-than-impressed eye over Hawkridge.

"Jacoby! We have discussed this!" Jacquetta appeared in a swirl of blue that matched her eyes. "Miss Jacobson and *His Grace* the Duke of Hawkridge."

The would-be butler's face didn't shift.

"Isn't the captain a duke?" he asked skeptically.

"Lord Thane is the second son of a duke," Jacquetta corrected him. "Be a dear and go help Bryson with the flour delivery, will you?"

"Of course, my lady." The unlikely servant bowed so far forward that his nose was in danger of scraping the tiles in the foyer.

Jacquetta waited for him to go, cringing at the slam of the door that must lead down the servants' stairwell.

"I'd apologize for Jacoby," she said in a conspiratorial whisper. "But quite honestly, this is an improvement. You should have seen the look upon my sister Marie's face when he complimented her—"

"We understand," Jane said sharply.

"Are all of your servants so colorful?" Hawkridge asked from behind her, amusement rolling off him in waves that seemed to fill the small foyer of the townhouse.

"Only the ones who were formerly employed on the *Agamemnon*," Jacquetta said, rubbing a hand over her face as she led them through the townhouse. "Honestly, setting up house is more tiring than dismantling a criminal enterprise."

"And you've decided to expedite the process by sourcing your household staff from an ex-pirate ship?" Jane kept her voice level, but she knew her friend would hear the amusement in it.

Sure enough, Jacquetta shot her a grin over her shoulder as she opened a door and ushered them through. "The *Agamemnon* is a respectable privateer vessel, nowadays," she said. "Only Jacoby and one of the galley helpers have joined us here. And, of course, the notorious captain himself."

The one who looked very much a pirate blackguard, reclining on the sofa with a glass of madeira. Grayson's hair was even longer than the last time Jane had seen it, falling over his eyes at a rakish angle. No cravat, shirt unbuttoned, he looked entirely out of place in a proper London sitting room, and yet also unmistakably the lord of his new castle.

Jane noted the moment his eyes landed on Hawkridge, and his entire relaxed persona changed. No, she reminded herself—she only noticed it because of her training. To a casual observer, Grayson remained relaxed on his own sofa, a half-smile curving his lips as he slowly straightened and leaned forward, not standing.

But Jane saw the way his hand tightened around the stem of his glass, the sharpening of his eyes, and the slight divot between his eyebrows. His free hand edged closer to his waist. Jane wondered if he had a weapon stowed there even now, or if it was a habit he'd yet to divest himself of. In any case... If she noticed all these small cues, she was certain her irritating but competent companion did as well.

"Hawkridge."

Jane felt Hawkridge at her shoulder. She shifted to the side, expecting him to move past and offer his hand or a bow or something.

Instead, he replied, equally measured, "Thane."

Lovely. A prick-measuring contest.

"Tea should be along any moment," Jacquetta said, ignoring the two men.

She motioned toward the chaise adjacent to the sofa before taking a seat beside her husband. Jane poised herself on the edge of the chaise, comfortable but straight. Hawkridge, of course, couldn't be bothered to sit. He took up a post behind her, his hand annoyingly close to her back as it came to rest on the curved back of the chaise.

"Lovely," Jane said. "How much has the duchess told you about our quest?"

"Mission," Hawkridge muttered.

Jacquetta's bright turquoise eyes flitted between the two of them. Jane didn't miss how her friend tightened her jaw, holding in a chuckle.

"She had us to tea yesterday. The duchess wanted to meet my new husband in person," Jacquetta said, eyes gleaming wickedly.

Jane allowed her lips to curve in amusement. "I am sorry I missed it."

"It was not a spectacle," Grayson muttered before swigging back his madeira.

"That was exactly what it was," Jacquetta countered. "In any case, that was not your question. As to the quest, the duchess gave us only the briefest sketches. I am, after all, on temporary leave from the Lady Knights while we reacclimate to London."

The emphatic roll of her eyes told Jane exactly what her friend thought about that.

"Her primary concern is not Remington," Jacquetta said. That aligned with Jane's own assessment of the man as a mere puppet or minor player. "But rather, with the secret society of which he is a member."

Jane let out a careful, measured breath. "Secret society."

It was Grayson who grimly said, "I am afraid so."

"When we last met with the Duchess of Guilford, she didn't know who Remington's accomplices were," Hawkridge said, voicing exactly the thought that had been in Jane's head. They were failing at this quest even more miserably than they had been a few days prior.

"Nor does she now," Jacquetta said quickly. "Grayson—Well, you'd best explain it."

All eyes went to Grayson.

He shifted in his seat, setting aside his wine and straightening, his face grim and serious. That was enough to have Jane's stomach churning. There was a plot to assassinate the queen; that was chilling enough. But for a man like Grayson to have that grim, worried look upon his face…

"I don't know Remington personally," he began. "But he was among one of Delaurier's contacts. Not very bright, honestly. He made mistakes that ought to have ended with a round in his head or a knife in his back. Yet he is still alive. That alone tells me that whoever is his benefactor, whoever sent him on their behalf to interact with Delaurier, is powerful."

Jane's mind was already calculating possibilities. But before she could ask or Grayson could continue, a deep voice rumbled from behind her, tickling the fine hairs on the nape of her neck.

"What sort of deals was he making?" Hawkridge asked.

Grayson cut him a look that even Jane had difficulty reading. "The dangerous kind."

Jacquetta sighed dramatically. "How enlightening. Everything Delaurier did was dangerous."

Grayson opened his mouth, probably to chastise his wife, but tea conveniently arrived instead. Once they all had a steaming cup, Jacquetta's with cognac dashed into it, Hawkridge's black as Jane's opinion of him, Grayson continued.

"Guns. Explosives. Exotic poisons that are difficult to trace," he said bluntly. "It was not Delaurier's usual business. We smuggled illegal goods, but the kind that maximized profit and minimized interest from officials. It's easier to pay off an excise officer to look past French lace than it is to overlook muskets."

Jacquetta tilted her head to the side. "So, he must have been paid well for the risk."

Her husband nodded, the corner of his lip curling as he looked at her with clear admiration.

Just for a second, Jane felt a little twitch in her chest, a familiar, uncomfortable flicker of feeling that she'd felt too often on their journey across the Atlantic aboard the *Agamemnon*. She was happy for Jacquetta, she reminded herself. She even liked Grayson—his ruthless practicality was appealing to her. But that hint of jealousy, that little spark in her chest reminding her of what she did not have...

"How does this fit with the supposed secret society?" Hawkridge said, his deep voice cutting through the slurry of emotions in her chest, effectively bringing Jane back to the moment. For the first time ever, she felt a wave of gratefulness toward the duke.

Grayson's eyes moved away from his wife, up over Jane's shoulder. "Like I said, Remington is stupid. He ought to have been disposed of. I think the very reason he was used as an intermediary was because they considered him disposable. When we were in port in Southampton last year, he came drinking with some of my crew. I kept my own counsel, but I heard enough.

"He boasted about his *affiliation*, about passing through some sort of grotesque initiation. I have word out to the two members of my crew that were there that night, who are still in my employ. But one is visiting family in Scotland and the other is in the West Indies, so it may be some time before I have any more to tell you."

Jane drummed her fingers across her knee. "It certainly sounds like some sort of secret society," she said, voicing her thoughts carefully. "Anarchists? Revolutionaries? They must have some sort of creed."

Grayson nodded. "Agreed. But I don't know what it is. When I overheard all of this, all I was interested in was how many days until I was out. I wanted to stay the hell away from anything that could get me mixed up in trouble or time added to my..."

He stopped abruptly, leaning back with mock casualness.

Hawkridge, Jane realized. Grayson had already shared a lot about himself, more than he'd shared with anyone other than Jacquetta, Jane would have wagered.

Hawkridge cleared his throat behind her, ready to speak, but Jane forestalled him to spare Grayson. "Thank you. That gives us infinitely more information than we had when we crossed your threshold."

Grayson's dark eyes watched her for several long seconds before they rose over her shoulder. Jane could practically feel the intensity of the two men appraising each other. Though Grayson's eyes remained fixed on Hawkridge, she knew his next words were for them both.

"These are not men like my former employer, interested in money above all else. They are running a multi-tiered, well-funded, dangerous enterprise, that is certain. But the similarities end there. The men— and perhaps women—are operating in support of principle. And that is infinitely more dangerous."

Jane understood exactly what he meant. Men who acted for money wanted to be alive to spend it. Those who acted for a cause were willing to fight whether they lived to see the outcomes of their sacrifice or not.

She didn't turn to try to read Hawkridge's expression. But it must have satisfied Grayson, because her friend's husband lowered his chin an inch. A nod of acknowledgment.

Jane took a fortifying sip of her tea.

Jacquetta still had her blonde head tipped to the side, thinking. Her brow puckered; an idea had entered her mind. Jane braced herself instinctively.

"We can help you," Jacquetta said slowly, her mind still turning. "Grayson, you are perfectly poised to make a connection with this society. You could go to Remington and manage an introduction. He's not a smart man, and you are already acquainted—"

"No."

Grayson's voice was sharp enough that Jane turned in her seat, avoiding her friend's eyes.

"You do not get to tell me no," Jacquetta said, her voice dripping with honey sweetness.

"Then what is the point of being your husband?" Grayson countered.

"I am a lady knight. Just because I have chosen to marry a disreputable—"

Jane felt the tickle of warmth at her ear a split second before she heard his words.

"Perhaps we ought to leave them to it," Hawkridge whispered in her ear.

As much as she hated to agree with him, his words held wisdom. Jane had been trapped on a ship with Grayson and Jacquetta for two months. This was likely to escalate to yelling and flying objects, and end in the two of them doing something disreputable on that sofa.

They said their goodbyes, earning terse adieus from their hosts, and slipped out of the townhouse. The pirate butler, Jacoby, was nowhere to be seen, but Hawkridge's phaeton was fetched without too much fuss, and then they were on their way back to her parents' home.

This time, Jane stayed on her own side of the phaeton.

"We need to search Remington's study," she said, following a map in her mind as Hawkridge steered them down the streets of Mayfair. She counted the blocks until she would be free of him. "My sister has been invited to Ascot with Lady Sheffield on Thursday afternoon, so we will need to arrange—"

"I will do it," he cut her off, not even bothering to look in her direction as he did so.

Jane clenched her teeth. "We will be more efficient if we search together."

"We will be more likely to get caught." Again, he did not spare her a glance as he turned to the right.

Jane grabbed the side of the phaeton to keep herself from lurching sideways into him. She whipped her head back, thinking she must have lost track... No, she knew precisely where she was. "This is not the way to my home."

A slight wrinkle of amusement at the corner of his eyes. "I am taking a detour."

Jane did not bother to swallow down her annoyance. "Why?"

Hawkridge was fully grinning as he said, "I anticipated that I would need the time to bring you to heel."

"I am not a dog." She did not have a temper, but egads—he seemed determined to root one out of her.

"Damn near as intractable," he said, darting her a glance.

Jane started to boil over. "How dare you—"

"Remington is dangerous. If I get caught, I can defend myself." He was so irritatingly assured, so perfectly certain of his right to command.

"I can defend myself perfectly well," she snapped. She wanted to reach into her boot, pull out the knife hidden there, and stab him with it. "It is not your charge to protect me from danger. My entire career is danger."

"Your entire career," he scoffed. Another snide commentary about her age.

"You trust the Duchess of Guilford. That means you should trust me."

Jane knew the argument had landed, because he finally shut up. Working with him was going to be utter agony. Her logical mind was trying to regain control, even as her heart pounded in her chest with rage. *Analyze him,* her mind said. *Stab him,* her anger countered.

He is just a man. Clever and smart, but a man nonetheless. He had his weaknesses, his ways of being manipulated. She needed to deduce what they were and use them to her advantage to complete this quest as quickly as possible. The more time she spent with the Duke of Hawkridge, the more likely her hair was to turn a silvery gray to match his.

"I will stand guard," she finally said. "If Remington returns, I can create a commotion in the street."

Hawkridge scoffed again, but some of the force was gone from it. "Throw yourself in front of another moving carriage?"

So, he hadn't liked her tactics in front of the Pendleton. A little smile of satisfaction climbed her face as she filed that information away in her mind.

"If necessary," she said. "Something loud enough that it will give you time to get out of the house."

"I quiver to imagine."

He turned the phaeton again, and Jane vaguely recognized her street.

"Then don't. Trust me, instead," she said simply.

Jane could tell it went against every instinct in his irritatingly handsome head. But finally, as he reined in the team, he answered.

"Fine."

CHAPTER SEVEN

T HEY'D FOUND NOTHING useful in Remington's study. Despite the fact that they'd had multiple sources, and their own observations, attesting to the man's sloppiness. There also had been no cause for Jane to cause a commotion, near death or otherwise.

But Roland would have gladly taken death over attending a charity soiree given by Lady Mary Elizabeth Winston-Weatherby. He'd gladly sign over all the property not entailed to his dukedom to the Benevolent Youth Society, if it would have spared him.

Instead, he stood beside a glass bowl of ratafia deep enough to drown himself in, with little Jane Jacobson on his arm, and the eyes of half the *ton* glued to the pair of them.

This isn't going to work.

It was as if they were standing in the center of the ring at a circus. They shouldn't even have been an oddity. There were men here with wives young enough to be their granddaughters. But in the recesses of his mind, where the ill-used logic resided, he knew it was not their difference in age that earned them the attention. It was the unlikely pairing of their personalities—he, the wayward duke absent from London entirely for the last ten years; she, the wallflower sister of an otherwise glittering social family.

The whole thing practically screamed of an arrangement of convenience. But they'd agreed to pretend to be in love.

No, the ruse absolutely was not going to pass.

Roland turned to tell Jane as much, only aware that she was still there by the slight pressure of her hand on his arm. But when he looked down, he was blindsided.

Her smile was absolutely radiant. It reached the corners of her eyes, showed all her straight white teeth, softened her warm brown eyes. And it was all for him.

Hell.

He refused to let her be a better agent than he. Roland forced his eyes to soften, half of his mouth to lift. He leaned down, close enough that only she could hear him. He did not know what to say, only that the eyes of everyone in that room were fixed upon them.

"Two can play this game, little mouse," Roland heard himself say.

Jane stiffened, and a sweet little blush that he knew was not one bit fabricated climbed up her cheeks.

"What are you doing?" she said through her teeth, her smile faltering slightly.

"Lovers whisper sweet nothings in one another's ears," he said, his mouth still just above the shell of her ear. She was so small, he had to lean down significantly to do so. The gesture couldn't be missed, even by the most unobservant attendees.

Jane turned her face up to him, conveniently moving her head so that her ear was decidedly out of his reach.

"We are not lovers," she said in a harsh whisper.

"We are madly in love," Roland said, knowing it would grate on her.

No one was close enough to hear their exchange. For all that they looked like a lovestruck couple exchanging whispered endearments, this was a battle.

"We are supposed to be speaking with Lord and Lady Remington," she said.

To compile a list of possible accomplices.

Roland heard the second half of her sentence without her needing to say it aloud.

"Then let's go introduce ourselves." He was tired of being stared at like a prize hog. If he was forced to attend a charity event, pretending to court the tiresome little mouse, he might as well have some liquor in his hand and be advancing the cause.

"We *are* advancing the cause," Jane said.

Roland stifled a groan. He hadn't even realized he'd said that part aloud.

"Every moment that we are together *whispering sweet nothings*, we give more plausibility to our courtship. This allows us to investigate Remington and his... affiliations without anyone suspecting us," she explained. Logical, patient. Like she was talking to a five-year-old.

She was speaking to him as if he was a child? Roland almost laughed aloud.

"Besides," Jane continued, "if you were paying any attention at all, you would have noticed that Lady Remington just excused herself to the ladies' retiring room."

Roland forced his face to stay neutral, even as he swept her hand into his and raised it to his lips, pressing a kiss to her delicate fingertips.

"Then why are you still standing here?" he whispered tersely.

Jane managed not to yank her hand back, but he could see the frustration in her eyes. Her smile no longer reached the usually soft orbs.

"I shall meet you in the conservatory in half an hour," she said, dipping a curtsy before she walked away.

Roland wished he did not notice the way that her hips swayed in her pale pink gown as she sashayed away. He certainly did not imagine twirling the lone brown curl that had escaped from her chignon around his finger. And most of all, he was not contemplating if his little mouse would squeak when he kissed her lips instead of her hand.

AS USUAL, NO one noticed Jane when she slipped into the retiring room.

She'd been concerned that her very public courtship with Hawkridge would make her a curiosity. But it seemed that without him at her side, she was just another wallflower once again. That suited her perfectly well. No one minded their tongue around a wallflower.

But despite the quarter hour she spent pretending to powder her nose and nibbling syllabub, Lady Remington and her two friends revealed nothing. They chatted about their new modiste and about the difficulty of securing invitations to the Duchess of Sudbury's upcoming ball. Jane managed to keep the smile from her face when she heard them mention the difficulty of securing a reliable governess—why, the elder Miss McGovern had spent a mere Season as one before marrying her employer!

Jane knew that Red would have been mightily amused to hear that line of discussion.

When the trio finally departed, Jane sighed. She'd gained no new information, other than where Lady Remington preferred to buy her gowns. Jane's own mother would never sanction the expensive French modiste, but Jane would pass the information along to Miranda anyway. Perhaps Jacquetta could look into it, given her status as the new daughter-in-law of a duke.

Jane checked the small gilt clock in the retiring room before she departed. She had ten minutes before she needed to meet Hawkridge in the conservatory. She used that time to drift along the gallery, pretending to take in Lady Winston-Weatherby's collection of portraits. She caught snippets of conversation as she did, tucking bits away in her mind for later.

Lord Avery was taken ill and had returned to the country, but his young wife remained in town.

The younger Miss Christchurch was marrying hastily, without

having even reached her debut season.

The Marchioness of Clydon was the center of yet another scandal, but her husband was as besotted as always.

Jane never knew which tidbit would prove useful later, so she memorized it all. By the time she reached the conservatory, she was near bursting with information, though none of it was relevant to her current quest.

She wandered between the verdant plants bathed in moonlight, waiting for Hawkridge to appear.

She waited five minutes. Then ten.

After fifteen, her logical brain began to reason that something might be amiss, or he might be in a fruitful conversation with Lord Remington.

After twenty, her temper was attempting to strangle her logic and making a very good job of it.

Jane counted down from one hundred, promising herself that if she reached zero she would leave the conservatory and hunt down the Crown's most irritating agent.

100... 99... 98...

What sort of imbecile couldn't read a clock?

... 45... 44... 43...

Enough was enough. She would send word to Miranda tomorrow. This quest was a disaster.

... 19... 18... 17...

She was almost to the end of the row of plants. Her slippered feet were usually soundless, but now she was practically stomping. She prepared to spin, the toe of her satin slipper planted...

... 3... 2... 1...

"For the love of—"

"Have you taken leave of your senses?" Hawkridge said, catching her forearms to keep her from falling.

But it wasn't enough. She was off balance, her legs sliding under her, the delicate silk strap of her slipper snapping.

If Hawkridge hadn't been there, she'd have fallen face-first into a shrub.

If Hawkridge hadn't been there, I wouldn't have slipped at all.

She started to lean down to assess the damage to her shoe—

Except she couldn't.

Hawkridge held her firmly in place, his large hands gripping her forearms tightly against the slipperiness of her white silk gloves. But that was not the only place where they touched.

Her feet were barely beneath her, barely holding her up. Which meant that it was Hawkridge's body that supported hers. Her face was even with his cravat, his chest and throat covered by the elegant flourish. But Jane would have sworn she could feel his heart beating a wild staccato in time with her own.

Suddenly, the prim pink muslin dress she'd worn felt much too thin to be anything other than scandalous. Her breasts were pushed against his chest, right against the silk of his waistcoat. But no number of layers could disguise the taut, muscular chest beneath. Her breasts pebbled, straining against the thin layers of her chemisette and gown.

Desire rolled through her—that hateful attraction she'd stifled so successfully until Hawkridge stumbled into her life. Jane didn't even realize she had let the soft moan escape her lips until she felt the swell of him in response, his hard length pressing against his trousers and into her belly.

She ought to have jerked away. Later, she'd wonder why she hadn't, and would have to conclude that someone had spiked the ratafia with extra liquor.

But in that moment, Jane shifted her hips. Just a bit, just a hint of welcome that her body offered, though her mind would never have allowed it.

"Well, well, well, the little mouse knows more than she lets on." Hawkridge chuckled.

Though the primal, womanly part of her savored the rumble of his chest beneath her breasts, the logical part won out when he said those words.

She wrenched her hands away, stumbling backward over her shoe but managing to catch herself without assistance this time.

"I am not a mouse," she snapped, shaking her hands as if that could rid her of the remnants of his touch.

Hawkridge's eyes were darker than usual as he tilted his head thoughtfully to the side. "Maybe not," he said softly.

That sounded ominous.

Jane tore her eyes away, focusing determinedly on her shoe. She didn't care to see his expression, to look at that smug face for one second longer.

"Where have you been?" she demanded in a harsh whisper, lifting the hem of her dress to get a look at her slipper.

Surely she imagined the duke's sharp intake of breath as the curve of her calf was revealed.

"I was held up."

The slipper was ruined, at least for tonight. Until she could get it back home to her maid. Which meant her night was over as well. A night in which nothing new had been gained.

She didn't even try to keep the frustration from her voice. "Held up by what?"

"Remington."

Her gaze snapped back to Hawkridge. "Tell me."

He stared at her for a long moment. She half expected him to tell her to beg. But eventually he sighed, shrugging his shoulders.

"He's as buffoonish as Thane and the others made him sound. But if he has loose lips, he's either learned to keep them closed or they only ail him when he imbibes heavily," Hawkridge said. He sounded as defeated as Jane felt.

"Well, then." Jane sighed. "I suppose that is us done for the night."

Hawkridge frowned. "What do you mean? You dragged me to this charity soiree, and the auction has not even begun."

Jane blinked in disbelief. "My slipper."

He blinked back at her.

With an even heavier sigh, she ripped it off her foot and held it up to him so he could see the dangling strap. Egads, she hoped it didn't stink.

Thankfully, Hawkridge's nostrils did not flare, though his eyebrows rose. "I am not overly familiar with women's shoes. The strap is broken, so…"

"So it will not stay on my foot," Jane said, as if she was talking to a child. It felt like she was!

"You cannot dance, but surely you can stand around while we make idle conversation with Remington."

Jane could not believe what she was hearing. It was true, she could move slowly, a few careful steps at a time. If her sister or another of the lady knights had been in attendance, she could have borrowed a hair ribbon or something of the like and fashioned a temporary solution. But as it was, it was her mother and father who'd escorted her and Roland here.

She might be able to convince her mother that the strap had snapped innocently. After the suspicious looks her father had given when Hawkridge game to formalize his suit, she wasn't quite as sure she could convince him.

"This evening is over. I will tell my parents I'm feeling unwell, and we will depart," she said firmly.

She tried to brush past him. But, of course, her damned shoe slowed her down.

Hawkridge caught her arm. "Another half an hour. I think I can get something out of Remington."

The determination in his face gave her pause. She recognized the expression; she'd seen it on her fellow lady knights' faces. She'd worn it herself many times over the years.

With a long-suffering sigh, she inclined her head. "Half an hour, not a minute more."

THE DAMN SLIPPER was the same shape as her foot. What was the point of the strap, anyway? Maybe she couldn't dance, but she could certainly stand and sip ratafia with the other ladies while he tried to wheedle information out of Remington.

Roland offered his arm, which Jane took begrudgingly. By the time they reentered the music room, where the auction, the culmination of the charity event, was to take place, her lovesick smile was back in place.

He inclined his head toward her mother and father taking seats on the other side of the room. But he did not steer her in their direction. Instead, he moved toward the back of the room, positioning them near the doors.

More and more guests were filtering in, finding seats or drifting to where refreshments were laid out. The deep crystal bowl of ratafia was getting low. Roland took advantage of his height to scan the crowd, but Remington was nowhere in sight.

Jane hung dutifully on his arm, a contented smile on her face. She didn't attempt to move away from him, even though he could feel the tension in her arm. Whether she liked it or not, her mishap with her slipper meant she was stuck at his side.

But as the minutes passed, the truth became clear.

Remington wasn't here. Which meant he was somewhere else in the house, maybe even having an illicit conversation or conducting a deal of some sort. Roland needed to find him. The need to act, to find something useful out of this cursed night, flooded his veins.

He tugged his arm free of Jane's grasp. "I am going to go have a look—"

She tumbled backward, the motion too sharp, losing her footing in the too-loose slipper.

He tried to catch her, but this time he was too late. She careened sideways, straight into the footman holding the new punchbowl full to the brim of ratafia.

Roland felt the horror climbing his own face in the fractions of seconds as the footman's feet slid out from under him, the pink fortified punch flew into the air—and doused the Duke of Hawkridge with sickly-sweet ratafia.

He'd slammed his eyes closed instinctively. He heard other guests exclaiming over Jane, helping her to her feet.

When Roland opened his eyes, droplets of ratafia were still dripping off his brow.

"Now may we depart?" his little mouse said, the smugness in her voice sounding distinctly un-mouselike.

Roland growled.

If she was the mouse, he'd be the jungle cat.

CHAPTER EIGHT

THIS TIME, JANE did not encounter anyone she knew as she breezed through the hotel's lobby and snuck up the staircase. Her heart thumped in her chest, but it was not the wild beat that had overcome her when she found the duchess's summons.

Was it only her being called to report? That seemed unlikely. Another, more heartening thought occurred. Perhaps after the fiasco at Lady Winston-Weatherby's charity soiree, Miranda and her counterpart had finally realized what foolishness it was for Jane and Hawkridge to work together.

At this juncture, Jane was ready to give up the quest altogether. This was Hawkridge's last mission? Fine—he could have it. She was only twenty-three years old. She had a lifetime of worthy quests ahead of her.

She repeated that logic in her mind as she ascended the stairs. But her chest protested—what about the queen? Her queen needed her. Was she really so selfish that she would allow her personal feelings to hinder an important quest?

It is not my decision, Jane reminded herself as she lifted her hand to knock on the door of the duchess's suite. Miranda was the one in charge, and Jane had always preferred it that way. It gave her mind space to focus on the quest at hand.

But despite her swirling jumble of emotions, Jane was not surprised when the door swung open and she entered to find Hawkridge already seated before the Duchess of Guilford. Cartwright ushered her toward the remaining open seat.

Miranda wasted no time on pleasantries. "Report."

Hawkridge was silent. In fact, he was staring determinedly at the table rather than meeting the eyes of either of their superiors.

Coward.

Jane sat straight as a board, pursing her lips as she exhaled and began. "Lord Thane offered background on Lord Remington and his associations with some sort of fanatical secret society. We have reason to believe that he is a member."

Cartwright leaned forward over the table eagerly. "Who else?"

Miranda only raised her dark eyebrows expectantly, waiting for Jane to continue.

"Our search of Remington's study was fruitless. Whatever evidence there is, it must be kept elsewhere. We attended Lady Winston-Weatherby's charity soiree and interacted with both Lord and Lady Remington, to no avail."

It was a concise summary, factual.

"Nothing. That is what we have," Hawkridge said derisively. "This courtship scheme is getting us nowhere. Miss Jacobson and I would be best served to work separately and see what we can find through our own methods. We do not work well together."

He stared right at her, as if daring Jane to refute his claims.

She could not.

But the Duchess of Guilford was unsatisfied with silent acquiescence. "Jane, what is your assessment?"

Jane kept the deflating sigh that threatened trapped tightly in her chest.

"Despite the information we have gained, we have not made substantial progress in identifying possible conspirators," she said evenly. She hoped the duchess would not press her on the second part.

Why? her inner voice asked. It was pure fact that she and Hawkridge did not work well together. They were completely at odds. She employed a rational, measured approach. The rakish duke was all bluster and motion. She ought to be offering that opinion to Miranda unfettered.

But the words didn't quite reach Jane's lips. Her own shame and failings, she could bear. Failings were a chance to learn and improve. But the prospect of deriding Hawkridge, on his very last mission, before these esteemed colleagues... She was becoming too soft-hearted. She certainly had no issue pointing out his deficiencies to his face.

"Nothing." Cartwright shook his head, pushing away from the table and going to stand at the window.

Hawkridge's eyes followed him. "A change of tactics is in order."

"You're damned right," Cartwright said sharply, turning back to pin the duke with a fierce stare.

Jane's heart skipped a beat. This was not the Cartwright who had frequented her childhood home, sipping port with her father. This was a high-ranking member of His Majesty's secret service. In that flash, Jane could see why. The command, the menace, the intensity—they were striking.

Hawkridge must have noticed it too. He straightened in his seat, the casual, cocky demeanor he usually wore melting away.

"Ahem," Miranda coughed delicately. Neither of them stopped their staring contest, but Jane turned back to the duchess. "The footman inside Remington's household went silent two days ago. We have checked in on his family, who are well enough, but he appears to be missing."

Jane watched Hawkridge swing back to face Miranda. Cartwright didn't move.

"The last information he passed to us were copies of two letters between Remington and the Earl of Maltby. They are coded, but the references are innocuous—to both the plan to assassinate Her Majesty, and the secret society itself."

The duchess passed letters across the table to both Jane and Hawkridge. They read the decoded letters, then exchanged their papers wordlessly to read the other missive.

When both sets of eyes rose from the lines of text, Miranda spoke again.

"Whoever is leading the secret society, whether it be Maltby or someone else, has one goal—to kill Queen Charlotte. The death of the princess has led to nothing less than a crisis of succession, as you both well know. Whoever does eventually inherit the throne, it will certainly be a grandchild of our fair queen."

The words hung in the air. It was Hawkridge who worked it out first. "Princess Charlotte was close to her grandmother."

The Duchess of Guilford nodded. "It follows that another child, the future heir, would be as well."

"But the queen cannot influence the future king or queen if she is not alive," Jane finished, sadness ringing in her voice.

"Hell!" Hawkridge exclaimed, shooting out of his chair.

He stalked several paces away, raking a hand through his silver-streaked hair then rubbing it over his mouth. His low growl of frustration filled the room.

Jane blinked repeatedly, trying to understand. He had a temper to match Ethelreda's, that was certain. But this connection, to the princess, to the queen... It seemed personal. It was emotional. And emotion was dangerous; it clouded reasonable decision-making.

"What the hell are we going to do about it?" Hawkridge said, a deflated demand.

Miranda and Cartwright exchanged another glance. The latter nodded.

"The Earl of Maltby is giving a house party in the country," Miranda said.

In these trusted quarters, Jane didn't try to keep the surprise from her face. Miranda gave her a grim smile.

"Yes, it is quite early in the Season to expect anyone of substance to desert London. Which lends itself to our suspicion that this house party is nothing more than a ruse to disguise a meeting of the secret society," she explained.

Hawkridge stepped closer once more, gripping the back of his empty chair. "Those are the conspirators, then, whoever attends."

"Some, yes," Miranda agreed. "But surely others will be used as cover, to legitimize the gathering. Your charge will be to decipher who is conspiring with Maltby, and who is an unfortunate bystander to his treachery."

Jane tilted her head to the side, furrowing her brow. It did not make sense.

"My mother will never accept an invitation this early in the Season, not with my sister entertaining so many offers here in London," she said.

The duchess nodded her agreement.

"Not like it matters."

Jane and Hawkridge both swung their eyes back to the window, trying to decipher Cartwright's gruff words.

This time, it was Jane who pieced it together first. Even so, it was not a fully formed thought in her mind, but rather an accumulation in her gut—an instinct, Hawkridge would have insisted.

"Early as it is, Maltby is only inviting married couples to join him. Every other matchmaking mama is too intent on keeping her son or daughter here in London for the next month, at least," Miranda said, her voice calm, as if she were discussing something mundane—the weather, perhaps.

Not Jane's very future.

"Therefore, your courtship must end in favor of something more substantial. We have already obtained a special license on your behalf from the Archbishop of Canterbury."

So matter-of-fact. It ought to have appealed to Jane, the logic in it.

Only married couples would attend Maltby's house party. Which meant Jane and Hawkridge would have to pose as a married couple.

But for a maiden, a gently bred young woman like Jane, there would be no way to put aside the charade when Remington, Maltby, and their conspirators were caught.

She would be the Duchess of Hawkridge.

Miranda picked up a stack of papers, straightening them and then returning them to the table. She was nervous, Jane realized. She'd never seen the Duchess of Guilford with so much as a hair out of place, let alone a nervous compulsion.

That was the enormity of what was being asked of them. Her and Hawkridge.

For the first time, Jane remembered that she was not the only one being asked to enter into this inescapable arrangement.

She turned to Hawkridge, who was still bent over the chair, gripping the back hard enough that the knuckles on his large, powerful hands were snow white.

"Say it." His voice was harder than she'd ever heard it, his intense, dark gaze fixed on Miranda. But it was not she who responded.

"Marry the girl, Hawk," Cartwright said plainly.

"You must both consent," Miranda followed up quickly. "This is a very serious request. You have both risked your life time and again for England, so I know you will pay the ultimate price. But I will not pretend this is the same. Unfortunately, we do not have the benefit of time—"

"I will do it," Jane said, interrupting the Duchess of Guilford for the first time in her tenure as a lady knight.

It was what was required to complete the quest. She would do it, and be proud.

Hawkridge jerked his chin in her direction, and his dark gaze pinned her to the spot. Slowly, his eyes traveled down her face, to the tip of her toes just poking out from beneath the hem of her dress, then back up again.

Adept as she was, Jane could not read what was behind that expression. It certainly wasn't excitement. But nor was it acceptance.

"So?" Cartwright barked, his rough voice cutting through the tension.

The duke's eyes stayed on her. He stared straight into her brown eyes, searching them thoroughly. Jane wished she knew what he was looking for, so she could attempt to offer it to him.

Anything for the safety of the queen, a voice squeaked within her mind.

Hawkridge laughed acerbically, as if he'd heard it. Then he pushed the chair away with enough force that it toppled over. Before it came to rest on the floor, the door had already slammed shut behind him.

CHAPTER NINE

S *SSCRRAAPPPPE.*

The sound of the heavy wooden chair legs scraping across the threadbare carpet was dreadful. The only occupant in the room, the ancient Lord Pemberley Worcester, had lost his hearing decades ago. Even back when Roland's father was alive, Worcester had been an old man. Now, he was a rotund antique topped with a fluff of snow-white hair. Most importantly, he was snoring loudly.

Roland had found the quietest, most disused, shabbiest corner of White's. This room at the back of the building was one of the last remaining to be renovated. The window he'd pulled his chair up to face? It looked out on the mews and rubbish bins.

Perfect. It suited his mood.

He threw his long body down into the chair, propped his feet up on the windowsill, and pulled the flask from his breast pocket. He couldn't rely on a footman to find him in this corner; best to bring one's own libations.

He had another flask in his hip pocket.

Hopefully by the time someone young stag bucked up the courage to say something to him—on a dare from his mates—Roland would be thoroughly foxed.

It was the only suitable response to what the Duchess of Guilford had proposed that afternoon.

I will do it.

Not the only possible response, though.

His little mouse had agreed to trade her life away without so much as a quiver of her lovely, plush lips. What did that say about her? Or worse… what did it say about him?

Jane Jacobson, Lady Knight, all of twenty-three years old, was willing to leg-shackle herself to him for the rest of her life in the service of her queen and country. Meanwhile, he had every logical reason to want a wife. After twenty years of service, he was about to retire to his estate and actually play at being a duke. Marrying a respectable woman and producing heirs ought to have been high on his list of priorities.

But the thought of an arranged façade of a marriage to Jane made Roland nauseated.

He staved off the feeling by taking another gulp of whisky.

"I am shocked they still honor your membership, seeing as you haven't stepped through the door for at least a decade."

Roland slowly lowered the flask away from his lips, replacing the stopper. "Nonsense. I pay my dues on time. I donated to the restoration efforts. And since I returned to London proper, I've been here almost nightly."

Cartwright was much less noisy as he moved a chair next to Roland.

"Of course I don't mind if you join me," Roland muttered.

"You've turned into a grumpy old geezer, haven't you, Hawk?" Cartwright rasped a cough as he withdrew his meerschaum pipe and lit the tobacco.

"You're the one putting me out to pasture," Roland said.

"I'd like to put you there with a nice filly to keep you company."

Roland's gut clenched. "If this is some sort of harebrained scheme to saddle me with a wife to try to get me to go willingly—"

Cartwright blew a thick cloud of smoke in his face. "It's not that, and you damned well know it," he said. "What is your objection? Do you not find the young lady attractive?"

Another swig of whisky. "I never said that."

"Then what?"

"It's asking an awful damn lot, even for you, Cartwright."

The other man lowered his pipe, letting it dangle from his fingers loosely as he propped an elbow on the edge of his chair. The set of his eyes, above that bushy salt-and-pepper mustache, was serious.

"For once, Hawkridge, your duty to the Crown and your duty to your dukedom are aligned. I think that is an awfully convenient circumstance," Cartwright said. "A rational man would jump at the opportunity."

Roland uncrossed his feet, leaning forward to peer out the window at the rubbish and equine excrement. "And when have I ever been a rational man?"

His superior huffed out rings of laughter-tinged smoke. "Very rarely, I'll admit."

They lapsed into silence—Roland sipping from his flask, Cartwright puffing away. The melodic baritone snores of Lord Pemberley Worcester were the only sound.

Roland did not object to marriage in principle. He'd simply never considered it an option. He was an agent of the Crown, always abroad, always doing something dangerous. He'd bedded enough women across the Continent and beyond to fill an assembly room. But none of them had ever been more than a passing interest.

Miss Jane Jacobson… She was not what he would have imagined as his duchess.

But once he imagined it, it was difficult to stop.

It may have been the whisky, or perhaps the tobacco permeating his senses, or even the melodic cadence of snores that lulled him into the waking dream.

Jane laid out on his bed, the rich brown of her hair fanning out and blending with the maroon coverlet. He'd drag his fingertips along the back of her knee, down her delicately curved calf. Then he'd replace his fingers with his tongue. She'd moan for him, high-pitched and sweet. When he lowered himself above her, his entire body would swallow hers up, claiming her as his own...

Roland jolted upward, upsetting the flask and sending it tumbling into his lap. There were only a few droplets left to stain his breeches.

He refused to acknowledge Cartwright's rumbling laugh as he straightened, looking around the room self-consciously. His cock was hard, the vestiges of his daydream still pounding through his veins.

Hell. He was going to marry the chit.

Roland tossed the empty flask aside and dragged the other free, already cursing himself for only having the two. He tossed back the contents of the smaller flask in three gulps, savoring the way his head began to pound and swim.

Then he collapsed back in the chair and waited for oblivion to take him.

Lord Pemberley Worcester was still fast asleep.

CHAPTER TEN

"**P**ULL!"

She aimed the first smoothbore flintlock shotgun and fired.

In the next breath, she swiped up the American-made rifle and fired again.

She dropped that one as well, deftly grabbing the pistols from her waist and firing one after another.

All four clay plates lay in shattered shards on the grass.

Dominique peeked up from behind the enclosure of wooden boards surrounding thickly packed hay. "May I come out now?"

"No, again," Jane said without even looking up. The pistols were already reloaded and back in their holsters. She reached for the rifle next.

"I think ten rounds is enough for one day. You haven't missed a single plate," Jacquetta observed drily from where she stood, arms crossed, five yards behind Jane.

"Keep talking, and you'll be throwing the plates next," Jane threatened.

The next round was nearly identical, except that Dominique's tosses were getting progressively weaker. Soon enough, Jane would be shooting at squirrels on the ground.

"She is done!" Jacquetta called across the field without waiting for

Jane's direction or permission.

Dominique's relief was audible, even all those yards away.

"Come, let's have some tea," Jacquetta said. She was busy adjusting her scarf, but when she looked down, she found Jane had dropped down into the grass instead. "What are you doing?"

"I need to clean them properly," Jane said. The brass clasp of her cleaning kit was already open.

"Why is she sitting in the wet grass?" Dominique huffed, hands on her hips, her breath swirling around her in the cold spring air.

"It is not wet, it is damp," Jane corrected her, dipping the cloth in a bit of oil.

"She insists upon cleaning her guns, and that this is the place to do it," Jacquetta quipped.

Jane was certain her friends were exchanging glances over her head. The tenor of their voices was informative enough. But she kept on cleaning.

"I will not risk damaging Miranda's Aubussons," she said.

The Guilford estate, an hour's ride outside of London, was the closest thing to a clubhouse the Lady Knights had. There was a round table here too, though grander than the one tucked into a dressing room at Miranda's London mansion. It was also the only reasonable place for Jane to practice her shooting.

After the events of the last few days, she desperately needed to shoot something—or someone.

She also needed to be outside, in the fresh air, where she had some space for her thoughts. Another cloying drawing room and she would lose her mind. Even if that meant her derriere was a bit damp.

"If you two plan to dump your married-lady platitudes upon me, you'd best make yourself comfortable," she said, caressing the long barrel of her rifle.

When Jacquetta and Dominique had arrived at the estate within an hour of her, she knew that Miranda must have someone watching her parents' house. Jane glanced toward the sky—her colleagues were still exchanging leaden looks—and marked the time. She had another hour before she'd need to start back for London. Her parents thought she was with Jacquetta. That, at least, was the truth. Even if they were shooting rifles and pistols rather than taking tea in Windsor.

Finally, the two other women dropped down to the grass as well. Dominique carefully arranged her cloak to protect her dress as much as possible. Jacquetta's thick velvet pelisse was not fit for sitting on the ground, but she looked more worried about the ominous clouds overhead than concerned for her expensive garments.

"Dominique, which one of us should begin with the married-lady platitudes?" Jacquetta sniped, her voice laced with annoyance.

Feigned annoyance. What lurked beneath it was pity, and Jane wanted none of that.

"Jane," Dominique said gently. "You do not have to do this if you don't want to."

"Pfft!" Jacquetta teetered sideways with the force of her own exclamation. "She most certainly does! Have you met Jane Jacobson? This is precisely the sort of thing she is telling herself she *must* do."

Dominique drew in a slow breath, fortifying her defenses before countering the more hot-tempered Jacquetta.

"Our charge here is to help her weigh her options, not presume she has already made one," Dominique said, her voice deceptively flat.

Jane shook her head, rolling her eyes for no audience but herself. "As much as I'd enjoy seeing which one of you goes for blood first, there is no need. I have made my decision, I understand the gravity of it perfectly well, and I am fine."

"Except that you've shot forty plates in two hours," Dominique pointed out. She had, after all, been the one tossing them.

"It has been too long since I practiced." Jane set aside the lovely American-made rifle, a special requisition by the duchess. She moved on to the shotgun. Not her favorite weapon, but useful at times.

"This quest to save Queen Charlotte is of the utmost importance. We are talking about the stability and future of England. No price is too great, we all know that. We knew it when we joined the Lady Knights. If I am willing to risk my life in Her Majesty's service, then sacrificing my hand in marriage is nothing."

"Sacrificing your maidenhead as well," Jacquetta added.

"I have no maidenhead to sacrifice," Jane said. This was the tricky bit. She'd known this conversation would emerge eventually. Short of dodging her friends' presence entirely, it was unavoidable. Especially after they'd each made such satisfying love matches.

"Pardon?"

"—come again?"

Jane cleared her throat, keeping her eyes trained on the methodical motions of cleaning and polishing the engraved handles of her dueling pistols. "When I was sixteen, before my debut, I spent a summer with my cousin Franny in Cornwall. I met a young man there, and we engaged in a short-lived amorous affair. It ended poorly."

"It ended poorly," Jacquetta repeated. "That is all you have to say?"

Jane's gaze snapped up. "What else would you like, Jacquetta? Should I detail how many tears I shed? Or perhaps a recounting of how I felt when the banns were read for his engagement to another woman?"

Damn, damn, damn. If there had been pity in Dominique's eyes before, now it was in Jacquetta's turquoise ones as well.

"It was a long time ago," Jane said.

Surprisingly, there was no great wave of emotion. The wound was there, sure enough. But it had scabbed over—in the last few years especially. Her work with the Lady Knights was infinitely more meaningful and important than an adolescent tryst gone wrong. Marrying the Duke of Hawkridge was a natural extension of that. Her role as a lady knight was the most important thing about her, and marriage to Hawkridge would not change that—it would only aid it.

"Besides, as the Duchess of Hawkridge, I will have access to even more rings of Society than ever before," Jane said.

"You won't be able to hide against the wall," Dominique pointed out, her dark eyes considering her friend closely. The pity seemed to have faded from them, thankfully.

Jane nodded. "I have considered as much. I will always be a quiet, reserved person, even as a duchess. I may not be able to hide, but I will still be able to listen. It should prove interesting to hear what the ladies of the *ton* will say when they are trying to curry the favor of the Duchess of Hawkridge."

When Jane glanced up from her pistols, Dominique's dark, thoughtful gaze hadn't budged. Jacquetta was busy worrying her lower lip but, for once, was silent.

"What about…" Dominique caught her breath, as if she could not quite believe what she was about to say. "What about love?"

Jane laughed at that. "I have no illusions about love. If I am going to marry, then to do so in service to my queen is the best possible proposition."

Dominique's nose wrinkled, but she didn't retort right away. Jacquetta, meanwhile, nearly combusted with the thought she could no longer hold in.

"What does Hawkridge have to say about all of this?" she asked.

Jane's stomach clenched. Then released.

Then her chest fluttered.

Egads! Being attracted to Hawkridge before had been inconvenient. Now that she was to become his wife, it was damn foolishness.

"He will accommodate himself to the notion, I am certain," Jane said—and she was.

Hawkridge might have stormed out. He might have hated the idea. In fact, that much was clear—he did not want to marry her, was appalled at the very notion. But that was fine. Because if there was one thing that Jane was certain of after her brief, fake courtship with the Duke of Hawkridge, it was this—he was loyal. To his queen, to England—which meant there was only one choice he could in good conscience make.

As she tucked her rags and implements back inside her cleaning kit, Jane took several deep breaths to try to settle the fluttering in her stomach and chest.

One could only hope he would be as loyal to his wife.

CHAPTER ELEVEN

Lady Tiara's Tidbits
The toast of London teatimes

Esteemed readers! You thought this Season was off to a slow start...
You could not be more wrong! Not even Ascot's most astute gamblers
had money on this filly.

The recently returned Duke of Hawkridge—a contemporary of
my mother's, if I recall—has been snagged from the Marriage Mart.
Care to guess who will be holding court as the next Duchess of
Hawkridge? None other than the fair Miss Jacobson.

No, no, dear readers. Not that Miss Jacobson. Though one can be
forgiven for forgetting the elder Miss Jane Jacobson, who until recently
was more likely seen hugging walls than dancing at balls.

Just what magic did this plain Jane work upon the wayward
duke? Rumors have abounded about why the elusive duke has so long
neglected his title. Was he simply waiting for true love?

More than one source reports these two were looking very cozy
riding in His Grace's phaeton through Mayfair. While few of us can
forget the adoration upon the duke's handsome face at Lady Winston-
Weatherby's charity soiree. Perhaps the Season has begun with a love
match.

It should be no surprise, then, that our besotted couple have al-
ready absconded from London. Though why they have chosen to visit
the Earl of Maltby, rather than the duke's ancestral home, remains a
mystery. Perhaps there is more to this unlikely union than meets the
eye...

You do know how I love a good twist.

Roland married Jane on the first of April, in the year eighteen hundred and eighteen, before precisely twelve witnesses at St. George's in Mayfair. The bride wore a pale rose-pink gown that complemented her classical English coloring. Her spectacles were nowhere in sight.

The vows rolled off his tongue with ease, considering how much whisky he'd drunk to come to the decision to marry Jane at all. She was even more composed. Her eyes shone with adoration so perfect, he wondered if she'd been practicing it in front of a mirror.

But had she also contrived some way to make her pulse leap like that when he gently held her wrist between his thumb and forefinger to slide on the ring? Jane was meticulous, but even that seemed excessive when the only one who would feel it was him.

Slowly, his gaze traveled up from her hand, along her exposed pale forearm. No gloves today. He could see the delicate hairs rising as her skin pebbled. It was cool in the church, so early on a dreary April morning. That was why her fingertips trembled.

Her hand dropped away.

The service continued. As did Roland's gaze. Up over the puffed, translucent taffeta sleeves, then to the fine silk bodice of her gown. Tiny roses were embroidered in gold and white across her breasts, though a fine linen fichu hid the delicate curves from his eyes.

The linen was what gave her away. It, too, trembled—the only tell, visible to his eyes alone, that the sunny, lovestruck demeanor was not real.

She was vulnerable.

He'd never thought of her as anything other than annoying or competent.

Or beautiful.

This other side of her was lovely as well.

His gaze snagged on her lips, thinner than was fashionable, but the perfect, dusty rose pink. Roland wondered who had selected her gown, if they'd done it intentionally to match those irresistible pink lips.

When he reached her brown eyes, he got one second, one breath—less—to see her true feelings. Her vulnerability.

Then she fixed her mask back into place, blinking as if she was trying to hold back tears of joy, biting her lower lip as if overwhelmed with love.

Roland ignored the tightening in his gut.

None of this was for him, he reminded himself.

For the dukedom. For Queen Charlotte. For England.

But when the priest made his final pronouncement, and Roland lowered his lips to Jane's... he was selfish enough to realize that moment was all his.

Her lips were as soft as he'd imagined, and twice as sweet. She might be wearing rose, but she tasted of honeysuckle and tea. He'd happily drink her nectar for the rest of his life.

Hell, what am I thinking?

I'm not.

He was tasting, licking, sampling. A chaste kiss in a goddamned church, before her parents, siblings, and a few friends. But it spun his world on its axis.

The slight tremble of her lower lip against his tongue was exquisite. Roland wanted to make her tremble with desire, not just nerves. He wanted to slide his tongue past those sweet lips and taste the corners of her mouth, swirl his tongue around hers, see how intoxicating and heady her taste was the deeper he went.

He wanted it all. He wanted her—not just as his wife in name, but as a lover in his bed.

But they were standing in a church. Married for the sake of their service to the Crown, not affection or desire.

And when the priest spoke again and they turned to greet their guests as the Duke and Duchess of Hawkridge, Roland found himself more profoundly shaken than ever before.

CHAPTER TWELVE

S HE WOULD ALWAYS remember that kiss.

The look in Hawkridge's dark eyes when he realized that she was nervous. None of the sharp teasing or cocky humor, just... empathy.

Jane knew he did not want to marry her, that he detested the entire notion. What she did not expect was that he might feel as nervous as she.

But the kiss...

That kiss.

It had completely unraveled her.

Sixteen-year-old Jane Jacobson had sworn she'd never be taken in by another young man. She wondered if the Duke of Hawkridge had ever been described as a young man. He exuded such strength, such powerful command of himself and any situation. Pure, masculine magnetism seemed to ooze from his pores. Despite herself, the long-dead part of her that had wanted, desired, *lusted*, was now fully alive and making irritatingly persistent demands.

She didn't have time for this folly.

This marriage was a means to an end. That end was the Queen of England's life. She could not possibly allow something as trivial as attraction to distract her.

Be practical.

Focus on facts.

She was now wed to the Duke of Hawkridge. She'd kissed her mother and father goodbye. In a moment, Hawkridge would join her in the carriage and they would return to his London house. Very soon, they would depart for the country for the Earl of Maltby's house party.

None of those facts required her to take him to bed.

In fact, she'd specifically requested a separate bedchamber—to which Hawkridge had told her the townhouse and Hawkridge country estate were already set up to accommodate as much.

Hawkridge will expect heirs eventually.

The last of her trunks landed on the back of the carriage. She heard the straps being affixed. The deep rumble of Hawkridge's voice. Then he swung himself into the carriage and landed on the seat beside her.

Later, her inner voice squeaked. Later, after the queen was safe, they could discuss heirs. Today, she needed to keep her mask in place long enough to get behind a closed door.

Then Hawkridge pulled her into his lap.

"What the—"

His long, masculine forefinger pressed against her lips.

Ridiculous. A finger was a finger. It could not be *masculine.*

"Hush, little mouse—our act is not concluded yet," he crooned, easing his hand away from her mouth only to settle it on her hip. To hold her in place, Jane realized.

"We are alone in the carriage," she whispered back fiercely, trying to wiggle herself loose.

A mistake. That only ground her legs and bottom against his...

"We need to keep up the ruse until we are safe behind the doors of our private quarters. We are a love match, remember?" As he spoke, his eyes drifted down to where one of the few loose curls grazed her collarbone. His hand followed, fingers skimming her flesh and sending a delectable shiver—

"Stop it!" she whisper-cried, swatting his hand away. "No one can see us inside the carriage. There is no need for me to be in your lap."

"Ah, but what about when that door swings open? Do we want the footman to see a blushing, disheveled bride clearly taking advantage of a few minutes alone with her husband? Or would you rather he run off and whisper to the other servants about your scowl?"

"I am quite certain that proper young ladies do not... *canoodle*... with their new husbands before even making it to the bedchamber," Jane countered.

She gave up trying to free herself. The pressure of his powerful hands bracketing her hips made it impossible. She also ignored how possessive those hands felt, and how her blood thrummed in response.

"You clearly know less about besotted brides than you do about spy craft." He laughed, and the rumble of his body against hers did deliciously dangerous things to her composure.

Jane forced her hands into her lap, balling the fists tightly together. She'd sit here, but she wouldn't touch him any more than was necessary.

But Hawkridge leaned forward until she could feel the heat of his breath in the shell of her ear.

"No bride of mine would be primly sitting by or scowling on our wedding day. And you can be assured that my servants, and all of London, know it," he purred.

Then he nipped her ear.

"Hawkridge! Have you taken leave of your senses?"

He laughed again, deep and melodious. So easily, that laugh came to him. Jane could even learn to enjoy it, if she wasn't so damn angry at him.

"Roland," he said. "Married couples do not call one another by their titles."

Of course, that laugh had only succeeded in seating her more firmly against him. And now she could feel his rising need. She refused to acknowledge her own. Instead, she turned to her good friends—facts and rationality.

"That is patently untrue. I've heard plenty of women address their husbands as such."

"Not us, little mouse."

If he didn't want her scowling, he'd do well to leave off with his infuriating nickname. But then a thought occurred to her. "If I agree to call you Roland, you must promise to never call me that again. Jane. That is my name."

He looked thoroughly put out by that demand. But he did, eventually, acquiesce. A fractional inclination of his stubborn chin, but enough to satisfy her. For now.

She opened her mouth to bring up the next matter—she had a list of items she wanted to discuss and get in order before they departed for the house party. Talking about their quest would keep her mind off her traitorous body.

But as her mouth opened, so did the door of the carriage.

They'd arrived.

And the blush on her face when the footman found her sitting snugly in Roland's lap was entirely unfeigned.

※

ROLAND GRINNED WOLFISHLY as his bride slid out of his lap. "Good day, Jackman."

The footman blinked, flushing nearly as brightly as Jane.

Roland deposited his petite, comically speechless wife on the seat beside him and climbed out. She followed, taking his proffered hand. He was ready when she tried to jerk it back, placing it in the crook of his arm instead and leaning down to press a kiss to the top of her head.

"Defenses up, wife," he murmured into her silken curls.

He spared her the embarrassment of sweeping her into his arms on the street. If he really were in love with her, he'd have been cognizant of his new wife's feelings and introverted tendencies.

The doors swung open as their feet touched the first stair.

Roland groaned. Every single member of his staff was lined up in the sweeping entry hall to welcome him and his new wife. Jane would persevere, he knew. But the lines were beginning to show at the corners of her eyes and mouth. Not of mirth, but fatigue.

They stepped over the threshold, out of view of any interested eyes watching from the street. Roland did not think; he acted. As always.

He slid his arm around Jane's waist, gently sliding his fingers into the crevasse between her arm and side. In one perfectly synchronized movement, he caught her behind the knees with his other arm and swung Jane up into his arms.

Her first reaction was to smack him in the chest.

Roland coughed hard as the sharp pressure forced the air from his lungs.

Jane, at least, looked horrified when she realized what she'd done. It was a small consolation as he wheezed, trying to compose himself while also not dropping her on her arse on the parquet floor in front of his entire household. Theirs, now.

"Your Grace, are you well?" his butler, Erickson, asked. Concern warped the man's lined face. "Fetch His Grace some tea!"

A maid near the end of the receiving line jumped to attention. Roland waved them off, still coughing.

"Not... necessary," he sputtered. Jane was staring up at him, something like remorse upon her face. One delicate hand reached up, ever so slowly, as if she would cup his chin. As if she truly did care if he was well. Her fingertips quivered, then dropped back into her lap.

"The duchess and I will retire," Roland managed to say, coughs gone but throat still scratchy. So much for a powerful, impassioned declaration like he'd planned.

Several of the maids blushed. A footman snickered. That was something, at least.

The housekeeper stepped forward, her staid face unmoved. "Shall we send up some luncheon, Your Grace?"

"No. Do not disturb us unless called. We mean to start our honeymoon. Immediately." Roland caught the widening of Jane's eyes a second before she burrowed her face against his chest. Whatever reaction she was having to his words, she'd decided the best course of action was to hide it.

That, perhaps more than anything, spurred Roland's feet around Erickson and up the curved staircase. He was halfway to the first floor when he remembered.

Pausing, he let out a long, sharp whistle that echoed through the townhouse.

Jane jumped in his arms, snapping her head up as she looked around wildly, before those enticing brown eyes landed upon him in accusation.

"Sorry," he muttered.

But a heartbeat later, his summons was rewarded.

Several of the maids ducked and cried out, even though the sharp talons were nowhere near their heads or hair. Roland did not so much as twitch as those same talons landed upon his shoulder, their points digging into the fabric of his tailcoat. They were made with an extra layer of padding just for this purpose.

Jane did not squeak. No, his little mouse knew better than to out herself to a bird of prey.

But her eyes widened and her nostrils flared as she took in the inch-long talons and the razor-sharp beak.

"What is that?" she said.

Roland continued up the stairs.

"Hawkridge—"

"Roland," he corrected her, turning down the first hallway. "Surely you've seen a peregrine before," he said, a laugh tugging at the corner of his lips.

Her brow furrowed, and those very kissable lips turned pert. "Outside. Where they belong."

"Careful, Jane," Roland tutted. "Guinevere has been my lady much longer than you."

He kicked open the door to his chambers. Their chambers, now.

Growing up, his mother had held court in this sitting room while his father tended to retreat to his study downstairs. Roland hadn't been back in London long enough himself to have any attachment to it. It was just another room, in the house that he'd been avoiding for the last decade.

He kicked the door closed behind him, and Jane immediately slid from his arms. Then she was several feet away, back behind a sofa, until there were three full yards separating them.

Escaping him or the falcon, he wasn't sure.

Guinevere could handle the disappointment. Judging by the desire burning in his gut—and his cock—Roland wasn't sure that he could either. He rolled his shoulders, trying to ease the tension.

The falcon seemed annoyed by the nervous movement. She ruffled her feathers up, tilting her elegant head to the side, then abandoned him in favor of the perch in the corner of the room.

Jane's metaphorical feathers were ruffled as well. And just like Guinevere, she was already plotting her escape.

"Which rooms are mine?" she asked, glancing between the two doors leading off the sitting room where they stood.

"Those," Roland said, nodding over her shoulder. "Your bedroom is through there, as well as a dressing room. Mine are that way. The sitting room is shared."

Jane edged backward, closer to her door. "We will not be disturbed?"

"My staff know how to follow orders."

Her fingers curled around the handle. "Good. I shall retire for the night."

"It is barely midday." Roland nodded to the low table and comfortable, plush chairs. "Take luncheon with me."

Not a question. If it was a question, he could be denied. A statement… Well, she could argue, but he wasn't asking her for anything that she could then withhold.

Her brown curls bounced as she shook her head. "No."

Roland sighed. Fooling his staff would be more difficult than he'd anticipated. "I can have a tray brought to your room—"

"I am not hungry," Jane said sharply.

Roland only stared.

"I ate a big breakfast."

He doubted that. Nervous people did not eat big breakfasts.

"Good day," Jane said, opening the door, "Roland."

His name on her sharp little tongue went straight to his gut, lower, to the burning desire in his loins.

Then she closed her door in his face.

HAWKRIDGE.

Roland.

Her husband.

And a falcon.

When had her life turned into the punch line of some schoolyard jest?

A loud, grumbling sound emanated from her midsection.

Even her stomach was mocking her.

She couldn't call for a bath. She couldn't call for food. The staff was under the impression that she and Hawkridge were ensconced in their room, consummating their marriage on every available surface.

Jane undressed herself. Her mother had had her trousseau delivered directly to Roland's home. Thanks to her mother's foresight and

Roland's industrious staff, the armoire held an assortment of clothing. She removed her gown and undergarments, choosing a simple pale peach nightgown.

Simple as it was, it was the finest sleeping garment Jane had ever possessed. Her mother had not missed the implications of Jane's new situation. She was a duchess now, and she ought to be dressed like one.

The delicate silk-wrapped buttons started between her breasts. Jane found herself counting as she slipped them through their loops.

She'd reached twenty-five when she ran out of buttons.

The buttons stopped just above her navel. What a strange oversight. This garment must have been relegated to the modiste's assistant, who had neglected to finish or been distracted. Jane sighed. It was no matter. No one would see her in it—

Oh.

Oh.

It was not a mistake.

Jane took three quick steps so that she was standing before the tall mirror on the dressing table. The peachy silk was nearly sheer, skimming over her curves with tailored artistry. Her peaked nipples were clearly visible. The apex of her legs... She shifted to the side, watching as the artfully draped fabric parted to reveal the tangle of dark curls.

Not a nightgown meant for sleeping. No, this was meant for something else entirely. A wife, on her wedding night and many nights beyond. A beloved wife, in a happy, blessed love match.

A woman who did not exist.

But Jane could not tear herself away from the vision in the mirror.

Seemingly under some power other than her own, her hand drifted downward. Over the buttons, counting them again. Still twenty-five. Then to where the silk parted to show glimpses of her legs.

She watched in the mirror, eyes tracking her own fingers as they slipped between the soft drapes and skimmed over the thick curls. Then she wasn't seeing her own fingers at all. The elegant hand in her mind was much larger, the fingers stronger and more experienced.

A whimper slipped from her lips as she grazed her fingertips over the bundle of nerves hidden in curls at the top of her slit.

Will you squeak for me, little mouse?

One delicate finger slipped inside. It wasn't enough. No, no, she needed more. She needed those long, powerful hands.

Another finger.

Her eyes were fixed on the mirror, watching her body respond. But her mind was filled with images and memories. She could feel the strength of his hand covering hers in the phaeton, imagined it was curling around her fingers as she stroked herself toward climax. The heat of his mouth as he'd kissed her in St. George's was spearing through her still, driving the burning between her legs.

She wanted her husband like she'd never wanted a man. But only here, alone in her bedroom, in a hunger-induced haze of lust, would she ever come close to admitting it, and only barely to herself.

But as pleasure crashed over her, waves of satisfaction turning her legs to water, only one word slipped from Jane's lips.

"Roland."

CHAPTER THIRTEEN

T HEY WERE HALFWAY to the Earl of Maltby's Hertfordshire estate when disaster struck.

It was not the fact that when the carriage careened abruptly sideways, Jane's slight body was flung forward into Roland's lap. Nor was it the heat that flooded her body or the surge of wetness between her legs. Jane could manage all of that. For the last two nights, the full duration of her marriage thus far, she'd managed for herself each night. If she imagined Roland's hands and mouth upon her while she brought herself to climax...

Well, she did so for the purpose of allowing herself to focus on the quest at hand rather than her body's infuriating response to her new husband. Attraction was simply another normal bodily function, Jane told herself. It was the same as eating or stretching—a compulsion that could be taken care of manually.

The real disaster occurred after she'd settled herself back on her seat and Roland climbed out to see what was amiss.

The door of the carriage swung open, revealing her husband. His gray hair sparkled silver where it was studded with the sprinkling mist that hung persistently over the English countryside. His eyes, those soft sea-blue eyes that could turn sharp or laughing in an instant, just looked tired.

That was not a good sign.

"What is it?" Jane asked, straightening her spine to meet whatever verbal blow he was about to deliver.

"Would you prefer the good news or the bad first?" Roland said, cocking one brow over his handsome, angular face.

"The bad," she said without hesitation.

"The axle on the right rear wheel is broken," he said, his face unmoving.

Jane wrinkled her nose, turning to look out the opposite window—the one not blocked by her husband's impossibly wide chest.

They were in the middle of nowhere. The middle of Hertfordshire, to be more accurate. This delay would cost them valuable time. They were already arriving to the Earl of Maltby's party a day late. It had taken them that long to arrange the wedding and the subsequent invitation to join Maltby.

The mist that had coated the glass panes of the carriage windows in fine droplets all morning was not letting up. Jane hoped that Roland's "good news" was something more than the fact that the weather had remained a sprinkle rather than a downpour. At least she'd had the foresight to coat her spectacles in the special soap concoction she'd devised to prevent them from fogging up.

"And the good?" she asked, sighing already with resignation.

"I have unusually fine taste in carriage horses."

Jane's eyes snapped to him. "And you happen to have a saddle, as well?"

Amusement entered those mesmerizing eyes of his—their center flicked a silvery blue that mimicked the shining of his hair in the rain. "You've never ridden without one?"

Jane scoffed. "I am a proper young lady. Of course not."

Roland's grin only widened. "I will make sure you do not fall off."

The resignation morphed into horror.

"You cannot be suggesting—"

"We must make haste. We've wasted enough time getting to

Maltby already. If we ride double, we'll make it before suppertime. Even by country hours." Roland glanced over his shoulder as he spoke.

Jane couldn't see past him, but she guessed that the footman or driver was already at work readying the horse for them.

She bit her lip hard. He was right. She knew he was right. But the idea of being pressed up against Roland for the duration of the ride—the next several hours, to be precise—was utterly horrifying.

No escape from his strong muscles, nor his spiced spirit scent…

"Have you something sturdier in those trunks?" Roland said, already taking her acceptance as a given and turning his attention to her attire.

Jane pressed her eyes closed, forcing herself to count slowly back from twenty. Inhale on the even number, exhale on the odd. It was one of a dozen breathing exercises she'd developed and taught to her fellow lady knights, for managing one's emotions in intolerable situations such as this.

Being a lady knight meant maintaining her composure under even the most intolerable circumstances, Jane reminded herself. *I am a lady knight.*

"Fine," she said, climbing out of the carriage and into the mist.

THEY'D EXTRACTED A thick, silk-lined cloak with a hood for Jane. Roland already had his greatcoat and topper, which would have to be sufficient. Within a quarter of an hour, he swung his leg up and settled himself behind his wife on the sturdy bay gelding.

The horse shifted under his weight, but Roland held firmly to the reins as he adjusted his seat. Jane was so slight that her addition hardly made any difference. They wouldn't be able to gallop all the way to Maltby's estate without tiring the horse, but a steady clip through the rain would see them there before nightfall.

Every one of those hours was going to be pure torture.

Roland had spent the last two nights with his cock in his hand, imagining Jane in that rose-colored gown she'd worn on their wedding day. More precisely, he'd imagined peeling it off her layer by layer. He knew her trousseau had been delivered to his house. Were there any wonders awaiting in the polished armoire that stood in the corner of the duchess's bedchamber?

Based on the loneliness of the past two nights, Roland wondered if he was fated never to know.

They'd kept their interactions with the servants to a minimum, keeping mostly to their respective rooms. Hopefully, all that his staff saw were two newlyweds, more interested in spending time behind closed doors than out in Society.

The fact that they'd barely exchanged a sentence... Well, hopefully no one had noticed that, either.

All of that must change once they arrived at Maltby's estate. It was a kindness to them both, really, that they hadn't had to playact the last few days. Once they dismounted from this horse, they would both have to give the performances of their lives.

Roland let the horse walk for the first quarter mile, letting all of them settle in. But at that pace, they'd never reach their goal. With a silent apology to Jane—and to his own manhood—he urged the gelding into a trot.

Even with a smooth-gaited horse, there was no helping the rocking. Jane's hips slid back against his own, and her bottom pressed firmly against his crotch. As the horse lengthened his stride, she slid forward an inch, then back again.

Roland's cock was already dragging its head up from a bedraggled slumber. By the third time Jane's perfectly round little arse pressed against him, he was hard and ready.

Fuck.

This was going to go on for *hours*.

Roland had always known he would die in service to the Crown. But he hadn't imagined it would happen quite like this.

"Tell me about Princess Charlotte." Jane's voice cut through the sound of hooves, sharp as a knife. It wasn't a request—it was a demand.

She couldn't help but feel his desire, Roland knew. *Fuck, fuck, fuck.*

He swallowed hard. "I beg your pardon?"

"To pass the time. Tell me about your quest—mission—with Princess Charlotte."

Her voice sounded as strangled as his own. She was just uncomfortable riding without a saddle. At least the billowing cloak covered her legs. And she hadn't balked at the notion of riding astride. She really was something, his little mouse.

Roland could admit that he'd underestimated her.

Young and less experienced them himself, yes. But no one could doubt Jane's commitment to her position as a lady knight. She'd married him, for God's sake.

For the sake of queen and country.

Which meant, naturally, that the tight timbre of her voice was entirely due to the discomfort of her current position rather than any physical attraction engendered by their closeness.

"I asked the duchess for a dossier about you," she said, facing forward. Roland couldn't see her face, not with the hood of her cloak up. "Before we wed," she added.

"I see," Roland said slowly.

"I never met the princess," Jane continued. "I thought, given the circumstances of our quest, that you might have interesting insight to share regarding the princess and her relationship with the queen."

Roland sighed, a slow, measured attempt to control the quiver in his chest. "I've never had any dealings with the queen directly," he said.

Jane shifted slightly, rubbing her shoulder against his bicep. Even that small motion, even while they discussed the young woman who'd torn his heart to bits, was enough to set desire fanning through his limbs and down to his loins.

"And the princess?" she asked softly, her words almost lost to the increasing pitter-patter of the rain.

"After her infamous flight across London to escape the Prince of Orange, I was assigned to her as personal protection. Until such time as an agreeable royal match was completed."

If Jane had meant to distract him, she'd succeeded. He no longer noticed the ache of unbridled lust in his cock. No, now all Roland could feel was the suffocating pain in his chest.

But whether she'd meant them to or not, he found that the words somehow moved past the knot in his throat. They were suddenly spilling out of him.

"It was a lonely time for her, confined at Cranbourne Lodge. But Her Highness never complained once. She was the epitome of kindness, even to those of us whose sole purpose was to be her jailors."

Jane's shoulders shook slightly at that. "I'd hardly describe an esteemed agent of the Crown as a jailor."

Roland felt a smile play across his face at that.

"I suppose not," he agreed. "But she certainly had no reason to entertain me. I am old enough to be her father. Hell, maybe even her grandfather."

"You are not *that* old."

She was right, of course. But making a jest of it always helped to ease the pain.

Jane was quiet for a moment. Roland wished he could see her face or even her profile. But it was so well hidden beneath her woolen cobalt hood, he had only the tilt of her shoulders to judge her reactions or mood.

"You loved her."

Her voice was a whisper on the wind. His sad, bruised heart

swelled to hear it.

"I did," he said, feeling the cavity that held his heart expanding and making room.

Jane's voice... There had been emotion in it. The need to tease her, to make her work for the next sentence, had evaporated entirely. Not forever, Roland was certain. But that hint of emotion in her three whispered words awoke something in him that he wasn't even yet ready to acknowledge.

"She is the closest thing I ever had to a daughter," he said, voice clear even as swirling, unexpected emotions filled his chest.

Jane turned then, enough that he could see her lovely face. Her hand landed on his knee, holding her steady as she twisted to look at him.

Roland bit his tongue, determined to let her speak, hungry for whatever words she was about to bestow upon him.

But Jane said nothing. She swept those brown eyes, warm even in the dreary damp chill of the countryside, over his face. What was she searching for? Did she turn back around because she'd found it? Or because she had not?

She settled back against him, her hand leaving his knee and knotting in the base of the gelding's black mane instead. After several minutes of silence, she spoke again.

"Your affinity for the princess is why you were so intent on this quest," prim and proper Jane said, firmly in control once again.

Roland cleared his throat. "Yes. After Princess Charlotte's death..." A tremor racked through him.

"It affected all of us, I think," Jane said. No emotion, but a softness. Sympathy. Or empathy, perhaps.

"England has already lost her princess. I will not allow our queen to be taken as well," Roland said, nary a tremble or quiver in his voice.

Almost imperceptibly, Jane relaxed deeper against him.

Above their heads, a sharp screech cut through the rain. It seemed that even Guinevere was in agreement.

CHAPTER FOURTEEN

"WELCOME TO MALTBY Manor," the earl said, bowing before Roland with a courtly flourish.

The misting rain had turned to a drizzle and then a downpour in the last hour before they arrived. She now stood in the central entryway of Maltby Manor, dripping wet, while two dozen other guests dressed for an elegant supper looked on from the terraced levels of the manor.

It was not precisely the entrance she'd hoped to make as the new Duchess of Hawkridge.

Roland, at least, was undeterred. He shook off his wet topper, handing it over to a Maltby's butler with a wide grin. "Our carriage snapped an axle just past Hatfield."

He shrugged off his greatcoat next. Despite his having been riding for the last five hours, his perfectly tailored clothing was pulled tight over his lean, muscular body. The man would probably look just as at home in no clothing at all.

A maid stepped forward to help her with the ties of her cloak. But Roland waved them away, and his hands landed on Jane's shoulders instead.

"Of course, I couldn't leave my bride to sit alone in the rain," he said. His fingertips lingered to caress her shoulders even as he handed off the dripping garment. "You'll forgive our bedraggled arrival; I couldn't bear to be parted from her, even for a few hours."

His fingertips traveled down her spine, and his warm hand settled into the small of her back. The Earl of Maltby watched them with barely cloaked interest. Jane was sure he was noting the blush climbing up her neck. She averted her eyes, tilting her head slightly in Roland's direction. She may be a duchess, but she'd been a wallflower first. That was how Maltby would expect her to behave.

"I could do nothing else," Maltby replied, flashing too-white teeth in a smile that Jane was certain was meant to be welcoming. But it still sent a shiver down her spine. At least she could pass that off on the March chill. "Adair! Two more seats for supper!"

Roland's gravelly laugh filled the entry hall. "Oh no, Maltby. You'll have to do without us for tonight," her husband said, effusive smile in place. "A hot bath is in order. And after that, I intend to feast in private." He added a wink.

The ladies on the first floor tittered, and the men laughed bawdily.

Jane stilled the impulse to drive her elbow back into his gut. She already knew how useless that was; he was pure muscle there. If she wanted to have any impact, she'd have to aim lower. In either case, she could do nothing with so many onlookers other than to blush even more ridiculously.

Maltby's dark eyes sparkled, though the gleam seemed more menacing than entertained to Jane. But there was that bright smile again.

"Of course, of course," their host said, waving a hand to summon servants forward. "My housekeeper will see you to your rooms. I'll have one of the footmen wait up for your carriage and bring your trunks up as soon as they arrive."

"All our thanks," Roland said, increasing the pressure of his hand on her back, guiding her forward.

Maltby turned back to his guests still lining the ornate filigree railing that encircled the first-floor terrace where it looked down on the open entry hall. "To feasting!" he called, raising the glass that had somehow appeared in his hand.

Jane's face burned brighter as she followed the housekeeper up the stairs, then up another flight, Roland's hand ever-present on her back.

It would be no chore to bring down the Earl of Maltby. She already hated the man.

***

"ARE YOU CERTAIN you have no other accommodations?" Roland said, rubbing his hand over his mouth.

He'd spent five long hours with Jane's perfect arse pressed against his cock. He hadn't lied to Maltby. He wanted a hot bath, to stroke his cock while picturing his sweet wife, and then to gorge himself on supper. In that order.

But it seemed that God Himself was intent upon aiding their quest. Mission.

How much easier it would be to keep up their ruse as the love-addled newlywed couple if they shared a single chamber... and how much more torturous?

"I apologize, Your Grace," the housekeeper said, though there was no apology in her voice. "But the house is full to bursting. Her ladyship assumed that you would not mind."

Exhaustion had made the housekeeper brazen. But from what Roland could tell, she spoke the truth. Lady Maltby believed he and Jane were a love match. What trouble was a single bed to a newlywed couple who were madly in love?

Emphasis on *mad*.

Because that was what would happen to Roland if he had to lie in that bed beside Jane and keep his hands to himself. He would go insane.

He could not let Maltby's housekeeper see his discomfiture. She probably thought he was griping about the fact that they were in a mere bedroom, rather than a suite with attached dressing room and sitting room. He needed to build upon that, rather than let her realize his real concern was the lack of separate bedrooms.

But where he faltered, Jane stepped in.

She trailed her fingers along his arm, curling her fingers around his and squeezing reassuringly.

"This is fine, my love. We have everything we need." She glanced meaningfully back at the bed.

The housekeeper pretended to sneeze, but Roland caught her rolling her eyes. It did not matter. She was fooled. He forced a smile to his face. Looking down at Jane, at eyes a few shades darker in the evening light, it wasn't even difficult to do so.

"You are right, wife. Thank you, Mrs. MacMillan."

The housekeeper needed no further urging. She promised to have water sent up for a bath, then disappeared—leaving Roland and his lovely, crafty new wife entirely alone.

She dropped his hand instantly, turning to look at the bed longingly.

"We can take turns sleeping in the chair," she said, her nose wrinkling as she glanced at the lone wingback chair in the corner by the window.

"I've slept in worse places," Roland said, sighing. But that did not make it an appealing proposition.

"We are professionals," Jane said slowly, eyes still trained on the bed. "We can sleep in the bed together without…" She swallowed hard.

"We are husband and wife," Roland heard himself say.

Even he had no idea what he meant by that.

When he glanced at Jane, her back was stiff as a rod. "So, we can share the bed," she said, voice wooden. "For sleeping."

"I…" Roland's voice came out squeaky.

Hell. He was the mouse now. He might as well open the window and throw himself out of it. He'd left Guinevere outside to find her own way—few hosts wanted to accommodate a falcon, even for a duke. Maybe she'd take pity on him and lead him to whatever sheltered alcove she'd found for the night.

Before he could cross to the window and wrench it open, a knock rang out. The maid—with hot bathwater. Jane retreated behind the tall folding screen that hid the chamber pot and copper basin for bathing.

"Thank fucking God," Roland muttered as he went to answer the door.

CHAPTER FIFTEEN

J ANE WAS THANKFUL she'd packed cosmetics. She dabbed rouge onto her cheeks, trying to lift the color from sallow to lively. Though she supposed after all the ribald comments Roland and Maltby had exchanged the night before, none of the guests would be surprised to see her eyes heavy from lack of sleep.

When they'd both bathed—behind the safety of the privacy screen—and eaten supper, they'd fallen into bed in borrowed night-gown and nightshirt. By tacit, silent agreement, neither had looked too long at what was or was not revealed by the ill-fitting garments they'd been lent. But while Roland fell asleep almost instantly, his soft snores filling the too-small room, Jane had lain awake into the wee hours of the morning.

Every time he shifted, she skittered across the bed, trying not to touch him.

That horseback ride had completely shredded her nerves. Every part of her had been wet by the time they arrived at Maltby Manor. Especially her lady parts.

But her husband, it seemed, was not so similarly afflicted.

Of course, she'd felt the hard press of his cock against her bottom for the duration of the ride. But, as she kept reminding herself, it was a biological response. What man could ride like that for hours and not have a physical reaction? What was more telling was how easily he slept beside her. He had no problem at all, with his hands folded neatly over the tight muscles of his abdomen.

He didn't want her.

He never has, she reminded herself. Egads, he'd only agreed to this marriage out of his loyalty to the late princess.

She could hardly be disappointed that he was delivering on the promises made by his countenance and distaste from the moment the match had been proposed.

But after that kiss at the altar... and the way he'd pulled her into his lap in the carriage, caressing her for no one's eyes—

No. That had been for his staff. All of it was a show. All of it.

She was a fool for entertaining any other notion, however briefly.

Her husband did not want her.

What she wanted... That was immaterial.

This was a quest. Her priorities were: investigate Maltby, topple the secret society, and save the Queen of England. In that order, and to the exclusion of all else. Including her own foolish physical desires.

So, she was not at all disappointed to find that her husband had departed early to join the Earl of Maltby for a ride across the estate. No, not at all.

Rather, she was thrilled. Their trunks had arrived in the night, and so she had her own clothing on, her penknife tucked into her boot, and a sharp set of lockpicks threaded into her hair when she left her room to join the other ladies for a bit of embroidery.

"GLORIA, THAT GOWN you wore to Lady Brisbane's ball was divine. You must share that modiste you've been hiding away."

"Yes! I shall have to resort to following you every time you leave the house! Six months is quite long enough to keep her to yourself."

"Hear, hear!"

"That is the biggest secret of all." Silence and dramatic glances. "It is not a 'her.' But a man!"

"A man! Forsooth!"

"How can a man make something so perfectly fit to a woman's body?"

"Unless he—"

"Yes, I have heard he was a bit of a rake back in Paris." Gloria, the Countess of Leicester, giggled.

The wives in attendance—a total of twelve, including Jane—had been harassing the lady about her modiste for the last quarter of an hour. Before that, they'd discussed tonics. The things these women were willing to put into their bodies... Jane had nearly gagged.

But they'd left her alone, content to let her set stitch after stitch while she listened in silence and sipped her tea. Altogether, it was not a bad first public outing as the Duchess of Hawkridge.

Until the men arrived.

They came through the door a boisterous bunch, tailcoats already missing, several cravats hanging loose. Not Roland's, Jane noted, her eyes tracking her husband as he moved across the room. He walked with Lord Chatterley, a man in his mid-thirties who had been active among the *ton* for years. His wife, a pretty blonde with a sharp tongue, sat to Jane's left.

The group crossed the wide hall, hardly acknowledging the gaggle of ladies tucked onto the sofas and settees in the opposite corner. When two footmen carried in a wooden stand with several gleaming sabers and swords, their attention was turned entirely.

Except for Roland's.

She *felt* his eyes. The blue-gray sparkled like diamonds at this distance, and they were fixed on one thing—her. All the other gentlemen were busy selecting blades, lifting them high to admire the hilts, cutting amateur swipes through the air to test their weight.

But Roland fixed his eyes upon her, inclining his head in what might have been a respectful nod, were it not for the infernal burning of those eyes. He might not be attracted to her in truth, but he certainly knew how to make a show of it. Jane's stomach twisted within her, her response all too uncomfortably unfeigned.

"Duchess," one of the women breathed, meaning heavy in the singular word.

Lady Maltby, Jane realized. She forced herself to turn away, to tear her eyes from Roland's. But her pulse was still jumping as she unsteadily let out, "Yes?"

"We should all wish to be so lucky," the lady of the house said, her needlework resting untended in her lap.

Jane blinked. "I beg your pardon?"

Lady Chatterley scoffed beside her. "The duke is besotted with you."

Jane's eyes flicked between the ladies and Roland. He'd turned away, held a blade in his own hand now. But Jane still had the impression that he was watching her.

"The feeling is entirely mutual, it seems," Lady Maltby said quietly.

Jane whipped her head back, meeting the other woman's eyes. They were dark with understanding. For a second, Jane was completely disoriented. She was *not* besotted with Roland Hawkridge. And she certainly should not be exchanging knowing looks with Lady Maltby, the wife of a traitor. But... that was precisely what she ought to be doing. All of it. That was the quest.

She stabbed her needle down into the taut fabric caught in her hoop, hoping the other women would pass her strange behavior off as nothing more than the nerves of a lovestruck wallflower.

Lady Maltby laughed softly. "Marriage suits you, Duchess."

Jane offered a tight smile. "Jane, please."

"Of course, Jane," Lady Maltby agreed.

Jane was relieved when the lady of the house turned her attention back to her own embroidery, and the conversation shifted to the entertainments scheduled for the next few days.

It was not until several minutes later, when she heard the clash of metal on metal, that Jane realized what was happening across the hall.

Roland had rolled up his shirt sleeves, revealing his muscled forearms for all to see. The cravat was gone entirely. This sort of casualness would be unheard of in London. But a married man, in the country among friends? What was a bit of sparring but part of the entertainment?

And the ladies were certainly entertained.

Every one of their gazes was riveted upon the spectacle. Whether Roland had chosen Maltby as his sparring partner or been invited, Jane would ask later. Perhaps it was meant to be an honor, extended by their host to his most illustrious guest. In any case, everyone was watching.

Even on the tiered walkways that surrounded the hall, from the first and second floors, servants stopped to watch.

Roland was the superior swordsman. It took Jane less than a minute to realize it. Every movement was precise, honed, and graceful. His powerful thighs rippled beneath his tight breeches, which clung to his buttocks as he spun and parried. Even his misses were intentional, leading Maltby on so that he would think himself well matched with Roland.

Let him win, Jane urged silently.

Roland was a cocky bastard, but he was an agent first. He had to realize the benefit of letting their host win the bout.

Jane glanced sidelong at the other ladies. The appreciation in their eyes as they watched her husband sent an entirely new emotion winding through her body—jealousy.

They'd never made any agreements about fidelity, she realized then. Roland was as serious about the quest as she—Jane knew that now. Despite his hotheaded, instinct-driven methods, he was committed. Their conversation about Princess Charlotte had convinced her of that. He would do nothing to put their image of besotted newlyweds in jeopardy.

But what about after the house party? After Maltby and his conspirators were caught and the queen was safe?

What would happen then? Would one of these ladies welcome her handsome husband to her bed?

Over my dead body. Without realizing it, Jane had shifted her posture, setting her embroidery to the side—so that her penknife, tucked into her boot, was within easy grabbing distance.

Jane blinked, hardly seeing the spectacle in front of her.

She'd never harmed an innocent person. Ever. She'd killed, yes. More than once. She'd maimed and scarred when necessary. All of it without flinching, in the service of her queen and England. But for her own sake—never.

What was coming over her?

Then Maltby cut a jab dangerously close to Roland's throat, and fire burned in her gut, her chest, her entire body.

She was on her feet. How had that happened? She'd entirely lost control of her body.

Roland had fallen to one knee.

Maltby cried out in victory, then offered the duke a hand and pulled him to stand, clapping him on the shoulder.

It is fake. It is all a ruse. All of this is pretend.

She repeated it like a mantra.

What is fake? her all-too-logical mind demanded. The sparring? Her marriage? This feeling in her chest?

She had no answer.

Roland crossed the hall, sweat dripping from his temples. He extended a hand, a rakish half-smile lighting his face.

"Come, wife."

So she did.

CHAPTER SIXTEEN

ROLAND HAD NO notion what was wrong with Jane, but every instinct inside of him was screaming. She needed comfort and care. More than anything, she needed out of that room with all of its prying eyes.

He led her from the hall, not set on any direction, only on getting her out. They turned the corner and ran into a spiral staircase. He had enough presence of mind to note how odd it was, totally out of date to the manor around it. But there was no door to bar the way, so up the stairs they went.

The staircase ended in a perfectly square room with tall ceilings stretching high above their heads. But Roland hardly noticed it—his eyes were intent on Jane.

"What is wrong?" he asked, catching her forearms and holding her steady.

Jane blinked, her clouded brown eyes heavy with emotions. Roland had built a career upon his ability to read people's expressions, see the cunning in their eyes. But with Jane, it was as if all of that experience melted away to nothing. She blinked again, and her eyes were clear.

"I am fine," she said, wriggling her shoulders.

"Your face says otherwise." He let go of her arms, stepping back so he could study her face more clearly in the filtered light from the tall, narrow windows above their heads. *"Said* otherwise," he corrected himself. Her calm, composed mask was firmly back in place now.

He watched as she took a slow breath in, then exhaled it even more slowly. She repeated it, down to the second. It was a measured way of calming herself, he realized. *How clever.*

She skated her eyes down his body, from where their gazes had met, down over his shoulders and abdomen, to his knees and toes, then back up again. Checking for injury, Roland realized.

"I was in no danger," he said slowly, watching her features for any sign of a reaction.

Was it possible that his little mouse actually cared about his well-being? Probably only insomuch that his injury or death would jeopardize the quest, he thought. She was eminently practical, and having an incapacitated partner would be inconvenient. Though it would allow her to work on her own.

He caught her gaze again, determined to discern which it was.

"Where are we?" she asked, avoiding his eyes and looking around the room instead.

Roland spared a glance toward the walls, though only a glance. He was much more concerned about Jane than which room they'd stumbled into.

"Is this meant to be a solar?" Jane asked, looking around.

Her face was unreadable. Or rather, there was no emotion in it other than professional curiosity. Roland stifled a sigh and looked around as well, noting the comfortable furnishings. The tall, narrow windows started above their heads and stretched upward toward the conical roof. Below them, rows of bookshelves lined with leather-bound tomes and other ephemera covered the four walls.

"I suppose so," he agreed. It certainly had all the trappings of a solar—the huge, carved fireplace, the Tudor-style tapestries.

"Maltby Manor was built less than a hundred years ago," Jane said, eyes tracking upward to the dark sapphire-blue ceiling painted with hundreds of gold stars. "The solar is about three hundred years out of fashion."

Roland rolled his eyes. "Maltby is very enamored of his own grandeur."

But to have a place like this built especially for himself was also meaningful. This place was special to Maltby. Which meant...

"We need to search it," Roland and Jane said in unison.

"I will start on the bookshelves," she said, already halfway across the room. "You—"

"The desk," he finished for her, hardly even annoyed that she was trying to order him around. The excitement humming in his veins was too powerful.

They'd stumbled upon this chance, and they couldn't waste it. There must be something here. Roland's instincts were screaming about the importance of this room. The desk in the corner was small, but oriented to face the fireplace. Not as ornate as the one he'd glimpsed in Maltby's study, but more personal. If the study was where estate business was conducted, this little writing desk was for personal use. And perhaps more nefarious purposes as well.

He stared at the desk for half a second, eyes roving over the various drawers and compartments. He let his instincts guide him. Maltby was cack-handed. Roland reached for the center-left drawer. There was something about that center that always felt comforting, even to brigands.

The soft whir of pages flipping caught his attention. On the other side of the room, Jane was meticulously going through book after book. She was already halfway through the top shelf. Why she'd started there, when she had to stand on tiptoe just to reach, Roland didn't understand. She'd have gotten through more books, faster, if she'd started where she could easily reach.

He opened his mouth to tell her as much, then slammed it shut again. They didn't have time for arguing. They'd made a bit of a scene by running off. The other guests would chalk it up to their barely contained newlywed amour. But if Maltby had seen the direction they went—and they must assume he had—he'd come to check on his solar before too long.

Roland had nearly finished with the desk when he heard the footsteps.

"Jane," he whispered sharply, shoving the last compartment closed, unsearched.

She was already back in the center of the room, lowering herself to the chair. Roland glanced over her shoulder to the bookcase she'd been searching, but everything was as perfectly in line as it had been before. His little mouse was nothing if not neat and tidy.

"Come, hold my hand and pretend to be reassuring me," she said, offering her tiny palm.

"I have a better idea." He bypassed her hand. In one movement, he scooped her up out of the chair, then dropped himself into it and deposited her in his lap.

Roland didn't give her time to argue. Maltby's was more than halfway up the winding staircase. He wrapped his hands around her waist, his long fingers almost able to encircle her petite form, and dragged her body against his as he kissed her senseless.

This was not time for demure kisses before a priest. Maltby had to catch them in a moment of passion. Despite her insistence to the contrary, Jane had been worried when he allowed Maltby to best him in their sparring match. Whether concern was personal or professional, Roland did not know. But for Maltby and his guests, it had been the naïve concern of a young wife.

And what would a reformed rake such as Roland do to console his wife, to assure her of his voracity and wellbeing? He'd bend her over the sofa and make her—

Not the time for that, his befuddled brain reminded him.

But passion was the objective, and it took shockingly little to loosen it within him.

Roland's hands couldn't stay at her waist. He wanted to touch her everywhere. He stroked his thumbs up over her ribcage, sliding them along the underside of her breasts. Jane quivered in response. God above, if she was this responsive with all her layers of clothing between them, what would she be like when he finally stroked her bare skin?

And her mouth… If her body was responsive, her mouth was claiming. She was as thorough in her application of kissing as in everything else. She swirled her tongue around his, curling and twisting without a hint of reluctance. She nibbled along his lower lip, then his top. Roland was in control of the embrace, exploring every dip and curve of her upper body, but Jane ruled that kiss. She nibbled and sucked, nipped and tortured with her delightful little tongue. Little mouse, indeed.

She was enjoying this performance as much as he.

If this was for show, Roland would happily perform every day for the rest of his life.

Maltby's footsteps stopped. He'd reached the top of the staircase and now stood at the threshold to the solar.

But neither of them stopped, though Roland was certain that Jane marked their adversary's approach as precisely as he. She kept the pressure on his lips; her tongue danced around his as she dipped and explored every corner of his mouth. His cock was hard, nestled beneath her legs. He couldn't help grinding it up against her, wanting to see if she would return the motion.

She did. She even let out a strangled little moan.

"Ahem."

Jane jerked away from him, nearly jumping out of his lap. Roland caught her waist again, holding her steady as she swayed. The horror on her face looked entirely genuine, and the flush on her cheeks turned to a blush of embarrassment. Her lower lip was trembling. So were her hands. She looked like she wanted to bury her face in his chest.

She was playing her part well.

So would he.

With the slowness of a cat stretching upon waking, Roland eased her out of his lap and then stood beside her. He wrapped an arm around her waist and tucked her in at his side, where she could easily hide her face and avoid Maltby.

Roland, on the other hand, turned to their host with a wolfish grin. "I beg your pardon, Maltby."

The other man watched them with dark, discerning eyes. His nearly black hair was loose over his brow from the sparring, giving him the look of a younger man for all that he was nearly Roland's agemate. If it was meant to be disarming, he'd done well. But Roland knew better.

"I am the one who ought to be begging yours," Maltby said, raising one eyebrow in measured amusement. "I've interrupted a private moment."

Roland tightened his grip on Jane. She squeaked. He gave her an indulgent smile that she didn't lift her eyes to see.

"You have such a fine space here," Roland observed. "Forgive me. I got a bit carried away with comforting my wife."

The corner of Maltby's mouth lifted in a wry smile. "She did appear distressed."

"She is quite young," Roland said. Jane poked him in the side, where Maltby couldn't see. Roland didn't even flinch. "She'll learn that her husband is quite capable of taking care of himself."

He winked at Maltby, who was now watching Jane. His gaze was... not quite predatory. But Roland didn't like it. There was too much interest in the man's eyes. Not attraction—interest, when there should have been none. Jane was a pretty wallflower from an unremarkable family. The most interesting thing about her to Maltby should have been her marriage to Roland. But that was not how the other man looked at her. It turned Roland's stomach. He found himself tugging her even tighter against his side.

Maltby seemed to realize he was staring, as he shook his head slightly and refocused on Roland.

"The other ladies have retired. I have some business to attend to myself. I shall see you both at supper?" he said, stepping away from the door. But not to go back through it; to allow their passage out of the solar.

So, this room was important. He was not willing to leave them alone here.

Part of Roland demanded he make an excuse to remain, to try to finish the search. But that rare logical impulse stilled him. They couldn't make their interest too obvious.

"Of course," he said with a grin. "Come, my love. We will take advantage of the afternoon to ourselves."

He released Jane enough to catch her hand, then led her past Maltby and down the stairs. But despite the fact that the entry hall was deserted, and Maltby had not followed them down the staircase, Roland found himself holding her hand tightly until they were behind the locked door of their room.

CHAPTER SEVENTEEN

S HE'D DONE EVERY single breathing exercise in her repertoire thrice. After all of those failed, Jane pleaded a headache and pretended to take a nap. Roland, meanwhile, had sat in the lone chair in their bedroom and read a book.

Jane had thought he might be pretending as well, but every time she dared to glance in his direction, his eyes were moving reliably from left to right. Once she lay down, she pointed her back to him so at least she wouldn't have to keep control of her facial expressions.

She was completely undone.

Every promise she'd made herself, every claim to chastity—all of it came crashing down when Roland had pulled her into his lap and really, truly kissed her. In that moment, Jane had believed that it was real. With his hands stroking her breasts and his mouth pliant under hers, she'd known only the raging inferno of her own desire and that Roland matched her every move.

Back in their room without an audience to perform for, Jane wasn't as sure.

Roland acted on instinct. It drove her insane, but it also was effective at times. Her idea of holding hands demurely was nothing compared to the passionate embrace that Maltby had discovered them in. It was a hundred times more convincing. Roland's instincts had been right.

It was logic, not instinct, her stubborn mind tried to argue. They were meant to be a lovestruck couple who could not keep their hands off one another. Of course they wouldn't be chastely holding hands. They would be making love on the sofa. Roland had simply worked that out faster than she.

If she had not been so focused on keeping her burgeoning desire for Roland at bay, she would have seen that logical line of thought herself.

Egads, he was managing to muddle every part of her mind.

Perhaps the smart, logical thing to do would be to bed him and be done with it. It must be done eventually; they were man and wife, after all.

That is not your rational mind talking, a voice that sounded decidedly like Jacquetta said.

She fought the urge to roll onto her back and pummel the pillow with her fist. She was supposed to be napping.

Really, she ought to be discussing a strategy with Roland. But she couldn't bring herself to look at him without going all mushy inside. Ridiculous. She was a lady knight! This was a mission to save the Queen of England! She could not be so thickheaded!

Roland was not nearly as bothered as she. Was that his experience showing? How often had he reminded her that he'd been in service to the Crown for twenty years... almost her entire life? He'd probably seduced women every other week. He was that damned good at it.

But I'm his wife.

Not the one he chose. The one he took of necessity—out of duty to the Crown. The same as she had. Whatever was between them physically...

No. Nothing was between them physically.

All that mattered was the mission. Quest.

He was even infiltrating her mind now!

Jane squeezed her eyes shut and began counting backward from one hundred. She could not think about this. She could not think about him.

... 98... 97... 96...

Despite all odds, she finally drifted to sleep.

WHEN SHE WOKE, Roland was gone.

She found the scribbled note on his pillow easy enough. He'd gone down to peruse Maltby's library—the official one, not the one tucked into his private solar—before supper. He would send a maid to her if she did not wake in time to ready herself. That bit felt useless to include. She'd either wake up herself and see the note, or the maid would wake her up. But Jane didn't have much time to think about it either way.

A soft knock rang out—the maid come to assist her with dressing.

When Jane descended an hour later from the second floor to the first, where the dining room was located, she was at least breathing evenly.

Until she caught the looks upon the other ladies' faces.

The dress had been a mistake.

Jane never would have selected such a thing on her own. Her role was to blend into the other debutantes and be utterly forgettable. She wore pastel colors, preferably muslin. She did own a few silk ballgowns, but they were understated and simple. The goal was to look unremarkable, not poor. She wore her hair as all the other *ton* ladies did, with the same fashionable curls loose at her temples. Her mother had offered her jewels to borrow, but Jane left those to her sister Josephine. She preferred to have the maid weave flowers into her hair. They were less ostentatious, but preserved the sense of gentle femininity that comforted men and women alike into loosening their tongues.

The sapphire-blue silk whispered softly as she entered the sitting room. Most of the guests had already arrived, and couples were dressed as elegantly as if they were attending a dinner party in Mayfair.

She was a married woman now. She was entitled to luscious, jewel-toned gowns.

Then why did she feel like such a fool?

Because everyone in the room was watching her. It was the exact opposite of the effect she'd worked to achieve for the last four years.

Jane's mother had selected the gown for her trousseau. Sapphire silk cut in a low, square bodice showcased what little bosom she had. The puffed organza sleeves were dyed the exact same shade as the gown itself, but they were sheer. Her slim arms, from the curve of her shoulders all the way down to her elbows where her white gloves began, were entirely revealed.

She shivered, but not from the cold. The bright fire blazing in the sitting room's hearth had chased away all of the April chill. The delicately beaded silk chiffon overskirt, also perfectly matched sapphire, was purely decorative. Jane had even donned earrings. Simple diamond teardrops, but still.

The neckline wanted a necklace, the maid attending her had said. But Jane had demurred. She hadn't even brought one with her.

"Your Grace," Lady Maltby said with her wide hostess's smile, stepping forward and taking Jane's hand. "I shall say it once more— marriage suits you very well."

Jane blushed madly. Her neckline was low enough that she was sure everyone could see the color climbing her bosom, with no necklace to distract from the crimson flush. But Lady Maltby's smile only widened.

"You even blush prettily," she said. "How long have you been hiding among us, fooling us into thinking you a wilting wallflower?"

Her tone was teasing, but alarm bells sounded in Jane's mind. She cast her eyes down, avoiding Lady Maltby's gaze.

"My mother selected this gown," she said quietly. From beneath her eyelashes, she scanned the room again, even knowing what she would find. Roland was not there. Nor was Lord Maltby.

"Then your mother has excellent taste," Lady Maltby declared. She looped her arm through Jane's and led her over to where two other women and their husbands waited. "I was just telling Her Grace that her gown is divine. It even puts your modiste's creations to shame, Lady Leicester."

"The color suits your hair," Lady Chatterley said before sipping her sherry. Not quite a compliment, Jane noted. But after the last few days spent interacting with the woman, it was about what she expected.

Gloria, the Countess of Leicester, was burying her strained smile in her wine glass as well. Her husband, however, raked his gaze over Jane appreciatively.

"You should see what her modiste is charging, Gloria. It cannot possibly be more than yours," he declared.

Lady Leicester's face colored; her cheeks instantly turned ruddy. Lord Chatterley, the chap who'd been so chummy with Roland earlier in the afternoon, laughed politely.

Only Lady Maltby did not appear inclined to entertain the inappropriate comment. She turned her eyes back to Jane.

"Where is that handsome husband of yours, Jane? He had us all quite in a dither this afternoon," she said with a conspiratorial smile.

Jane's pulse quickened, but she ignored it. "I believe he was perusing Lord Maltby's library. He's a bit of a bibliophile. I'm afraid in our..." She paused and looked away again, feigning embarrassment. "Our minds were quite distracted in our packing, and he forgot to bring his usual favorites along."

The innuendo earned her rounds of laughter, male and female alike. The anxiety in Jane's stomach eased slightly. She was not used to playing this role. But she supposed that if she was to have a career with the Lady Knights after this quest, she must accustom herself. She couldn't hide on the walls any longer. She was a Society wife now, a duchess. She must learn to use that to her advantage in her investigations.

"When we were newly wed, we hardly had time for books," Lady Leicester said, tossing her dark curls back from her face. She placed her hand on her husband's knee and fixed Jane with a smug look.

The Earl of Leicester jerked his knee away as if his wife's hand burned him. "I say, Gloria. What has gotten into you?"

He stood up and stalked away.

Things were not well between the earl and countess. Jane wondered briefly if she would be able to use that to her advantage somehow. Either now, for this quest, or for a future one. But before she could contemplate it further, Lady Leicester surged to her feet and pushed past her. The other ladies might have missed the glare on the woman's otherwise pretty face, but Jane had not.

Lovely. She'd made an enemy already. Not that Jane cared what the Countess of Leicester thought about her, but she needed the trust of those attending the house party if she was to wheedle information from them.

She waved off Lady Maltby's offer of sherry and turned toward the wall by instinct. Settings like this always unnerved her. She preferred to have her back against the wall so that no one could sneak up on her. In a place like this, a manor house full of snakes hiding in the grass, it felt especially prudent.

Besides, Maltby was not the only one she wanted to avoid sneaking up on her. There was the matter of her own husband, as well.

As if summoned by her thoughts, Roland appeared in the doorway with a book in hand. Jane found herself admiring the way his long fingers curled around the spine of the leather-bound brown tome, and his thumbnail unconsciously caressed the gold-embossed lettering.

His eyes found her immediately, through the sea of guests. The group had swelled in the intervening minutes. Jane didn't need to count heads to realize that he was the last to arrive. They were now a complete party.

Roland was halfway across the room to her when Maltby intercepted him. "There you are, man! I thought about sending your lady wife to fetch you, lest you miss the first course."

Lady Maltby joined her husband, her voice loud enough for all the guests to hear. "If you'd done that, we'd have seen neither of them for supper, nor the rest of the night."

The brash comments were met with hearty laughs. Roland took it in good humor, flashing that easy grin and kissing Lady Maltby's hand. Jane watched from her station against the wall.

She was not sure what to make of the whole spectacle. Such blatant ribbing was not appropriate in the ballrooms of London during the Season. But she was not a debutante anymore. She was a married woman. This was a house party with only married guests. Things were bound to be more casual. But this…

Perhaps this too was a ruse on Maltby's part. By playing up the ribald comments, making her and Roland the center of attention, he could provide further cover for the covert activities. The members of the secret society were here, Jane reminded herself.

She scanned across the room, considering each gentleman and lady wife. A secret society bent on murdering the Queen of England was unlikely to have any female members. Men were all selfish pigs, once one got down to the heart of things. But that did not mean that the wives were not complicit.

Jane had found that women were rarely oblivious to their husbands' nefarious activities. It was part of what made the proposition of the Lady Knights so effective.

The ladies always knew.

The doors to the dining room opened, Lord and Lady Maltby leading the pack.

Jane waited for Roland to come and fetch her. For once, she had a partner. She would sit beside him at the table.

While in London it had seemed so far-fetched and downright irritating, she could not deny that here in Hertfordshire, it was a relief.

"Pardon my tardiness," Roland said, offering his arm. His book had disappeared.

"Of course." She smiled primly, slipping her hand around his black broadcloth-clothed arm. "Did you find what you were looking for?"

A loaded question.

By the squeeze of Roland's hand on top of hers, she knew he understood it. "I did find some titles which might interest you," he said casually. "Perhaps tomorrow we will find a minute to ourselves so I might show them to you."

Of course, that only made Jane want to feign illness and run to the library immediately.

Instead, she sat primly in her chair beside her husband and waited while the small army of servants began the carefully orchestrated dinner service.

She was lifting her wine glass to her lips, turning her head to listen to the conversation between Mrs. Hawthorne and Lady Leicester, when she felt the heat of his breath caress her ear.

"You look beautiful."

She didn't dash any wine down the front of her dress. That was about all that she could say for herself. She had absolutely no control over her facial expression or the trembling of her fingers.

Jane forced herself to set down her glass, lest she drop it in her lap.

"Blue suits you," Roland said, catching her hand as it retreated into her lap.

"Thank you," she murmured, fixing her eyes on one of the wall sconces over Lord Chatterley's shoulder.

Roland's fingers circled her wrist easily. He pressed his thumb against the inside, where her blood was pounding riotously. She opened her mouth to tell him that was the wrong way to take her pulse—he needed to use his fingers or he'd confuse it with his own.

Roland Hawkridge certainly knew that, Jane chastised herself.

Besides... she was relatively sure that everyone within spitting distance was able to hear the pounding of the blood in her veins.

She forced herself to focus on the conversation happening beside her. The two women were discussing the latest Society papers that had been delivered that morning. News was always a few days—or a few weeks—old by the time it reached the country. Jane had her own set of scandal sheets waiting in the bedroom so she could peruse them.

Gossip columns were notorious for their lies, but if one was keen, they could glean quite a bit of truth.

Jane wondered what the gossip columns had said about her and Roland.

"Lady Burbank—"

Roland dropped her wrist. But instead of pulling his hands back into his own lap, he slid one beneath hers so that his wide palm cupped her upper thigh.

"I thought she was married to his—"

He stroked his thumb back and forth. Back and forth. Was he moving closer...? No, she must be imagining it...

"—indeed!"

His thumb dipped in between her legs, caressing her inner thighs through the suddenly irrelevant layers of her dress.

This was madness. No one was even looking at them. Maltby was busy talking with Leicester. The ladies were all talking to one another. Another course of food was in the process of being brought around.

"What are you doing?" Jane whispered, using the clatter of a plate to cover her words.

Roland's soft laughter skittered over her.

Jane realized that if any of their dinner companions looked over, they would see the Duke of Hawkridge and his new duchess with their heads together, whispering, as if there was no one else in the room. It was a perfectly orchestrated act.

Except for his hand on her leg. Between her thighs. The hand that no one could see.

"I told you how beautiful you look," Roland rumbled.

She opened her mouth once more, not sure what words were about to come out. Her lips were quivering terribly. But Roland spared her the struggle of trying or deciding.

"I cannot resist," he said. His thumb stroked higher.

Jane's heart was in danger of pounding right out of her chest. She turned to him, expected to see that wide grin in place. But Roland's eyes were intent, his face so serious.

"Tell me to stop," he whispered.

She swallowed hard.

She should tell him to stop. She should chastise him, turn away, and talk with the ladies on her other side. She should be able to focus. But with Roland's hand inches from her core, already trembling with need—with his eyes fixed so intently upon hers—what she *should* do didn't seem to matter quite so much.

"Duchess, do you know Miss Talbot?"

Jane blinked.

Lady Maltby, she realized. That was who had spoken.

She forced herself to turn to face the woman across the table, her entire body feeling unbearably stiff. Roland's hand retreated, coming to rest chastely on her knee. Well, there was nothing chaste about it. But in comparison to the last few minutes, that simple motion felt almost saintly.

"I have met her a few times. She is good friends with my sister," Jane said smoothly. Precise facts. She always found those the easiest when she wasn't sure what she was dealing with.

"She is engaged to…" Lady Maltby continued. Jane nodded along and responded appropriately. The conversation took only a small fraction of her attention.

All the rest of it was focused on the seat beside her. More specifically, on the rake of a duke who sat in it. On her husband.

For the first time, Jane thought she might have finally arrived at a different answer to the question that had been raging inside of her. The one she'd ignored, tucked away, refused to answer just to avoid the disappointment of it.

Did Roland want her as badly as she wanted him?

After that little show—

No, not a show. That had been for her, and her alone. The answer was no longer resoundingly clear.

Did her husband want her?

Maybe.

CHAPTER EIGHTEEN

H E WAS THE worst sort of scoundrel.

He'd never seduced a virgin. Not that he hadn't deflowered a few, in his day. But the women had always been eager participants, with their eyes wide open, and a clear understanding that there were no precontracts between them. Looking back now, Roland could see even those interludes had been mistakes.

But none so terribly predatory as what he'd done to his wife in that dining room.

She'd entered into an arrangement out of duty to her queen. This was professional to her. Maybe she'd kissed him back. Maybe there was passion there, beneath the cool, calm exterior she presented to everyone—him included.

But that did not give him carte blanche to touch her like that, for no reason other than his own hard cock and insatiable desires.

Hell. He was going to have to retreat to the stables and abuse himself soon. Either that, or his cock was going to explode from the torture of being in constant proximity to Jane and unable to do anything about it.

He may be a rake, but he was not a cad. He would not force his attentions upon her unless she really, truly wanted them.

Roland sipped on his brandy, pretending to be even mildly interested in the conversations happening around them. He was back in

Maltby's library with the other gentlemen. All except for Leicester, who'd excused himself at the meal's conclusion.

The ladies had adjourned to the spacious hall below, with its comfortable chaises to drink more sherry, but Roland had heard their footsteps heading up to the bedrooms a quarter of an hour before.

Meanwhile, he knew that the men would linger on for hours draining Maltby's decanters and smoking.

Focus, Roland admonished himself. Among these eleven so-called gentlemen were the members of the secret society intent upon murdering his queen. He would not allow it.

Leicester had peeled away, citing a headache. Roland found himself wondering—was he off to some nefarious purpose? Maybe he ought to have found a moment to speak with Jane, to ask her to follow him.

Remington hadn't even shown up at the house party, which was deuced strange. They knew the man was connected with Maltby, but he was not here. Why?

There were three locked cabinets in this very room. Roland had discovered them under the guise of searching for a new book. But there hadn't been time to pick the locks, and he wanted Jane with him when he did. They would stand less chance of being discovered if they could search together in half the time. They'd also have a better excuse if they were caught. Roland already had the jest—something about how he intended to kiss his bride in every room of Maltby Manor.

In the far corner of the room, Chatterley spoke with three other men. Among the attendees, Chatterley was the closest thing Roland had to a friend. He didn't trust the man, couldn't afford to. But he'd known John Chatterley since they were at Eton, and he hoped the man was one of those guests being used as cover. It would disappoint him more than he wanted to admit if his schoolmate was part of the secret society.

Secret society. They didn't even have a proper name for it. Roland had realized by now that Maltby wrote down very little. What he did was in code—like the letters intercepted between him and Remington.

Remington might be an idiot. But Maltby was not. He was a snake in the grass.

And he was slithering right over to Roland.

Maltby held up the half-full crystal decanter by way of greeting.

Roland tipped back the last splash of brandy and then held out his empty glass.

Once that was settled, Maltby settled into the chair beside him, leaving the decanter on the triangular table wedged between the two tall wingbacks. Roland observed him covertly, though his eyes were still across the room on Chatterley and his trio of companions.

Maltby had styled the dark curls back from his face, looking much more the elegant gentleman that he had that afternoon. He was quite good at transforming himself, Roland noted. He must be, if he could live the life of a lord while simultaneously plotting regicide. Roland had to assume that every action the man took was calculated.

The long drink of brandy was meant to put Roland at ease, as was the way Maltby propped his ankle up on the opposite knee and relaxed back in the chair. It was all so casual, as if they were friends rather than just peers.

Roland felt Maltby's dark eyes slithering over him, assessing his own stance and expressions. Then the other man's head turned to follow Roland's gaze.

"I am quite pleased that Chatterley suggested you join us this week," Maltby said, eyes on the aforementioned gentleman, who was now speaking animatedly as he regaled his trio of onlookers with a tale of his latest triumph at Newmarket.

Roland lifted his glass in salute to Chatterley, oblivious on the other side of the library. "As am I. Your estate provides a much more private retreat to celebrate with my bride."

From the corner of his eye, Roland watched Maltby's lips and chin move in a soundless chuckle.

"There were odds at White's that you would never take a wife," Maltby said drolly. "I am glad I did not take that bet. You are clearly besotted with your duchess."

Roland laughed genuinely at that, settling back in his seat. He didn't doubt that there *had* been odds on such a thing. "She is a treasure," he said with absolute sincerity.

Unexpected emotion clogged his chest. He drained his brandy and poured another dram.

He could tolerate a lot of liquor before his mind became muddled. But hopefully it would do something about the tightness in his chest long before that.

"You've been away from London so long, you are an enigma," Maltby said, swirling his brandy.

Roland scoffed. "On the contrary, I am a simple man, Maltby. I enjoy a strong drink, a bit of adventure, and full coffers, the same as any man."

Maltby's dark brow rose slightly. "A bit of adventure? Is that what you've been doing all this time abroad? Adventuring?"

Roland grinned raffishly. "Among other things."

"Profitable things."

Roland shrugged. "Sometimes."

"You are being humble, Hawkridge. Rumor has it you are as wealthy as the king himself," Maltby said. He was no longer feigning disinterest, but looking directly at Roland, dark eyes carefully watching for any reaction in his face or posture.

"Are you about to ask me to invest in a harebrained scheme? Is that the origin of this timely invitation to the country?" Roland did his best to sound amused—as if he'd entertained such propositions from dozens of other minor lords.

In truth, he'd heard more than a few during his travels. He imagined he was in a tavern in Jamaica, listening to the ridiculous business schemes of the fourth son of Baron Trelawny. A smile tugged at his lips at the ridiculous memory.

"I have no need of your money, Hawkridge."

Roland rested his brandy snifter on his knee and leveled Maltby with a direct gaze of his own. "What do you need, Maltby?"

He met those dark eyes and held them, feeling the calculation, the estimation. He'd done as much himself hundreds of times over the last twenty years. But always for good. This... this man was evil. There was no other way to put it that did not minimize the situation.

"Not here," Maltby finally said, breaking the stare. He shifted in his chair so he was surveying the room once more. Their ranks had thinned a bit—Chatterley was down to one companion instead of three.

"Where, then?" Roland asked, this time with no humor in his voice. He wanted Maltby to understand that whatever he was about to reveal, he would take it seriously.

"Ride out with me tomorrow."

Roland barked out a dry laugh. "I rode out with you today."

"Nevertheless," Maltby said softly, "I'd like to show you something."

Roland made a show of considering, narrowing his brows. But then he nodded sharply. "Tomorrow, then."

"Good." The Early of Maltby stood, straightening his waistcoat. He raked a hand through his hair, loosening the curls once more. He reached for the crystal decanter and lifted it to toast the remaining gentlemen. "Tonight, we drink!"

Roland forced that affable grin to his face as the rest of the group caroused and held out their glasses. He did the same. Now he could turn his mind to his other problem—numbing his desire for his wife.

CHAPTER NINETEEN

J ANE FOUND THE book sitting atop the dressing table. She recognized it instantly as the one Roland had been holding when he first joined the dinner party. How it had gotten up here… He must have entrusted it to a servant. Which meant there was likely no secret note or message inside of it, which had been Jane's first instinct upon sighting it.

To be certain, she lifted the tome and flipped through the pages, shook it out by the spine, examined it from various angles. It was exactly as it appeared to be—a book.

She recognized the emotion in her chest as she sat down on the edge of the bed—disappointment. This quest was progressing at a snail's pace, when the threat was imminently dire.

She glanced at the clock on the mantel. The ladies had retired, but the gentlemen were still smoking and drinking in Maltby's library. Perhaps she ought to use this time to poke around the solar again.

But she'd likely get caught. If not in the solar itself, then somewhere between here and there. The room she and Roland had been given shared a corridor with those assigned to several other guests. It would be too easy for her to be discovered coming or going, and she wouldn't have a plausible excuse. Not on her own.

If it was the middle of the day, she might have managed it. But with the husbands due to start stumbling back at any moment, it was not worth the risk. Nothing would happen tonight. Maltby was still here, drinking with Roland and the others.

She didn't ring for a maid, managing to get herself out of the sapphire gown all on her own. Her hair was a bit more complicated, woven with Bristol fairy. But she meant to wait up and speak with Roland, so time was on her side.

Hair finally loose around her shoulders, waves still thick and voluminous after several minutes of brushing, she moved to the armoire to retrieve her nightgown. Her gaze snagged on the sapphire chiffon.

For a moment, she was confused. She'd laid the gown across the chair... She turned back. *Yes, there it is.*

Then what was this? Had she missed some part of the ensemble?

Carefully, she nudged away the linen nightgown she'd been about to don and pulled free the delicate fabric beneath. Jane's breath caught in her throat as the garment unfurled before her.

Garment was a generous word. This was... hardly anything, really.

She'd thought the nightgown she donned on her wedding night scandalous? This was nothing short of wicked.

The bust was entirely made of creamy lace. Jane slipped her hands beneath the narrow straps, noticing just how much of her own fair skin was visible through the open weave. The lace continued down over where her breasts would be, gathering into a dark blue silk ribbon below the bust. There was one tiny bow that would be nestled just between her breasts. Then the lace and ribbon gave way to an expanse of chiffon—the same chiffon that had been embroidered and overlaid on the dress she'd worn to supper.

They must be a set. The gown for supper and this for... dessert.

Jane shook her head, trying to shake loose the images swirling in her mind. She got the negligee fully folded, halfway back into the armoire, when she heard Roland's words in her mind:

I cannot resist.

He'd called her beautiful in the gown. What would he think of this?

Would he be able to resist?

And the more important question—did she want him to?

Jane's body answered for her. Her shoulders shrugged away her chemisette. Then she was tugging the negligee over her head, adjusting the straps around her small breasts, smoothing the ribbon and the bow.

Looking down at her body, she caught her breath once again. She'd never seen herself like this... not even when she'd worn the scanty nightgown on her wedding night. She thought of herself as so many things—lady knight, elder sister, wallflower. But now, she looked every inch a duchess and wife. A woman.

If Roland truly wanted her, if he truly could not resist... this would be the night to prove it.

JANE COUNTED AWAY the minutes. She counted the number of fleurs-de-lis on the patterned curtain. She counted the individual bricks in the hearth. She would not allow herself to fall asleep. Although it defied logic, staying awake on this night felt equally important to all the nights she'd spent keeping herself awake on quests for the Lady Knights.

Except that this quest was purely for herself.

She'd left the lamp beside the bed burning, and one on the mantel of the fireplace, in addition to the banked fire. The room was warm, but still her skin pebbled in anticipation.

When she finally heard the footsteps in the hall, when the door finally swung open, every muscle in her body stood at attention.

Roland froze in the doorway.

Despite her promise to herself to remain relaxed, Jane sat up. She was instantly aware of how much of her skin was revealed. But she didn't reach for the coverlet. She lifted her eyes and looked at her husband.

He'd shucked his tailcoat. It hung limply over one arm. His once-crisp white shirt was rumpled, the top few buttons of his gray embroidered waistcoat unbuttoned. His cravat hung loose around his neck. She could see a triangle of tanned skin reaching down from his throat.

But Jane could not see his eyes. His entire face was cast in shadow.

Yet the room was small enough that she could see the bob of his Adam's apple, and the way his chest rose and fell as he dragged in a long breath. Then he stepped forward into the soft candlelight, closing the door behind him.

"Jane," he said, his voice a strangled thing.

She bit her bottom lip, waiting for him to say more. His eyes raked over her, lingering on her breasts. Even in the dim light, she knew that he could see the dark circles of her nipples through the lace. They were firm and erect, begging to be touched. Roland's hand twitched at his side. But then he curled it into a fist.

"I expected you to be asleep," he said, forcing his eyes back to her face.

Jane took an unsteady breath. "I thought there were things we needed to discuss."

Roland took a few steps toward her, tossing his tailcoat aside. Neither of them looked to see where it fell. Jane wasn't sure if she imagined it as she watched him sway slightly on his feet, crossing the room slowly to come stand at the foot of the bed. "I am in no state to discuss anything of importance right now."

That was brandy she smelled. She didn't mind. If she'd had any to hand, she'd have taken advantage of the liquid courage as well.

"Neither am I," she said. She let her hand trail down the neckline of the negligee, pausing at the little bow nestled between her breasts. Then she skated her hand lower, pausing just above her navel before letting it fall into her lap.

Roland tracked every movement.

Jane could not imagine a clearer invitation.

But still, her husband hovered at the edge of the bed.

Damn him, he was probably determined to make her beg.

No, her logical mind whispered back. He was foxed. Whatever games he was playing, they'd all melted away now.

"Come to bed," she said softly.

Roland didn't move. This was it, Jane realized. He'd made his decision. She'd been mistaken.

But then suddenly he was sinking down. Not coming to her, precisely, but sitting on the edge of the bed. Her bare feet were resting on top of the coverlet, peeking out from the bottom of the translucent chiffon, just inches away from his powerful thigh.

He reached one hand back to brace himself. As he did, his fingers skimmed over her calf. It was like she'd been struck by lightning—the impact of that one grazing touch set her entire body aflame. It was all the invitation she needed. She slid closer, so that her legs were tucked underneath her and her face, for once, was even with his.

Roland's eyes were shadowed still, but even so, Jane could see the war taking place on his face. What demons was he battling, she wondered? Desire, duty... indifference?

No, it could not be that.

She would find out now.

Tentatively, she reached out a hand and laid it upon his thigh.

Roland groaned. "What are you doing, little mouse?"

Jane leaned closer. "I told you not to call me that," she breathed.

"So, now you will punish me?"

His silver hair gleamed in the candlelight, bright as strands of diamonds. Jane could see the curls across his chest, revealed by his open shirt. They were still dark, unchanged by time. What about the rest of him? What she'd felt of his body was all toned, lean muscle. She tightened her fingers on his thigh, itching to feel and touch and take.

"I don't want to punish you," she said softly. She dragged her tongue over her lower lip.

Kiss me, her desire begged him.

"Oh, sweet wife, you do nothing but," Roland groaned, finally reaching out to touch her.

He cupped her face, drawing her closer still. Another few inches and she'd be pressed against him, with nothing but a scant layer of lace and his thin shirt to separate their bodies. She found herself leaning forward, trying to close the gap. But Roland's hand on her cheek held her still.

She didn't understand.

He wanted her—she could see it in every angle of his face.

He must.

But instead of kissing her, Roland dragged one finger across her lips.

Jane thought she must be losing her mind. She was imagining the *tap tap tapping* in the background. It must be some strange trick of the fire.

Her husband was going to kiss her now. Her eyes drifted closed, her lips pressed against the smooth pad of his thumb, she swiped her tongue out—

Suddenly, she jolted forward.

Roland was gone.

Or, at least, gone from the bed.

He was striding toward the window, covered now with those fleur-de-lis curtains she'd so mindlessly counted earlier in the night.

And she was alone.

Jane rocked back on her heels, her mouth falling open as she turned to follow him with her eyes.

She watched in open-mouthed confusion as he threw back the curtains and fiddled with the latch.

"Hell and damnation, how does this thing—"

Without thinking, her body operating totally outside of her emotions, Jane stood and walked around the bed. Roland was struggling with the latch, unable to free the mechanism. He was very drunk, she realized.

Anger flashed through her. Some brandy with the gentlemen, that was acceptable. But to get so deep in his cups that he could not function was irresponsible. What if Maltby had dropped some hint about the plot to assassinate the queen? How could Roland be so stupid?

She let the anger flood her veins as she shoved his hands aside and opened the window herself, freeing the mechanism and shoving her palm against the glass pane.

Anger was the appropriate emotion for the moment, she thought logically. It was also easier to bear than embarrassment.

The minute the window was open, Jane fell back to avoid the flash of wings.

The peregrine swooped into the room on a graceful flash of bluish gray. Roland was still swearing under his breath. Jane turned away from him, refusing to give him her eyes, her attention, or any other part of herself. Not after that humiliating rejection.

He'd held her at a distance, even when she damn near begged for him.

He was too busy letting in a damn bird to kiss her.

Because he did not want her.

Sure, maybe he desired her in some detached, philosophical way. He was a man; she was a woman. But he didn't burn for her the way she did for him. His entire body didn't jolt with each touch, tingle with awareness when she entered the room.

"Why is she here?" she said sharply, moving past him to close the window again. "She better be prepared to stay. I will not be shivering all night."

He didn't answer her question.

"She'll bide," he said quietly, crossing the room to where Guinevere had taken up a perch atop the armoire.

He rifled around in the pocket of his trousers, then offered a morsel to the peregrine. She nuzzled his hand affectionately and then took it into her sharp beak.

The damned falcon had more of his affection than Jane.

Without another word, she walked to the fireplace and doused the lamp, then back to do the same to the one at her bedside. In the space of a minute, their bedroom was doused in darkness.

Let him stumble around in his drunken stupor, Jane thought harshly as she pulled the coverlet up to her neck. She would not think of him at all.

"Goodnight." Roland's voice rumbled through the darkness.

Jane pretended she was already asleep.

CHAPTER TWENTY

ROLAND'S HEAD WAS pounding as he poured himself into the saddle the next morning. To his chagrin, Maltby looked as if he hadn't drunk at all. The sharp lines of his dark brows and hair were as crisp as ever.

He waited at the edge of the stable yard, kicking his mount into a trot before Roland had even come fully abreast.

"Where are we going?" Roland called out, adjusting his seat as he urged his horse forward as well.

The Earl of Maltby smirked at him over his shoulder. "You'll see," he said before whipping the reins and galloping away.

"Christ Almighty," Roland cursed, left with no choice but to ignore the pounding in his temples and urge his own horse to follow.

They rode at the breakneck pace for a quarter of an hour, through glades of trees, until they reached a sparse field. Roland felt the horse beneath him digging in as the path slowly sloped upward.

He did not know where they were going, but he'd been around Maltby enough now to know the man had a predilection for grandeur. Taking him on this long ride, up the sweeping hillside—it was all to make a big impression.

When he reached the crest of the hill, he couldn't help but be impressed. The Chilterns spread out before him, the rolling hills softened further by morning mist. Beneath their horses' hooves, the grass was green and gold, wet with dew. But as the miles stretched out, the bright green turned to dark emerald, and then shades of sapphire and amethyst where the distant hills undulated, dancing against the gray sky.

The two men stared out at the tableau in silence, the only sound their horses' huffs and their own heavy breathing from the exertion of the gallop.

"Is all of this yours?" Roland finally asked, though he was already certain of the answer. A man did not show off what he did not already own.

Maltby smiled, still admiring his own good fortune. "This land was gifted to my family by Henry the Seventh."

Roland nodded his appreciation. "The throne has been kind to you."

"At times," Maltby said judiciously.

Roland took a measured breath, steeling himself. Now was the moment. Now that Maltby had him here, he wasn't going to waste any time. It was just as well. Roland would rather have something real to report to Jane than have to discuss the disaster of the previous night.

"And at others?" Roland asked, ready for the response.

Maltby shifted in his saddle, turning that dark gaze to look directly at Roland. The better to judge his reactions.

"A foreign queen sits on our throne," the earl said.

The duke laughed, despite the ache in his head. "All of the Hanoverians are foreign, Maltby. Would you rather a Catholic king or a German one?" This was dangerous territory. Treason. But Roland kept his tone light, as if they were discussing rounders rather than regicide.

"I have no interest in deposing the king," Maltby said, his lips quirking slightly.

Roland exhaled slowly, loudly. "I am glad to hear it."

The earl inclined his head slightly, brows lifting as he said, "But I do have a vested interest in who comes to sit upon it next."

Roland raised one of his own brows in return. "The prince regent, I should think."

"You are correct, of course," Maltby allowed, looking back out toward the vista. Roland saw the tactic for what it was—an attempt to get Roland to relax his guard and show more of his true feelings. "And what about after that?"

Roland sighed heavily, although it pained him to do so. "His brothers. Or one of their children."

"One of *her* grandchildren," Maltby corrected him. There it was— the sneer. The distaste. Roland was satisfying whatever tests Maltby had set in his mind. Now the earl was letting his true feelings show.

"That is how succession works," Roland said slowly, as if he was weighing each word.

"How close she was to her namesake, our beloved lost princess." The sneer in Maltby's voice was unmistakable now.

Roland's gut twisted, and his hand lurched for the pistol concealed within his greatcoat. But he stilled it. He loosened the grip on his reins.

"We all grieve for the loss of the princess," Roland said. It was not commonly known that he'd been close to Princess Charlotte. But pretending to be indifferent caused a physical pain to slice through his chest.

Maltby turned back to Roland sharply. "I do not have time to grieve. I make plans instead."

Dangerous plans. Deadly ones.

"Plans for a new nation," Roland said instead.

"Plans for England," the earl said, conviction lacing every syllable.

Grayson Thane had been right. This was fanaticism.

"Your patriotism is to be applauded," Roland said. He was balanced on a knife's edge, every word dangerous. Now was when he would find out if he'd truly spoken the right ones.

Maltby cocked his head to the side. "I am glad you think so, Hawkridge. I wondered…" He paused, his shoulder twitching slightly in a silent chuckle. "It is no matter. I am pleased beyond measure to find we are aligned."

Roland let the silence hang between them for a few heartbeats, forcing his gaze back to the landscape before them. He traced the hills, the horizon, the fields, until he could trust his own voice enough.

"But to what end, Maltby?" he asked.

Maltby smiled then. It was like looking into the face of Lucifer himself.

"You will see, my friend. It is fortuitous that you are here now," he said.

Roland wasn't sure whether Maltby meant in England, at the house party, or sitting on this horse. "What do you want me to do?" he asked.

"Await further instructions," Maltby said, raising his chin an inch. A command.

He really was at the center of the intrigue, then. That was one question answered, at least.

"I'm no good at taking orders," Roland said, summoning that jocular smile he'd worn so often throughout his career.

"No, I suppose not. The errant duke, who has so long neglected his title and his duty. Just now, you'll have to put faith in those of us who have not." Maltby watched him closely as he spoke.

Roland let some of the frustration show on his face, earning him a conspiratorial chuckle.

"Be patient, my friend," Maltby urged.

"Another virtue rarely assigned to my name," Roland said wryly.

That earned him an acerbic laugh. "*Let us not become weary in doing good, for at the proper time we will reap a harvest if we do not give up,*" Maltby said, quoting the Bible. The devil cast one last wide look over the landscape, then turned his horse. "Come, before the ladies miss us."

Roland wanted more than anything to draw the pistol from his pocket and end this, now.

But that wouldn't achieve anything other than satisfying his own vengeance.

He'd play Maltby's lapdog for a bit longer. Long enough to find out everything he needed. Long enough to ensure that when the villain stepped onto the hangman's block, there would be no reprieve.

JANE DOUBTED SHE'D ever become accustomed to the married ladies' habit of taking breakfast on a tray in bed. Despite the hellish night, her eyes opened with the dawn. She'd feigned sleep until Roland left, mumbling something about riding out with Maltby. Then she dressed and went down to help herself to the breakfast laid out in the dining room.

After that, she positioned herself on one of the sofas in the massive entry hall, her embroidery in her lap, and willed herself to disappear into the scenery. It worked reasonably well. A maid carrying fresh linens nearly toppled her entire pile when Jane shifted in her seat and the sofa creaked beneath her.

A few of the gentlemen in residence passed through the hall on their way to various exploits. But it was the Earl of Leicester who sat down beside her.

"All alone this morning, Duchess?" he said, sitting without waiting for an invitation.

"I enjoy the quiet," she said pointedly.

After witnessing the little spat between Leicester and his wife the night before, Jane had no desire to further her acquaintance with the earl. It would only upset his wife further to find them sitting here speaking to one another, even if they did occupy a very public space within the manor. Jane had already given up gleaning any important information from Lady Leicester, but nor did she want the woman as her enemy in future.

"There's not much of that to be found at a house party," Leicester said, leaning back and hooking one ankle over his knee. "Nor in newlywed life," he added with a wink.

Jane cleared her throat delicately. "With all the other ladies abed and my husband entertained with Lord Maltby, I thought I would seize the opportunity for a bit of quiet reflection."

She could not be much clearer. But Leicester's smile only widened, and his gaze flicked down to her hands.

"And needlework."

Her patience was quickly wearing thin.

"I enjoy my needlework," she said, pursing her lips in an obvious show of annoyance.

Somehow, the blasted man took that for an invitation. He pushed away from the chair, coming to sit just beside her on the sofa and peer at her embroidery hoop.

"What is it you find so fascinating?" he murmured.

The hairs on the back of Jane's neck stood on end. Not in the way they did when her husband was near, teasing her senses. This was a warning.

"Is your wife feeling better this morning, my lord?"

Leicester laughed, the riotous sound filling the air and pressing in at her from every side. "I have long learned not to concern myself with Lady Leicester's little fits of ague," he said. "Someday, when you've been married as long as I, you will understand what I mean."

Jane couldn't figure out what his angle was. It was clear from the interaction between Lord and Lady Leicester last night that their marriage was stilted at best. That was not really so unusual in the *ton*. Most marriages were made for convenience rather than affection. Those that were made for affection often devolved once that initial attraction faded.

But that did not account for Leicester's behavior now. He acted as if he was attracted to her.

That was ridiculous.

No one had noticed Jane in the last four years. Not even the year of her debut. Now, she was a freshly married duchess in what the scandal sheets had all reported as a love match.

He could not honestly think she would be unfaithful to her husband, especially so early in their union.

Was this somehow related to the assassination plot? Maltby had ridden out with Roland this morning. Perhaps Leicester had been dispatched to cozy up to her and try to deduce just how dedicated she was to her husband?

Or maybe he was simply an ass.

Either way, Jane scooted as far as she could across the sofa until her hip was pressed firmly against the arm to the point of discomfort.

"Please convey my wishes for a speedy recovery to your wife," she said, jabbing her needle through the fabric and briefly imagining it was Leicester's skin.

"Where is your husband this morning?" Leicester asked, no longer bothering with the pretense of interest in her embroidery.

"He's ridden out with Lord Maltby," she said truthfully. No use evading—whatever Leicester was about, she was perfectly capable of dispatching him without Roland's help.

"I see." His smile deepened. "The light is so much better in the library. Perhaps you would allow me to escort you." As he spoke, he slid his hand across the polished wooden back of the sofa, behind Jane's shoulders.

Thank the Lord she'd been sitting up straight, or his smarmy hand would have been perilously close to actually touching her.

Jane straightened out her thread, adjusted the angle of her embroidery hoop, and stabbed the needle through the taut fabric, aiming directly for Leicester's—

"Leicester."

He leapt away before she could prick him. For a second, Jane questioned whether her sharp needle had actually reached Leicester's thigh, his reaction was so extreme. Then she saw Roland's face.

His voice may have been even and measured. But his eyes... She'd seen them laughing, plotting, hazed with drink. But she'd never seen them like this—with the promise of death staring directly out of them.

She rose to her feet, setting aside her embroidery on the sofa. Whatever came next, she wanted both of her hands free. Though from the danger emanating off Roland, perhaps she would have been better served to hold on to that needle.

In the time it took her to inhale, Roland's long strides had covered the space between them. He smelled of spice and sweat, and the subtle animal smell of horses clung to him as well.

Leicester stumbled backward, trying to maintain the distance between them, but with none of Roland's feral grace.

"I see you have been entertaining my wife while I was out," Roland said. She was ready for his hand on her waist, expected it. But the heat of him, like a blazing flame, was a surprise that rippled through her.

"I was merely making conversation," Leicester stammered. He glanced around wildly, searching for an ally or other witness. But the widening of his eyes told Jane that Maltby was nowhere to be found.

"My wife is plenty capable of entertaining herself."

Jane frowned, fighting to keep it at that rather than a downright scowl. She did not need Roland protecting her. She certainly did not need him making a scene that would only cause gossip amongst the other houseguests and might damage their cause.

She turned slightly in his half embrace, laying one hand on the lapel of his greatcoat. Lord, he really had come straight in from riding. He'd been looking for her—eager to tell her something. Jane's stomach lurched.

"I am well, my love," she said quietly, though still loud enough for

Leicester to hear. Let him think that she was soothing her husband. Let him be grateful to her. Perhaps she could use that to her advantage at some later time.

But Roland's gaze did not shift away from Leicester.

This temper of his was going to be the downfall of them both. He might call it instinct; Jane called it what it was—folly. No one really knew what the Duke of Hawkridge had been doing for the last twenty years during his travels abroad. But this moment made one thing clear—he was a dangerous man. If Leicester was in league with Maltby, as she guessed, then Lord Maltby would know it very soon. It could either aid their cause, or lead Maltby to shut them out entirely.

"Remember your place, Leicester," Roland said, gripping her hand on his chest.

The other man made a strangled sound that Jane could only surmise was an acquiesce. Then he darted from the room.

Jane waited until his footsteps faded away before she dropped her hand and stepped out of Roland's embrace. "You are overreacting—"

Roland did not let her go. His hand closed over hers like a vise, and the one at her hip tightened around the curve with proprietary strength.

"Not here," her husband said before dragging her away.

Twice, now, she'd been dragged out of Maltby Manor's grand hall by Roland. She was beginning to resent how comfortable he was in using the superior bulk of his body against her.

This time they didn't go to the solar, but a small butler's pantry. Roland opened the door, poked his head inside long enough to confirm it was empty, and then shoved her in.

She only waited for the door to close behind him to launch into her offensive.

"You have scared Leicester witless! He's probably running to Maltby right now to report that the Duke of Hawkridge is a danger—"

"Maltby already knows who I am."

Jane blinked, grabbing around for something to steady herself. Her husband's arm was the first thing. "How?"

Roland shook his head. "Not *that*," he clarified. "But I've given him plenty of reason to believe I'm sympathetic to his cause. After this morning, I expect some sort of invitation to be forthcoming."

Jane snapped her mouth shut, processing that information. But she still could not stop herself from whispering harshly, "I am perfectly capable of handling myself. Leicester—"

"Leicester was a second away from trying to slip his hand down your bodice," Roland snapped, glaring down at her.

The space was much too small for someone of his size. Even with Jane's diminutive stature, there was not enough room for both of them. She tried to back away, but there was a wall. She tried to shake out her hands, but realized she was still gripping the steely muscles of Roland's forearm.

"So what if he was?" she spat. "I can handle an oaf like Leicester in my sleep."

"So what if he was?" Roland repeated, his voice dropping to a deadly whisper. "You are *my wife*."

But Jane ignored the warning in those last two syllables. Apparently, she'd left her rational thinking on the sofa with her embroidery.

"Little that seems to matter to you! You want nothing to do with me!" she cried.

Instead of retreating back from her vitriol, Roland stepped closer. How could he get closer? They were in this tiny little space already, practically pressed together.

His hands bracketed her waist. Such strength in those large palms, the long fingers... When he closed them around her hips, the message was unmistakable. *Mine.*

"Is that what you think, little mouse?"

Jane opened her mouth to demand he stop calling her by that ridiculous nickname. But Roland slanted his lips over hers and stole the words away.

He stole every thought in her head. Jane's entire world narrowed to the place where their lips met. His tongue pushed past her lips, claiming her as his own without a second's hesitation.

Wrong, wrong, wrong.

That one kiss was all she needed to convince her of how utterly her logic and reason had failed her.

"You think I do not want this?" He slid his hand down her thigh, using his fingers to bunch the fabric of her gown in his hand until her leg was bare beneath his fingertips. "You think I have not imagined doing this?" He curled his hand around her bare hip, and those long fingers came dangerously near the building heat between her legs.

All of the desire from the last weeks flooded through her, like a dam breaking. Roland knocked it free with the swipe of his tongue and the stroke of his hand. All it took was one indication that he wanted her as much as she wanted him, and all restraint was gone.

"I have thought of nothing but this, ever since I felt your sweet body pressed against mine on that bloody horse," he said against her chin, before moving his mouth down beneath her jaw to devour the delicate column of her throat.

She was half a second from admitting that she'd burned for him long before that, but then his mouth disappeared. Jane's eyes popped open, and her chest heaved as she searched for him. But Roland was gone.

He was sliding down her body. He pressed a kiss to the dimple between her breasts, just above the neckline of her bodice. His hands didn't move at all. They tightened.

Both sides of her gown were rucked up in his hands, hands that held her firmly in place as he nudged the layers of soft fabric aside and pressed a kiss to the inside of her thigh.

"Little mouse," he murmured, nipping at the tender flesh. "Will you squeak for me?"

Jane expected his hand to fall away, to feel those glorious fingers she'd been dreaming about parting her and finally—*finally*—touching her.

But it was not his fingers that skated against her slit. It was his tongue.

Jane didn't know if the strangled sound from her lips qualified as a squeak, but she felt Roland's groan of approval. Felt it right there against the most private part of her body. Academically, she'd known that men and women engaged in such activities, but—

"Oh my God," she moaned, biting her bottom lip hard to stifle the sounds that built in her chest.

To hell with academics and logic.

Roland's tongue on her cunt was nothing short of heaven. It defied reality and logic, and she would happily never think of such mundane things again so long as he kept on doing *this*.

He tasted her like one would a delicacy. First, he ran his nose along the length of her slit, breathing her in. The warmth of his breath against her sensitive flesh sent shivers ricocheting through her body. Then came his tongue.

It was not the deep, possessive stroke he'd used to take her mouth. No, this was a taste. He was sampling her, delving his tongue deeper with each stroke, sliding it up and down the length of her sex, before finally twirling it around that bundle of nerves—

"Roland," she gasped, flailing around for something to hold on to.

His hands were on her hips, holding her steady, but she was desperate to anchor herself. Somehow, her hand landed in his hair. With the next swirl of his tongue around her love button, she dug her nails into his scalp.

"Just like that, my love," he said, chuckling against her, pausing a moment to nuzzle her dark curls.

"Roland, please," Jane heard herself begging, her hand in his hair urging his mouth back to its task.

"Is this what you want?" he asked softly, circling her nub with his tongue and then drawing it between his lips, suckling on it with delicious pressure.

Jane arched against him, wanting more, wanting it now.

"Yes, you like that," he said. "But do you like this more?"

His tongue slid down her slit, and his lips helped to maneuver aside her folds. Then he plunged his tongue inside of her, fucking her with the silken length of it. Jane whimpered, high-pitched little sounds she hadn't even realized she could make. It had never been like this. Not by herself, not with—

"You're going to come for me, my darling," Roland said. *Commanded.*

Even in this, he wanted to be in control, to boss her around. But damn him, she was powerless to stop it. His hands were rocking her hips forward in time with the movement of his tongue as he drove it inside of her again and again.

Jane pressed her hips together, feeling the pressure building. She could feel the climax, her breathing coming in ragged gasps.

But Roland pulled his tongue free. Jane nearly screamed with the loss.

"Hold on, my love," he said, easing one hand down from her hip.

He was as good as his word. Just as she was about to open her eyes, to break into a million pieces with the force of her need, his tongue landed on her love button once more. And that hand that he'd moved from her hip nudged apart her entrance. He slid one finger inside of her in time with sucking on her, and Jane was powerless before the pleasure.

Her climax crashed over her, the power of it stealing her breath. If she hadn't been pinned against the wall, Roland's strong hand on her hip, she would have melted onto the floor. He stroked her through it, wringing every last tremor of pleasure from her body until her legs were shaking.

Even then, when he drew his fingers free to caress her thighs and hips, his tongue continued with long, languorous strokes. Tasting her, licking up every last drop of her pleasure.

Finally, he let her skirts fall and rose to stand, returning his hands to her waist. They held her loosely now, but with no less possessiveness.

Her lower lip was trembling as she slowly raised her chin to look up into his eyes. They were as dark as ever, but the desire in them now—she'd seen it before, she realized. So many times. It had been there all along, even when she'd convinced herself otherwise.

Jane tried to find something to say, something that made sense. She'd even settle for some nonsensical turn of phrase. But she had nothing. Roland seemed to read her face, as his lips stretched into that rakish smile. Lips that were still wet with her pleasure.

He lowered those lips to hers, kissing her with slow, steady confidence.

She could taste herself on his tongue.

Suddenly, one climax was not enough. She wanted more—she wanted him. Not his fingers, but his cock, buried deep inside of her.

Jane skated her hand down from where it was curled around his neck, past the layers of clothing. He was still wearing his greatcoat. How was that possible, when she'd been bare before him not a minute before?

But Roland caught her hand before she could slide it past the folds of his coat.

"I thought I'd caught a mouse, but it turned out to be a jungle cat," he murmured against her lips. She could *feel* his smile.

Slowly, he lifted her hand up above her head.

"I'm not done tasting you just yet," he said, already moving his lips downward once again.

Her breasts, she realized as his free hand began to toy with the thin fabric of her bodice. She arched again, trying to move her hand so she could rip the damn thing off her body. She wanted nothing between them.

But Roland held her tight, pressing the back of her hand firmly against the wall, pinning it with his palm—

Then the entire wall moved.

CHAPTER TWENTY-ONE

"I SUPPOSE A secret society needs secret passageways," Jane said softly.

The fact that she could form such a coherent sentence had Roland wondering if he'd done as thorough of a job making love to her with his mouth as he'd thought.

They'd tumbled backward through a concealed passage.

He ran his gaze over Jane, quickly assessing her for any injury. But she was already nudging him aside to peer up at the panel in the wall where he'd pressed their hands. It looked entirely nondescript.

Jane skated her fingertips back and forth, then paused, pressing her fingernail down. A groove, Roland realized, though it was hard to see in the dim light of the passageway.

"A lever of some sort," Jane said softly, standing on her tiptoes and angling her head to try to get a closer look.

"It doesn't matter how it works," Roland pointed out, already dismissing it and turning around. "Look at this." Before him stretched a long, dark corridor only a hairsbreadth wider than his own shoulders. He had to stoop to stand, an uncomfortable angle that would surely leave an ache in his neck. "Do you think—"

He turned to ask, but Jane was still examining the makeshift doorway that had allowed them through. "We stumble upon a network of hidden passageways, and you are staring at the door."

Jane shot him a look of reprove, her lips thinning away to near invisibility. "We have yet to verify that this is a network of hidden passageways," she corrected him. "If it is, it would be prudent to study the entrance. It may help us find other entrances hidden throughout the manor."

Roland sighed heavily. He hated when her logic led her to being so irritatingly correct.

"We'll look at it on our way out," he said, tone conciliatory. "When it's firmly closed behind us, we can examine it at our leisure without danger of being caught in the passageways themselves."

Jane's eyes narrowed, and her pert nose tipped upward. But she must have deemed his logic sound, because she stepped back and closed the doorway behind her, leaving a small crack just in case the mechanism locked into place and sealed them in.

Always so prudent and forward thinking, his little mouse.

She peered down the corridor, wrinkling her nose as she did. "I cannot see past you. You take up the entire passageway."

Roland felt the smile tugging at his lips and let it have its way. "By all means, lead the way." He stepped to the side, pressing himself against the wall to let her pass.

The walls themselves were made of stone, roughly hewn, and grouted bricks that dug into his back at awkward angles. They were more or less straight until they reached his shoulder, then they started to curve inward to form an arch that met where his eyeballs would be if he weren't stooped over.

Oil lamps burned every few yards, set into the stone. While they were modern in function, the design looked like those he'd seen at Hampton Court. All of it was completely out of place for a manor house built in the eighteenth century.

Roland glanced back at Jane, catching her eyes making all the same assessments as his own. He nodded toward the end of the corridor, where the path split in either direction. "Shall we?"

Jane nodded, gathering her skirt in her hand to keep it from snagging on the uneven flagstone floor.

Even molded as he was to the curved wall, Jane had to press herself against him to get past. One hand held her skirt. The other hesitated at his shoulder. The easiest thing would have been for her to hold on to him as she maneuvered past. But her fingers curled, tentative.

"You're safe, little mouse," he said softly.

He didn't need to see her eyes in the faded light to know she shot daggers at him. But she did reach out and firmly grasp the front of his jacket, moving herself over and past him. If she was as affected by the way her breasts pressed against his chest or her thighs skimmed over his cock... Well, she at least was a consummate professional.

While Roland focused on reining in his cock, Jane moved slowly down the passage.

"What an odd choice," she said, dragging her fingertips over the rough wall. "It looks medieval, though that is impossible. Why go to the trouble of making the passageways look like a castle, when no one is meant to see them?"

Roland sighed grimly as he voiced the suspicion that had been building in him. "Someone is meant to see them—Maltby's collaborators. He wants to harken back to the days of old England. The true kings, whatever that is supposed to mean. He said as much this morning."

Jane cocked her head to the side, her eyes pensive. "It is meant to make an impression," she said slowly. "I wonder how many of the guests know about them."

They reached the end of the first passage, where it split off. Each paused, their minds turning with possibilities. But the sound of voices stole the need for a decision. Roland and Jane both moved with absolute silence even over the uneven ground. He spotted the source of the sound two steps down the second passage.

The stone had been cut away, and a metal grate with narrow vertical caps sealed over it. Even standing on tiptoe, Jane struggled to get her eyes high enough. Without asking, Roland slid his hands around her waist and lifted her.

She didn't protest. What could she do? Through the first metal grate they could see through to the other side, straight into Maltby's library.

From the height and viewpoint, Roland thought the grate must be set into the bookshelf itself. Some object partially obscured the view into the library, and that of any of the room's occupants who noticed the metal grate.

Although, from the raised voices, it would have taken a great deal to distract from the argument happening within.

"Marion told me! You were making yourself comfortable with Hawkridge's simpering little wife!"

"Who the hell is Marion?"

"My maid! Do you really pay me so little attention? We brought her with us from Hempstead!"

"So, you've set your maid to spying on me."

"She was fetching fresh herbs for my tincture!"

"You are not ill! Unless you consider waspishness catching, you ill-tempered besom—"

Roland eased Jane back from the wall, setting her carefully back on her feet. "I don't think there is much to be learned from listening to Lord and Lady Leicester's row," he whispered into her ear.

He watched her chin twitch back in the direction of the argument. Roland recalled what she'd said that day in front of the hotel, during their first official meeting. She'd commented that staying apprised of *ton* gossip and drama made her a better lady knight. He was starting to understand what she meant.

There was no immediate use for the knowledge that Lord and Lady Leicester were at odds. But if they needed to create a distraction, or an alibi at some point during the house party, it could be turned to their advantage. In the unlikely chance that Leicester was not involved in Maltby's schemes, but was an innocent bystander, it might even serve a later purpose once Jane returned to reign over the *ton* as the Duchess of Hawkridge.

"There is plenty to be learned," she countered when they were several yards away from the opening. "But logically, we have a limited amount of time to explore these passageways, and our time is better spent in that endeavor."

Roland made sure that when she glanced back over her shoulder, his grin was tucked well away.

They found three more spyholes, looking into an informal dining room, sitting room, and servants' stairwell respectively. All three areas were currently unoccupied, but the objective was clear enough. These passages allowed Maltby—and whoever else knew about them—to listen in on private conversations. Quite useful if one was trying to determine the loyalties of potential members of a secret society.

"Do you suppose this house party is meant for recruiting, rather than executing a plan?" Jane asked, her thoughts clearly having taken the same direction as his.

They'd reached a dead end and were now retracing their steps back through the passageways.

Roland waited to answer until they were well past the opening to the small dining room. "Everything we've learned has indicated the assassination attempt is imminent. It seems late to be recruiting... though I suppose that is exactly Maltby's intent where I am concerned."

They passed the library. Lord and Lady Leicester had retreated to elsewhere in the house, giving Jane and Roland peace to continue whispering as they picked their way back toward the door into the little pantry.

"From what I've gleaned speaking with the other ladies, they've all visited Maltby Manor before, except for myself and Lady Chatterley. So perhaps you are correct."

Roland stopped abruptly, turning slowly in the confined space. He did not hide his smirk at all this time. "Say that again, my love."

Her eyes turned murderous. Roland half expected her to reach for the little knife she had strapped to her calf. He'd noted it when he was busy kissing his way up the insides of her thighs.

Instead, she shoved him to the side and attempted to sidle past him in the minimal space.

Every brush of contact was a reminder of what had transpired between them mere minutes before. Despite the seriousness of the situation, Roland was as hard now as he had been when he felt her gushing climax on his face.

He caught her around the waist, pulling her tight against him. Her small hands turned to fists that connected with his chest, but Roland ignored them, kissing her hard instead. She tasted so goddamned sweet. He doubted he would ever get enough of the taste of her on his tongue.

He wanted to know every flavor Jane's sweet body had to offer. The taste of her pleasure on his lips once wasn't enough. He wanted to know how she tasted after a hard day of riding or sparring with a blade. He longed to lick every inch of her flesh fresh from the bath, shining and pink.

He was ready to release her, expecting her to fight back. But her fists flattened against his shoulders, and then she was clinging to him as hard as he was to her.

Hell.

For all her logic and reason, she was every bit as passionate as he was beneath the surface. He'd begun to peel back that calm and cool exterior. But was he ready for what was waiting beneath?

They both eased away, as if realizing in the same thought that a musty secret passageway was not the place for amorous embraces. But

Jane looked every bit as riled as Roland felt.

His breath was ragged as he forced an exhale, but there was nothing he could do for that at the moment. Short of taking her right there in the passageway, which was too dangerous to contemplate.

Jane's rich brown eyes were darker in the dim light, the color of freshly tilled soil. When she met his gaze, they softened instantly.

That's a nice change.

"We should return before we are missed," she said softly. "Lady Maltby has organized a tour of the chapel in the village. There is apparently an authentic Tudor tapestry on display."

Roland nodded. She was right, of course. But neither of them moved back toward the entrance through the pantry.

He reached for her hand, telling himself he would take it and lead her out. But once his fingers took hers, he found himself instead lifting their hands upward, so he could see them more clearly in the dim light coming from the vertical slats.

Even in the low light, the contrast of her alabaster skin against his deeper tan was evident. He'd been in India directly before his return to England, and the tan still colored his skin, even several months later. But Jane's was completely untouched. She was fresh and unmarked. Completely his.

He found himself wondering just how pale the skin of her stomach would be, where it had never seen daylight. Or the undersides of her breasts, where he wanted to drag his tongue and taste the subtle, sweet flavor of her.

She smiled softly. It should have come as no surprise to him that, in the end, it was Jane leading him out of the passage and back to safety.

CHAPTER TWENTY-TWO

THEY'D BARELY HAD a moment to speak privately after emerging from the labyrinth of secret passages. Lady Maltby and the other ladies were already assembling for their outing. They took luncheon in the village, and when the ladies returned in the afternoon to rest before supper, Roland was nowhere to be found.

Jane took a long bath, scrubbing her skin until it was pink and tingling, waiting for her husband. She lingered until the water was cold, hoping Roland would interrupt her. Now that she knew her desire was reciprocated...

But he didn't appear until a quarter hour before supper, when the maid was already in the room helping Jane dress. He changed behind the privacy screen and then escorted her downstairs to join the other guests.

Of course, the men and women separated at the end of the meal. The men were off to drink, smoke, and play billiards. Jane sipped sherry with the ladies, but excused herself after half an hour.

That had been a mistake. Once she was alone in the bedroom, time came to a standstill. She contemplated calling for another bath. But she was loath to disturb the servants. She pretended to read, not bothering to undress. She'd hoped that Roland would appear and do that himself.

But the hour was edging later and later, and still her husband had not appeared.

This is ridiculous.

She'd never waited for a man in her life. Even when things had gone awry... No, not even then.

She tossed aside the book, retrieved her slippers, and slipped out into the hall.

It was easy to avoid the rest of the houseguests. Most of the women had already come up to bed. She paused to listen at a few doors as she passed, confirming the sounds of movements within. Women were always harder to hear. They were used to being unobtrusive, had been trained to be so their entire lives. It was why they made such good spies—or rather, lady knights. It was simply a matter of weaponizing the proclivities bred into her since birth.

Men, on the other hand, stomped through life with all the entitlement of their gender. Which was how Jane knew that not a single gentleman with a room in this corridor had retired. The billiards game must have turned rancorous.

But that was not Jane's destination.

She moved on silent feet down the first flight of stairs, past the first floor where the dining and billiards rooms were located. The ground floor would be deserted, with even the servants starting to retire to the attics for the night. Which made it the ideal time to explore the secret passageways.

Jane found her way back to the butler's pantry with little effort. She pushed down the heat that flooded her cheeks as she entered the small room. It must be her imagination—she could not possibly still smell the musk of her own pleasure in the cramped space.

She pushed through the secret doorway. This time, she closed it behind her fully. She'd had enough time to examine the mechanism and was certain it would not lock her in. When she reached the end of the first passage, she turned right instead of left.

She counted each step she took, carefully constructing a map within her mind. She'd sketched out what they'd explored so far before her bath. But she wanted accuracy. How many steps, how many turns, what sounds and smells could be sensed from each passage.

Doing this herself was the only realistic way of getting it done at all, she told herself as she paused and peered into a room she hadn't yet seen from inside the passage or out. Roland was too damn distracting to her senses. When he was here, his huge, hulking form filling the space, she could hardly remember her name, let alone the important details that might save the Queen of England.

She was halfway down the third passageway of the night when she tripped.

Her knee hit the ground hard, sending her careening forward. She threw out an elbow to stop herself. It would hurt more, but if she braced herself with her hand at that speed, she'd likely break her wrist. All of those careful thoughts in the space of a breath. And not a single sound from her lips.

Jane remained on the ground for several long moments, taking stock of her injuries. She'd have bruises on her knees, certainly. Her elbow was likely skinned. She probed at it with the fingertips of her other hand, finding the fabric of her gown torn. But no moisture. She wasn't bleeding, at least.

With deliberate slowness, she rose back up to her feet. As soon as she did, she realized why she'd fallen.

The passage sloped downward. It was subtle but, with the uneven stones on the ground, dangerous if one did not take enough care. She glanced back over her shoulder, in the direction she'd come. She remembered the path she'd taken. She could find her way out easily.

You are injured, her logical mind said. *You will be slower and clumsier, more likely to be caught.*

Yes, a retreat was the logical course of action. But it felt as if there was a string pulling at the center of Jane's chest, urging her in the opposite direction. Down the sloping passage. She suspected Roland would call this instinct.

She relied on her instincts plenty. Not to the exclusion of rational thought, as Roland did. But that pull in her chest was so persistent...

Thirty paces more, Jane promised herself. If she had not discovered anything of note in thirty more paces, she would turn around and return to the safety of the bedroom, content with adding to the map she'd already begun earlier in the day.

As it turned out, thirty paces were more than sufficient. At fifteen, she reached the staircase. If she counted each stair, that got her to twenty-three. And five steps past that, she was no longer standing in the tight little passageway.

»»»«««

ROLAND MANAGED TO extricate himself when Leicester passed out facedown on the billiards table. The commotion—laughing and harrumphing—gave him an opportunity to slip out unnoticed, and he was not about to miss it. He'd nursed his two drams of whisky all night, waiting for an excuse to leave.

It was damned difficult. Maltby had fixed himself at Roland's side, seemingly intent on monitoring his every word. At one point, Roland had been ready to tell the man that he needed to go fuck his wife or he'd lose his mind. But he couldn't speak that way about Jane to a villain like Maltby, even if it was the truth.

They'd crossed their Rubicon.

Whatever else stood between them—differences in their professional approaches, beliefs about their own capabilities, pure hubris—the fact that they wanted each other desperately was startlingly clear.

But they each had a part to play. After all they'd discovered today, there was no doubt that everything they'd surmised about Maltby and his secret society was true. The danger here was very real. So Roland sipped his whisky and forced himself to leash his desire. He could manage it for a few hours. He could hold his need for her in check and give Maltby his attention, knowing that Jane was safe in the bedroom waiting for him.

He would join her, updating her on everything he'd learned as he undressed her layer by layer. Then he would make love to her. Slowly. He would explore every inch of her body, without danger hanging over them, at least for one night.

He left his empty glass on a side table and bounded up the stairs to the second floor two at a time. He tossed his cravat to the side in the same motion as he swung open the door—and froze.

Twice, he looked around the room, thinking his mind more addled by the whisky than was possible. Maybe Maltby had laced it with something. But by the second sweep, he realized his eyes were not playing tricks on him.

Jane was not in the bedroom.

CHAPTER TWENTY-THREE

S HE'D MADE IT as far as the first floor when she heard footsteps.

Jane looked around feverishly, but there was no door to be found. She was between the grand dining room and the staircase, with nothing but an expanse of wall from here to there. She was fast, but the cadence of the footsteps told her that even if she made a run for it, she would not make it up the stairs in time.

The shadows were her only chance.

She plastered herself against the wall, pulling her skirt tight around her legs so that even an errant breeze could not expose her. Thank the Lord she was so small; she'd have never fit in the narrow column of shadow otherwise.

Even so, it was a gamble. If the gentleman looked at her directly, there'd be no hiding. Only if he started up the stairs without looking down the other hall, keeping her in his periphery, would she remain hidden.

Another thought crept into her mind. Reach for the dagger strapped to her leg. Not to stab him—but the hilt was sturdy enough that if she hit him hard at the right angle, he'd be rendered unconscious. It was dangerous, though. If he recognized her before she could make her move, if he was fully sober…

But the space of a breath had the dagger in her hand. Better to be prepared should the situation go awry. Hiding was her first course of action. Talking her way out of things would be her second. The dagger was only for an absolute emergency.

Jane's muscles were taut and ready when the gentleman rounded the corner.

Her chest tightened immediately as she recognized his tall, lean form.

Her husband did not walk past her up the stairs without an idle glance. He froze, his foot firmly planted before the first step, and stared directly at her.

She opened her mouth to explain, but didn't get the chance.

Roland covered the space between them in three of those impossibly long strides. He scooped her up in his arms with equal efficiency, and his eyes flashed in the lamplight as he carried her to the stairs.

They darkened when they landed upon the dagger still clutched in her hand.

"Fucking hell," he swore under his breath, not breaking stride.

They were up the stairs and down the corridor toward their room. She could feel the emotion vibrating through him.

She wanted to believe it was desire.

But her instincts told her otherwise—though it defied all reason. What rationale could he possibly have for being angry at *her*?

Roland dropped her unceremoniously on the floor as soon as he stepped over their threshold. Jane managed to get her feet under her and not fall flat on her bottom. Roland kicked the door closed behind him, then caught it with his hand to soften the sound.

He was angry, but not completely gone to temper.

Yet when he turned his dark eyes back to her, she wondered if she'd misjudged that second part. "Why are you stalking the hallways with a dagger in your hand?"

Jane took a moment to set that dagger aside on the dressing table before replying calmly. "You were long with Maltby. I decided to take advantage of the gentlemen's occupation to further explore the secret passages."

"Alone. Without telling me where you were going." Roland jerked a glance around the room. "Without leaving any sort of note."

Jane's chin rose a fraction. "I do not report to you."

"We are supposed to be partners," he ground out.

He was trying to hold on to his temper. Jane could see the way his large hands closed into deadly fists. She could understand why other men cowered in fear before this accomplished agent of the Crown. But she was not afraid of him. He'd never hurt her. Of that, she was entirely confident.

At least not with his body.

But his words…

"And as partners, we both have roles to play. Yours was in the billiards room drinking away the evening with Maltby. Mine was to move in stealth."

Roland's hands opened. "What did you expect me to think when I returned to this room and found you gone?"

"That I was a capable professional going about my work."

"Or that you'd been taken!" He advanced across the room, each step punctuating a sentence. "That we'd been found out. That Maltby took you to torture you for information."

He was close enough now that she could smell the whisky on his breath. Anger began to uncurl itself in her own belly. "I was doing my job," she said again, stubbornly. "And I found something."

"I do not care what you found," he growled.

He was as feral a beast as she'd ever seen, his frustration caged only by sheer will—which Jane knew was about to fray away to nothing. She ought to retreat, to preserve their working relationship by stepping away until he regained his temper and could speak professionally.

But she did no such thing.

"You arrogant arse! While you were busy getting foxed, I found the meeting room where the secret society convenes. Torches, gold chalices, the whole ridiculous and nefarious thing!"

Roland stared at her. "I am not foxed."

Jane's mouth fell open in disbelief. "*That* is what you heard."

His brows narrowed, like silver bolts of lightning focused right on her. "I heard all of it. And you can give me a full accounting after I've bent you over my knee and spanked you for your insolence."

She knew he'd never actually try such a thing. But she still jumped back. "You are not my master."

Roland licked his bottom lip. "I am your husband."

Her hand landed on the bedpost. She gripped it hard, whether from anger or to keep herself upright, she didn't examine close enough to decide.

"Those are not the same thing," she said.

His lips curved wickedly. "And well I know it."

Damn it all, but she wanted to kiss that wicked smile right off his face.

"Good," Jane managed, her voice just above a whisper.

Roland's acerbic laugh filled the air.

"Good? There is nothing good about it. I cannot even have a sip of whisky without worrying that you will scurry off and get yourself killed!" The emotion in his voice speared through her.

She rose to meet him, straightening her spine to a length of steel. "I do not scurry. I am not a little mouse, or a duchess, or even a fucking wallflower. I am a lady knight."

She didn't curse. She was a lady. But even that seemed to be coming apart at the seams.

Roland stared directly into her eyes, no blink, no breath between them.

"You are my wife."

The intensity of those words pressed down on her. She forced a sarcastic laugh to match his. "Is this what I have to look forward to as a wife? A husband who gets belligerent when he's foxed?"

"I said it before, I am not foxed," he said. His gaze was as sharp as the falcon he kept as a pet.

Jane swallowed hard. "You certainly aren't the man who—"

"The man who what, my sweet? The man who made you come all over his face? The one who had you whimpering and begging for more?" He grabbed the bedpost as well, curling his fingers around the carved wood just at the level of her eyes, forcing her to think of when those same fingers had been curled inside of her.

"Bastard."

He gnashed his teeth. "I have been called worse."

"I shall be more creative," she promised.

He towered above her. Jane was grateful for every inch of space between them and hated it at the same time. She wanted to throw her body against his, pound her hands against his chest, and then torture him with a kiss as scorching hot as he deserved.

Roland licked his lips again. "Little mouse, duchess, wallflower, lady knight. You are all those things and more. My clever little mouse, sneaking around where no one suspects. My duchess, looking down on the other members of the *ton* because you know they are beneath you as well as I do. A wallflower... Oh yes, you are a beautiful ornament. An exotic Venus flytrap, waiting for your moment to strike. But before all of that, Jane, you are my wife. And I will protect you even if it means you hate me for it."

Her voice was little more than a whisper as she spoke. "I do not need your protection. I am not a child."

"No. You are all woman," her husband said, suddenly dangerously close. "*My* woman."

I belong to no one but myself, Jane wanted to say.

But as Roland's mouth slanted over hers, she knew that it would have been a lie.

CHAPTER TWENTY-FOUR

T HANK GOD ABOVE for gifting her husband with such large hands. They touched her everywhere, all at once.

The punishing heat of his mouth on hers set alight the inferno burning between them. There was no going back, and neither of them wanted to.

Roland cupped her breasts, teasing her with a few quick strokes. His hand traced down her spine before cupping her bottom through her gown.

Jane didn't even fight the squeak that he tore from her lips as he hoisted her up. Those wide, confident hands handled her as if she weighed nothing. It was intoxicating to give herself up to such power, more than any spirit she had ever drunk.

Her legs wrapped around his hips instinctively, digging her heels into the firm, lean muscles of his buttocks. She wanted that in her hands too—she was suddenly jealous of all the places he was touching her. His mouth tortured her neck while his hands massaged the soft mounds that filled his palms.

But she could touch him.

Roland was her husband. Hers, as much as she was his.

So, she shoved aside the broadcloth of his tailcoat, sliding her fingers beneath the silk panels of his waistcoat to tug on his shirt. She wanted to touch that skin she'd been dreaming about for weeks.

Roland seemed to hear her needs even though they lived inside her head. He lowered her back onto the bed, pulling his hands and lips away.

"No!" she cried out, bolting straight up. But Roland caught her eyes.

"Yes," he said with soft command. He stared directly into her soul, all the promise and reassurance she needed right there as his hands efficiently peeled away his layers of clothing until he was nothing but broad chest before her.

Jane's breath caught. He was perfect.

The planes of his chest were sculpted around each muscle— muscles honed from practical experience and use, not senseless boxing, as so many young *ton* pups did for exercising. One look at those hard, tight muscles and Jane knew that when Roland threw a punch, there was a villain on the receiving end of it. Even the gray interspersed among black that painted his chest—darker there than on his head of silvery hair—spoke of a body honed in service. He was a painting of duty, of long years spent sharpening his skill in the one thing Jane respected above all else.

He was a masterpiece.

Roland was watching her as she watched him, half of his mouth curving in that wicked grin once again. "Do you like what you see, wife?"

Jane exhaled a shaky breath. "Why are you still standing there?" she demanded.

Roland needed no further encouragement.

He dove upon her with the ferocity of a hawk swooping into the field to catch its prey.

First his hands had been everywhere—now it was his lips.

His mouth moved across the neckline of her gown, and his teeth tore at the fabric. It was positively bestial, nearly unhinged. Jane's core flooded with wetness at the sight of it.

Then she felt his hands at her back, urging her to arch beneath him. "Let me—"

"No," he said sharply, shoving away her hands.

Her arms fell back onto the bed, and she was momentarily at a loss.

"Touch me," Roland said between nips.

He urged her up again, tugging at the buttons of her gown. Her hips connected with his rigid cock straining against the confines of his trousers, and touching him was suddenly essential. Clinging to him. She had to hold on to his shoulders, to dig her fingers into that tanned flesh, just so that she could keep grinding her hips against his.

Roland groaned, tugging one arm away and then the other so he could slide down the sleeves of her gown. The chemise and stays were no impediment at all. Roland simply tore them away.

Rational Jane might have protested at the destruction of her undergarments. But this Jane, lost to the madness of his touch, was ready to let him shred her entire wardrobe. The burning in her loins practically demanded it.

This Jane was brazen.

She slid her hands into his hair, finding purchase even in the tightly cropped locks. She shoved his head down until his lips closed around her nipple.

"This," she moaned, arching her hips again.

Her breasts may be small, but they were so damn sensitive. Roland took her direction to heart. He easily cupped his entire hand around her other breast. While he circled his tongue around one tip, sucking with increasing pressure, he massaged the other. First broad touches. Then he dragged a fingernail around the perimeter of her areola, teasing the tight bud of her nipple until it was tight and hard as a bud in early spring.

She rocked harder against him, crying out with the need for more friction, more contact to that bundle of nerves at the apex of her dark curls.

"Such a needy, demanding little thing," Roland said against her as he lifted his mouth from one breast to the other.

Jane whimpered and thrust her hips upward in response.

She was going to climax just from the rubbing alone. Her entire body was encased in heat, and the feeling of his mouth on her breasts was edging her closer and closer to the precipice. Roland knew it, shifting so that she was grinding her bare slit against the corded muscles of his still-clothed thigh.

"Come for me, sweet," he whispered, his breath hot against the trail of moisture he left on her breasts.

"I can't," Jane moaned, even as she increased the pace of her thrusts.

"Yes, you can. You shall," he commanded before recommitting his attention to her breasts.

As if she truly was his to command, her body surrendered. Her climax ripped through her, and the cries wrenched from her lips were much louder than the squeaks and moans that had come before. As the sensation ebbed, softening, so did Roland's touches on her breasts. Until he was resting his head against them, idly stroking a finger along one outside curve.

Jane came up on her elbows, forcing him to sit up, trying to look down at the space between him. The slate gray of his trousers was soaked nearly to black where she'd ridden him. She felt the blush climbing her cheeks, but Roland grabbed her face between his hands and held her eyes.

"Do not apologize," he commanded. "Never be embarrassed for taking what you need. I will always—always—give it to you."

The sincerity in his words stole her breath. A second later, his lips took her mouth as well.

Even through the haze of lingering pleasure, she was keenly aware when his hand slid down between them. Not to stroke her, but to do away with the last remaining fabric between them.

The instant he was free of the trousers, Jane arched against him again. That same demanding thrust of her hips as before, but now with a very specific goal—him. She could feel the head of his cock nudging between her legs, trying to find her entrance. Without thinking, she slid her hand down, ready to part her folds and welcome him.

But Roland let out a long, rough groan and shifted his hips away.

"No!" she cried immediately, arching off the bed to reach him. Impossible. He was huge, every part of him, and he could hold himself away from her tiny form with only the barest effort.

"Jane," came Roland's strangled voice. "We must go slowly."

Her eyes snapped open from their heavy-lidded daze, fixing on his face. She dragged her tongue over her lips, then slid her gaze downward until she was staring at him. Every generous, beautiful, perfect inch of her husband.

"I am not a virgin," she said sharply, wrapping her hand around his shaft. Egads, he was *huge*. And she wanted him inside of her—now. "So do not treat me like one."

Roland drew in one long, ragged breath.

He didn't ask questions, didn't cut her a judgmental look. He covered her mouth with his, spearing his tongue into her mouth as his hand closed around hers and guided his cock to her entrance.

"This is what I want," she said as the magnificent head slipped inside of her. "I want *all* of you."

Roland groaned again. Even with her words of encouragement, that first stroke was so agonizingly slow. He slid into her inch by torturous inch, waiting to find some hindrance, expecting her to be unable to take him. Jane half expected it herself, so mismatched were their heights.

But in this, they were perfectly matched.

In the next breath, he was buried inside her to the hilt, filling every nook of her womanhood. He waited a moment—whether to give her time to adjust to his size or to try to regain some semblance of self-control, she did not know. Then he slid out again. Before he could go slow, be gentle, Jane closed her legs around his waist and slammed him back inside of her.

She watched in amazement and unbridled lust as the tether on his self-control snapped. He pounded inside of her like it was the end of the world, and she lifted her hips to meet every stroke. She didn't need to slide a hand between them and touch herself. The grind of his body against her own, the way he stretched her open and filled every part of her, was more than enough. She was already close to climax again.

And so was he, Jane realized as she clung to his shoulders and watched him. Just watching the angles of his face change with each thrust was enough to push her over the edge. His tight jaw, the holding back of his own pleasure—pleasure she had wrought—sent waves of bliss through her body.

Jane cried out, digging her fingernails into the muscles of his neck. But even as her own climax rocked her, she lifted her hips and demanded more. She wanted his surrender as badly as she'd needed her own.

She even opened her mouth to demand it from him, as he had from her. But there was no need. Roland's bellow filled the air as he lost control, and his cock expanded within her as he filled her with his own pleasure.

As the strokes slowed, she waited for him to roll away. This hadn't been about tenderness, she realized as the dregs of her climax ebbed. This had been about fulfilling the desire raging between them, silencing the anger and giving way to something much more necessary.

But instead of leaving her, Roland lowered himself. He planted a forearm on each side of her head, balancing his weight as he kissed her forehead, her cheeks, and finally her mouth. The kiss was still hot and demanding, even after the intensity of what had passed between them.

Jane drank it up like the sweetest, most intoxicating wine. He wanted more? She wanted everything he had to offer.

"Let us see what other sounds you make, wife," he said, already sliding down her body.

Jane closed her eyes and gave herself over to him. Rationality and logic could wait.

CHAPTER TWENTY-FIVE

ROLAND HAD NEVER felt as wholly complete as he did waking with his wife in his arms.

She fit perfectly in the crook of his shoulder, nestled against his chest. Her knee curved over his hip, dangerously close to his cock—which was already at attention, of course. But he'd already known from a week sleeping at her side that Jane was still and peaceful in sleep. Folded into the curve of his arm, even more so.

Today, they would have to talk. She'd demand an apology. He'd struggle to give it.

Because despite the voracity of their argument the night before, he still believed every word he'd said. He would never have peace of mind if she was constantly willing to put her life in danger without second thought. He would never stop protecting her.

He knew just as keenly that she would never walk away from her role as a lady knight. The professional, seasoned agent of the Crown understood that all too well. He was only resigning his post after his hand was forced.

But as a husband, the fear was paralyzing.

Jane was more than a partner assigned to him for this mission. She was more than a wife of convenience.

In a very short space of time, she had become *everything*.

It was damn unnerving.

She shifted against him, splaying her hand wide and sinking a little deeper into his chest. Her hair had come loose sometime during the night. They'd never bothered to fully remove the pins that held her normal, sensible chignon in place. One poked the underside of his arm even now.

When all of this was over, he'd spend hours tugging each pin from her hair and watching the mass of dark brown curls spill over her shoulders. For each pin he removed, he'd drag his tongue over another part of her body. He would tease her until the tips of her curls teased her nipples, then he would bring her to ecstasy.

Plans.

Jane made him want to have them.

She didn't make him want to manage tenants and estate accounts. But the proposition of her splayed over his desk, her wanton cries filling the empty halls of that huge, empty estate in the north... Those plans certainly made all the others much more palatable.

But none of that would be a reality if she got herself caught and killed by Maltby. That was what had set him off last night. Not finding her lurking in the shadows with her wicked knife—he had no doubt she'd used it with brutal efficiency, as she completed all necessary tasks. But after ruminating on Maltby's words, after sitting under the man's gaze for the evening and discovering the extent of those hidden passageways, Roland knew one thing for absolute certain—this business with Maltby was nothing short of deadly.

Alongside his love for Princess Charlotte, and by extension her mother the queen, something new was taking form. Roland could not quite bring himself to acknowledge it fully. But he did make a vow. Silent, and more serious than any he'd made before in his twenty years of service. He would not let the queen come to harm. And he would throw himself into the pits of hell themselves to spare Jane.

JANE'S MIND WAS intractable the entire day. They'd woken late, with no time to bathe. She could still feel Roland upon her skin, knew that if she stood close enough to him she'd scent her own pleasure lingering on his fingertips and in the silvery stubble on his chin. She prayed no one else in the house party was as astute in their observations.

The weight of the words that needed to pass between them pushed down on her more and more as the day dragged on. But they were never alone for more than a moment. She joined the ladies' entertainments, he the men's. Lord and Lady Maltby seemed determined to keep the two groups separate. Which fit with what Jane and Roland knew about the true purpose of this house party.

There was a brief touching of hands when they parted in the morning. Roland pressed a kiss to her cheek when they reunited for luncheon. But it was not until the hour before supper, when everyone started to filter up the stairs to dress for the evening, that Jane finally found herself arm in arm with her husband.

"You are flushed," she said, frowning at his ruddy complexion. "Are you well, Your Grace?"

She wanted to ask more than that, to demand what new development in their quest could set his cheeks burning like that. But there were too many others around, lingering as they also made their way upstairs.

But Roland flashed his easy grin, the color in his cheeks fading not a bit. "I am excited to see you, wife," he said with a meaningful glance downward.

Jane followed his gaze, wondering what—

Oh.

Heat and wet warmth surged between her legs. She was quite excited to see him, as well.

But this was not the time for wanton desire, she chastised herself. "Have you had a fruitful day?" she asked, struggling to keep her voice light.

"Nothing of new or pressing interest," Roland said as they reached the second-floor landing.

No new developments in their quest, then.

Jane hated this middle ground, this unbearable waiting. Roland had made inroads with Maltby. They expected something—some sort of invitation or initiation—imminently. But all they could do in the interim was play their parts and hope that Maltby did not change his mind about bringing Roland into the fold.

And where her marriage was concerned... That could easily be put off. She could step over the threshold of their borrowed bedroom, wrap her hand around the rigid length of Roland's cock through his trousers, and they'd be lost to passion rather than reason.

But they needed to talk. What did this development mean for their marriage? For their quest? They had agreed to play the besotted couple for the duration of the quest, until the queen was safe. Did this change that agreement?

What would happen once the quest was over, and they were left as man and wife?

So, instead of dragging her husband to the bed, Jane smoothed her skirts as she entered the room and let Roland close the door softly behind them. He was already shucking his tailcoat. Jane hesitated with her own clothing. If she took off even a stitch, there'd be no talking at all.

She paused by the foot of the bed instead, folding her hands neatly in front of her.

Roland paused halfway across the room, cocking his head to the side to consider her.

Good—he recognized the change in tone.

But before Jane could speak, there was that insistent tapping at the window.

They both turned. Roland was already halfway to the window by the time she spoke. The better for his lack of liquor, he opened the window to admit Guinevere.

Jane admired the peregrine as she swooped through the window and landed on Roland's forearm, rather than the roost she'd established atop the armoire. While at first she'd been put off by the wild animal in her bedroom, she'd grown to appreciate Guinevere's harsh beauty. The blue gray of her wings flashed in the light, much like Roland's hair and eyes. Her sharp beak and talons could be deadly, yet when she sat on his arm or shoulder, there was no violence in her— the same as when Roland caressed Jane with those powerful hands.

"You could leave it open for her," she said softly, still wary of spooking the falcon.

Roland ruffled her feathers slightly. "I've learned that lesson already," he said with his easy grin. "If we do that, she'll start bringing us presents."

"Presents?" Jane wrinkled her nose, envisioning the sorts of "gifts" the peregrine would find worthy.

"Precisely as bad as you're thinking," he said. "Once in Bermuda, she brought in a half-alive skink—and seemed to think I ought to have the pleasure of killing it myself."

Jane shivered and took an emphatic step back. She could admire the animal—from a distance.

"She won't harm you, little mouse," Roland said, amusement lacing his words.

Jane pursed her lips. Would he ever stop using that ridiculous nickname? But now was not the time for arguments.

"We respect each other. That is enough," she said.

She wanted to say more, but it seemed ill-advised to broach a potentially tense topic with those talons perched on his arm. Guinevere swiveled her head in Jane's direction, perhaps noticing the tension in her voice. She let out a soft chirp, then spread her wings and flew to her perch on the armoire.

No more delaying, then.

"Roland, we must speak."

He didn't respond. Instead, he turned his back to her and shut the window.

"Roland..." she tried again.

"I may be getting on in years, but my hearing is still quite good," he said, trying to maintain that faint amusement. But she could see the tension in his shoulders as he turned to face her.

Jane didn't know whether that ought to worry her or not. Was he tense because he knew he was about to disappoint her? Or was it because he was just as emotionally invested as she in the outcome of this conversation?

"What would you like to discuss, my sweet?"

Jane's hands tightened around each other. If he meant to disarm her by using the same endearments he used while making love to her, he was making a startlingly effective job of it.

"This development between us—"

"Bloody hell," Roland exclaimed, brushing past her in a flash.

Jane blinked behind her spectacles, spinning to see what had pulled Roland's attention from her so definitively.

She spotted it the second before he swiped it up off the pillow.

The note was crisply folded, the letters on the front in ornate calligraphy spelling one word: *Hawkridge*.

"Maltby," she said softly, stepping up to stand beside Roland. All other thoughts fell from her mind, her focus now narrowed to that one sheet.

"Indeed," Roland said, unfolding the note carefully.

Jane reached for his arm, trying to see. Roland shifted, holding it where she could read the three words.

The solar. Midnight.

"True to form, Maltby has not spared the theatrics," Roland said, flipping over the note. The paper was unadorned, but he still walked over to the lamp on the mantel and held it up to the flame, searching for any hidden messages.

"Invisible ink?" Jane asked, eyes following him.

Roland lifted the paper to his nose and sniffed for the telltale scent. "I do not think so. What purpose would he have for encoding a secret message to someone who isn't looking for it?"

Even so, he held the note out to her without being asked so she could verify for herself. Jane took it, but checked it out of habit more than desire. She trusted Roland's assessment.

"You will go," she said, though that answer was already a foregone conclusion.

Roland nodded, sinking down into the lone wingback chair. He motioned toward his lap, inviting her to join him.

For a second, Jane considered it. But she needed her mind clear. Even after a night spent making love to him—she'd lost count of the number of climaxes he'd wrought from her deliciously tortured body—she knew that sitting nestled so close against him would be too great a distraction to her logical thinking.

She sat on the edge of the bed instead and pretended she didn't see the flash of disappointment in Roland's eyes. They did not have time for personal feelings at the moment.

"I'll wait a quarter of an hour, then go down to the passageways," Jane said, mentally working through possibilities. "Perhaps half an hour, to ensure they are clear—"

Roland shot to his feet. "Are you insane?"

Jane blinked up at him in confusion. He could not possibly—

"You cannot go down into the passages," Roland said, huffing an acerbic laugh of disbelief.

Apparently, he could.

"We had this argument last night," Jane said tightly, pushing to her feet as well. He may tower over her, be large enough and strong enough to move her around at will. But he was not her superior.

"And I thought we settled that you will not put yourself in unnecessary danger!" Roland's voice was dangerously loud.

Jane darted a glance to their closed door, willing him to remember that they were never truly alone, even here.

"I am a lady knight," she said steadily. "My quests put me in constant danger. Manageable danger. I know how to protect myself, and I do not take unnecessary risks."

He had to realize she was logical about *everything*. He was the one who made decisions based on instinct and feeling.

She waited for the flash of his temper, but it did not come. He stared at her for several long moments, eyes locked with hers. Jane could practically see the cogs and wheels of thought turning in his mind as he formulated a response. Perhaps she was finally having a positive influence upon him, she thought smugly.

"Think about this logically, Jane," Roland finally said. "We saw no first-floor entrance to the passages. So even if we begin in the solar, we will have to make our way down to enter and go to the meeting chamber you saw—either through the butler's pantry or another entrance we've yet to discover."

He paused to breathe in, as if expecting her to argue. But Jane simply inclined her head, waiting to see where his so-called logic would lead.

"There are too many variables to account for. Maltby could give a little speech before leading us down. He might call for a toast. Who knows what the others will do? It may be a quarter of an hour before we go down; it may be an hour. If we do not estimate it correctly, you could be caught in those passages."

Jane bit her bottom lip. He was not wrong. But he was not entirely correct either.

"I accept your premise," she said slowly. "But I could watch from outside the passages. I can tuck myself into a corner or darkened room and observe who comes and goes. We need to know *who* is involved.

The more eyes we have on the situation, the better."

Roland stared hard at her.

She wasn't waiting for his approval. Jane was already thinking about which room would be best for her to hide away in, in order to stay hidden but also be well positioned to note the gentlemen as they moved through the house under the supposed cover of darkness.

But she found herself desperately waiting for him to agree—to recognize that she was capable and competent.

Finally, Roland inclined his head.

"The library would be best," he said.

The air whooshed out of Jane's chest. She let herself fall back onto the bed, catching the post to keep herself upright. Roland eyed the spot next to her, but eventually sank back into the chair so they could plot.

THERE WAS NO prickle of anxiety in Jane's gut. No flutter of butterfly wings twirling around her stomach. She'd descended into the calm well that always came to her when quests reached their zenith.

This was the moment they'd been working toward for more than a month. Tonight, they would have their definitive proof about Maltby and would know who populated his secret society.

Jane used the time between supper and midnight to write out a list of every single person in attendance at the house party, as well as all the servants she could recall. She organized them into various lists. All the men, then all the women. She made another that stratified the attendees by rank. She drew up a diagram charting familial connections between them. Then another accounting for known business connections. She would not miss a single detail tonight.

Roland sat in the corner in the wingback chair, with a book in his lap and Guinevere perched on his shoulder cleaning her feathers.

They'd made the silent agreement not to pass the time with amorous activities.

Before they'd been lovers, before they'd been husband and wife, Jane and Roland had been agents of the Crown. It was those roles they each slipped into as the clock on the mantel ticked down the minutes.

At eleven fifteen, Jane stood.

They'd agreed that it would be better for her to be in her hiding place in the library well before midnight, so that she would not accidentally encounter any of the gentlemen on their way to attend the gathering. But even so, Jane could see the hesitation in Roland's eyes as he crossed the room to stand before her.

He caught her hand, dragging a thumb affectionately over the knuckles. With his other hand, he cupped her chin and lifted it up to him.

"Be careful," he said.

A completely unnecessary reminder, but Jane appreciated the sentiment just the same.

She waited for him to release her chin, and was rewarded instead with a kiss.

It was the softest brush of his lips over hers. None of the fire of the night before, or even the urgency of the wee hours of the morning when he'd woken her with a hot trail of kisses from the mouth to the sensitive spot between her legs.

This was pure sweetness.

He dragged his tongue along her top lip, then her bottom one, tasting her with an exquisite lightness. His hands remained in place, no demand—he was simply enjoying the feel of her and the taste of her mouth.

Still, Jane's head was spinning slightly when he pulled away.

"We both come back to this room," Roland said softly.

"I promise." Then Jane slipped out the door on silent feet.

CHAPTER TWENTY-SIX

EVEN WITH THE invitation tucked into his pocket, Roland moved in silence. He wanted to hide his presence for as long as possible, so he might learn about the other gentlemen's involvement unobserved. But he did not encounter another person between the bedroom and the wide entry hall.

All the lights were dimmed. The servants were presumably all abed.

He'd watched Jane make her lists, the servants included. It seemed impossible that a man who thought as much of himself as Maltby would be concerned with the setup for the meeting. But it was possible one of the gentlemen acted in that capacity, rather than a servant.

Roland reached the bottom of the spiral staircase.

Now was the time to find out.

As he lifted his foot to the first step, he heard a soft exhale.

He spun quickly, one hand already reaching for the dagger tucked inside his coat, his fist at the ready.

Chatterley threw his hands up in open, unarmed defense.

Roland managed to stop just short of pulling his blade. He lowered his hands to his sides, shaking them out.

"Tense, are you, Hawkridge?" the other man observed wryly. If the light had been better, Roland was sure he would have seen a cocked eyebrow.

"Careful," Roland corrected him. He jerked his head in the direction of the stairs. "Do you think we're the only ones?"

Chatterley looked beyond Roland's shoulder. "I think they are waiting for us."

Roland nodded. He'd suspected as much. He and Chatterley were newly recruited. Everyone else was likely already waiting in the solar. He said a silent prayer of thankfulness that Jane had moved into place well before midnight.

"Shall we?" Roland stepped to the side, clearing the way for Chatterley.

His assessment of the man was conflicted at best. He'd hoped that his old schoolmate had been invited to Maltby Manor to provide cover for the nefarious activities. Now, he wondered what troublesome beliefs Chatterley held that had earned him an invitation to the solar.

He did not want this man at his back, not now. It would be too easy for him to slip a knife into it.

Chatterley seemed to have no such worries, because he shrugged and walked past Roland without hesitation.

He heard the soft voices as they rounded the last turn of the spiral.

The solar was lit with candelabra atop each bookcase, casting long spires of light down toward the center of the room. The room was filled with men—most of the attendees, Roland realized, without even having to count.

And every single one of them was wearing a mask.

JANE'S LEFT LEG was cramping, but she ignored it.

They'd selected her position within the library carefully. Since this room could be seen from within the passageways, she had to be carefully tucked into the spare bit of shadows that allowed her to peek out into the entry hall while also being shielded from view.

She'd leaned forward as far as she could, putting more of her weight on that left leg until the muscle began to protest. But the pain was nothing. In reality, it helped her focus, reminded her of the importance of the task at hand. Her pain was nothing compared to the life of the Queen of England.

She'd watched from the shadows as seven men crossed the entry hall and disappeared into the corner where the staircase to the solar awaited. Ten minutes later, Roland appeared. And less than a minute later, Lord Chatterley.

But while Roland and Chatterley were easy to identify, the others were not.

Those blasted masks.

It would make things more difficult, but not impossible. She'd already deduced two identities based on body type and hair color alone. She hoped Roland would be able to determine more in closer proximity.

Jane curled her hands into fists as Roland ushered Chatterley up the staircase. Whether it was a choice he thought through or one he made on instinct, she was glad that he hadn't given the man an opportunity to stab him in the back.

More than glad, Jane's mind chided her. *Yes, very much more than glad.*

But that was all the acknowledgment she could give her feelings just now.

When Roland's booted foot disappeared, she tugged the pocket watch from the deep recesses of her skirt and marked the time. It was one minute to midnight.

Let the real quest begin.

"Do I have to pay extra for the accessories?" Roland asked drolly before sipping the wine he'd been handed. He'd watched it poured from the same bottle as Maltby's own glass, and seen the other man sip first. It seemed unlikely he'd be poisoned, at least.

Maltby grinned wolfishly, a beast finally freed of the restraints of polite society.

"Pardon the masks, my friend," he said. "But they do add a layer of security."

Roland didn't comment, raising his eyebrows speculatively instead as he scanned the crowd. Ten in total including Maltby, Chatterley, and himself—which meant that two of the guests of the house party were indeed ornamentation.

Maltby was easy to recognize after a week spent staring at him. He was also the obvious leader of the group, moving between pairs and trios as they spoke in low voices. Chatterley had been handed over to a masked man whom Roland tentatively identified as Mr. Archer, who was apparently Maltby's second- or third-in-command. Roland hadn't spoken with the man personally, but he trusted his instincts. There were no servants present, though that didn't mean that some of them weren't aware of what was happening here.

What *was* happening here?

Roland was about to ask when Maltby cleared his throat. Every set of eyes, masked and unmasked, turned to him.

"Let us begin," he said.

But instead of commencing a speech, he turned in a whirl of black and started down the spiral staircase. Mr. Archer fell in behind him, then all the others. Roland and Chatterley were left for last, the hierarchy clear. They exchanged a glance, and once again Roland motioned Chatterley forward.

The other man squinted at him for a fraction of a second longer than seemed appropriate. Roland could not quite say what about that look gave him pause, only that his instincts marked it as worth noting.

He followed the line of gentlemen down the spiral staircase and through the hallways connecting the rooms that surrounded the open entry hall. Maltby didn't want to risk anyone peering down from the upper-level terraces, Roland guessed.

When they paused outside the butler's pantry, Chatterley's brow wrinkled in confusion. Roland mirrored it, though he kept his own face a bit more reserved, turning his lips up with wry amusement when the wall panel sprang free to reveal the secret passage.

"Very clever," he commented, loud enough for the masked gentlemen around him to hear. He hoped it might earn him a comment from at least one of them. The more he heard the voices, the better his chances of positively identifying them.

But despite some self-satisfied grins, no one spoke. Roland bit back his sigh of disappointment and crouched down to follow the others in the passages.

After several turns, he felt the ground sloping downward exactly as Jane had described. Then the staircase where she'd fallen. Though she hadn't told him about that part explicitly, he'd marked the scab on her elbow and the bruises on her knees. His mouth had touched just about every part of her the night before.

He didn't allow himself to think of Jane hiding in the library.

Their group was the same number it had been since his arrival in the solar. He'd heard no commotion. He had no choice but to assume that she was fine and proceed on. Even if she was not... she could handle herself. He truly believed that—even if it did not entirely relieve his worry.

The passageway widened gradually before suddenly opening into a room more than tall enough for Roland to stand fully. He didn't muffle his sharp intake of breath as he surveyed the chamber.

It must have been dug into the foundations of the manor itself. As he took a deep breath—as if steadying himself from the shock of the sight—Roland catalogued the scents. He detected clove and incense, a wisp of bitter almonds, all mixed with the unmistakable mustiness all subterranean rooms suffered from.

Be it fortunate or unfortunate, this was not the first room like this he'd seen in his twenty years of Crown service. Nor was it the first used for such nefarious purposes. He really had seen more than his share. For once, the prospect of never seeing something like this again seemed infinitely appealing.

At least there was not a body tied to the altar.

No, it appeared to be nothing more than a stone table.

There were indeed golden chalices around the monumental stone table, ten in total. One for each of the men in attendance.

It was difficult to be sure without examining each in daylight, but from what he could see, they were likely relics of the Catholic Church confiscated during the Reformation.

As he watched, Maltby swanned around the room, coming to stand opposite the entrance from the dank passage. Once he was at the head of the table, he held his arms out expansively.

"Welcome to our private sanctum," he said, glancing between the two unmasked men but ultimately landing his gaze on Roland.

What Roland could see of Chatterley's face from his periphery was unreadable. On his own, he let some skepticism line his eyes and mouth.

"A whole lot of show," Roland said, crossing his arms over his body.

The man to his right gasped. Another further down the table—Leicester, Roland thought—hissed like the snake that he was.

But Maltby's smile only widened. "The Duke of Hawkridge wants to be properly impressed," he said. "Let's do our best, gentlemen. Report."

Hawkridge could not help but be impressed by the efficiency, even as the full scope of the plot and its terror were revealed bit by bit. The call to speak moved around the table.

"We received word this morning that the queen has resumed her morning rides."

"Hyde Park and St. James's, though she was spotted in Regent's Park as well."

"Mr. Fitzherbert's butler sent word from their townhouse, which faces Regent's. She is accompanied only by her driver and a single footman, riding in an open conveyance."

"Our marksmen are training, though none of them have yet attained your level of precision..." This was directed at Maltby. So, he would be the one to take the shot.

Roland wanted to pull the pistol from inside his coat and end things here, now. To hell with everything else.

He'd succeed in killing Maltby, of that he was reasonably certain. But the nine others here? They'd skin him alive, and then they'd go for Jane.

He forced his hands to remain in place.

But Maltby had seen his expression, the brief flash of emotion on his face. He cleared his throat, holding a hand up. The man that was speaking, one whom Roland had yet to identify, froze instantly.

"What is it, Hawkridge?"

Roland tilted his head to the side, affecting detached casualness. "What do you call your"—he paused as if weighing the word—"cadre?"

"We are the Roses of Union," Leicester said, the sneer in his voice confirming his identity. "From the—"

"I understand the reference, Leicester," Roland said, his voice bored as he dismissed the earl and turned back to Maltby. "So, your plan is to kill the queen... and then?"

Maltby smiled malevolently. So did Mr. Archer at his side.

"Do not worry, Hawkridge. Should you decide to join us, you will learn in due course what precautions have been put in place to secure the succession moving in a favorable direction."

Roland didn't say anything else, merely tipped his chin down in slight acknowledgment. Maltby waved his hand, and the discussion continued. When each man had spoken, Mr. Archer moved to fill each golden chalice with wine, including the two empty spaces, presumably left open for Chatterley and Roland.

Once the wine was poured, all eyes turned to the two unmasked faces.

"Will you join us, Chatterley?" Maltby said, dark eyes nearly black in the low torchlight.

Roland felt the other man shift his weight back. Chatterley was moving instinctively into a defensive position. If he said no, a whole series of complicating events were sure to unfold. They might well knock the man senseless. Or worse, kill him to ensure his silence.

Roland sucked in a breath, readying himself to act.

But Chatterley cleared his throat and answered clearly, "Yes."

Roland's muscles eased slightly, even as disappointment rolled through him. Chatterley would be added to the list of conspirators, then—and punished accordingly, when the time came.

But there was no time to think on that, because all of the attention in the room was now on him.

"What say you, Hawkridge?"

He didn't pause.

He stepped up to the table and, without invitation, closed his hand around the golden chalice filled with deep red wine. "I say aye."

HE FOLLOWED THE trail of masked men up and through the corridors he recognized, as well as the ones that Jane had mapped during her individual foray. He marked each grate as they walked past it, reminding himself which room it opened onto and keeping a mental map of where he was within the manor.

They were exiting through a different door than the one they'd entered through in the butler's pantry. Maltby wanted to keep them off balance, even those he considered worth of joining his Roses of Union. But when the door swung inward to reveal the perfectly square nook situated at the base of the tower beneath the solar, Roland was not surprised. His sense of direction had told him as much.

He'd kept his face carefully neutral for the entire journey out. But when he passed through the door, cleverly disguised to look like a bookcase, he was face to face with Maltby.

Roland stepped to the side, allowing the others to pass behind him.

Maltby held his silence, waiting until the passage was empty and closing the door. Roland counted each body as it moved past his. He was sure that Maltby was silently doing the same—ensuring that no one had tried to hang back unnoticed.

Once Maltby was certain of that, he turned those dark eyes to Roland. "Hawkridge?"

"You are quite thorough," Roland said. A compliment from the newly minted member—and a truthful observation from the loyal agent of the Crown.

Maltby's eyes glinted with pride. "We are privileged to have a man of your power and prowess."

A duke with a sketchy background. Maltby intended to use him as a tool.

Roland would not give him the chance.

"Goodnight," he said, straightening his lapels and finally stepping away.

"Indeed, it is."

Roland could feel the man's eyes on his back as he walked away, following the corridor around the perimeter of the entry hall the same way all the other men had. When he turned the corner and was finally free of Maltby's gaze, his shoulders relaxed subtly, though substantial tension remained.

Despite the fact that he'd been all but initiated into Roses of Union, Roland was still frustrated with the lack of information. The queen was the target. The method would be assassination while she rode through the park. Maltby might be the one to take the shot. But when? How would the date be decided? What time of day? The queen had been spotted in the mornings thus far, but if the date was still weeks away, that habit might change.

He needed to talk it through with Jane and decide on their course of action. Perhaps she would see some damning detail that he had missed. Already he hated that he could not go back to the library and retrieve her. He was to return to the bedroom, and once there'd been no activity on the ground floor for a quarter of an hour, she would sneak back up to join him.

Roland knew those fifteen minutes would feel like fifteen hundred. He curled his hands into fists and forced his legs forward.

He was a yard from the staircase up to the first floor when he heard the sickening crunch of something heavy hitting bone.

CHAPTER TWENTY-SEVEN

J ANE DIDN'T NEED to squint through the darkness to know whom she'd rendered unconscious with the heavy marble and gold candlestick. His voice had been unmistakable as it slithered from the darkness.

"Wandered away from your husband once again, have you? Or were you waiting to continue what we'd started before we were so rudely interrupted—"

She'd been spared whatever other vile things Leicester might have said by the expediency of one of Maltby's ornate candlesticks to the side of his head.

But now she had to deal with him.

She sighed, returning the candlestick to its spot on the mantel and leaning down to hook her arms under his armpits, and then another male figure darkened the doorway. She recognized this one as well.

Roland blinked through the darkness. "What have you done?"

Jane shoved her spectacles up her nose. "Only what was necessary," she said grimly. "Come, help me get him into the library."

She couldn't see her husband well enough to tell if he rolled his eyes, but she did hear the curse he mumbled. At least she didn't have to worry about moving Leicester. Roland swept the man's unconscious body up as easily as if he was lifting her own slight form.

"Where?" Roland asked quietly, stepping into the dimmed room.

"The floor," she said uncharitably.

Roland didn't ask twice. He dropped the other man hard, giving no consideration to his head as it *thunked* against the Aubusson. Jane shoved a chair out of place and kicked up the corner of the rug so it was upturned and all too easy to trip on.

With a sharp nod of approval, she left the room and Leicester without a second glance.

Roland followed, and both of them kept silent until safely back in the bedchamber.

He rubbed a hand over the stubble on his chin. "What will he think when he wakes? Or when he is found?"

"If he has any pride, he'll say that he tripped on the rug and hit his head. If he'd care to tell them that he was attempting to paw at me and then suddenly was rendered unconscious, I think the logical assumption would be that my husband came to my defense and he was lucky to escape with minimal injury."

"I find your vicious streak quite tantalizing," Roland said, amusement dancing in his eyes.

Jane couldn't help the flush, or the little smile.

But she didn't take the implied offer. "Tell me everything," she said instead.

Roland did, carefully recounting every moment from when she'd disappeared into the hallway to when he'd found her clobbering the Earl of Leicester.

By the time he finished, they sat on opposite sides of the bed. Roland reclined against the carved wood headboard, his long legs stretched out in front of him, down to nothing but shirt sleeves and trousers. Jane still wore her gown, though she'd shucked her stockings and now sat with bare toes and crossed legs, leaning slighting into the bedpost as she parsed all of the insight Roland had gained.

She could feel his eyes on her legs, and between them, where the fabric of her gown pooled. But she forced herself to ignore that insistent heat for a few minutes longer.

"The parks," Jane said softly. "It will happen soon, then."

Roland paused, halfway to taking off his shirt. Apparently, he'd decided it was time to move on from the formalities to more enjoyable entertainments.

"How do you know? They did not mention a date or timeline," he reminded her, tugging the linen garment over his head.

Jane drew in a slow, careful breath though her nostrils to steady herself. "The daffodils. She is looking for the daffodils."

Roland stared at her, nonplussed.

"The queen. Another instance where it would benefit you to keep apprised of the goings on of the *haute ton*," she advised, feeling the superior smile tugging at her lips.

"Don't make me spank you again."

It was an empty threat—mostly empty. He had gotten in a few thumps of her derriere the night before, while buried inside of her. And Jane had liked it enough that she was tempted to tease him a bit more. But this was not a time for foreplay, despite Roland's hands lingering at the top of his trousers now.

"Ahem." Jane unfolded her legs, tucking them back underneath her and pulling her skirt down to fully cover her legs. "The queen likes to be the herald of spring. The daffodils are the first flower to bloom. She holds a grand garden party every year to celebrate and herald in what she calls the *true* start of the Season," she explained.

Roland's hands paused. "The queen considers herself something of an amateur botanist…" Understanding flickered in his eyes. "Maltby must know this."

Jane nodded slowly, her own mental picture of the plot clearing by the second. "If he didn't, I'm sure Lady Maltby informed him."

"Do you think she is an accomplice?"

Jane sighed heavily. "I hope not, but we cannot dismiss the notion. I find that I like the woman, at least more than the others in attendance. But in my experience, it is rare for a husband to get up to such nefarious activities without the wife having some inkling what is afoot."

"So we treat her as a co-conspirator until she is proven otherwise," Roland concluded logically.

Jane nodded wistfully.

"We need to get word to London." Roland sighed heavily, but swung his legs over the edge of the bed, reaching for his shirt to dress again.

"We cannot go now," Jane said, crawling quickly across the bed and catching his arm. Heat and desire reverberated through her. *Mistake.*

Focus.

"It would out us to Maltby if you ran away to London the night after he brought you into the fold. We have to be patient," she said, trying not to notice the way that his hand covered hers atop his forearm and tightened.

"We cannot leave the queen unprotected," Roland said, and there was surprise in his eyes that she would even suggest such a thing.

"We are not," Jane said quickly. "We will both send coded messages tomorrow. There are only two days left of the house party. If we post the letters first thing in the morning, they should reach London ahead of us by at least a day—"

Roland tried to speak, but she tightened her grip on his arm. "Maltby is here. You said yourself, he will be the one to take the shot. We must keep him in our sights, above everything else."

She watched as he slowly accustomed himself to her line of thinking, and his eyes softened. The slight lines around his eyes and mouth smoothed, and his silver brow un-furrowed until finally he rewarded her with a sharp nod.

"We write the letters now. I'll slip out at dawn and go post them in the village."

>>>><<<<

IN THE END, they took different approaches. Roland was decent at deciphering codes, but hated writing them. He was griping about it when Jane turned to the dressing table, returning a minute later with a jar of invisible ink disguised as cosmetics. He wrote a letter to his cousin—a nonexistent cousin who happened to reside at Cartwright's address—and then penned his invisible message to Cartwright on the back. Jane's letter was directed to her dear friend, Jacquetta Thane, née Lawson. Roland read it over several times, and would have sworn it spoke of nothing more than the delights of married life and the scenery in Hertfordshire. The code the two women used was invisible even to his trained eyes.

By the time they'd finished, it was four o'clock in the morning.

"There's hardly any point in sleeping now," Roland said, standing at the window.

Guinevere had come in an hour before, somehow seeming to know that they were still awake when she clicked her beak against the glass. The first shades of dawn were still absent from the horizon, but Roland could sense the coming sun nonetheless. So many nights he'd sat and watched in the dark that, by the age of forty-three, he spoke its language effortlessly.

When he turned back to face the room, Jane was perched on the edge of the bed, rubbing her eyes.

He chuckled softly. "Sleep, little mouse. I shall keep watch."

Her nose wrinkled. "Can you not think of a different animal-based moniker? Something slightly more fearsome, perhaps?"

"Mice are craftier than you think. Highly adaptable, as well," he said, enjoying the way she pursed her lips.

But he could not miss the weariness in her eyes even as she said, "I have stayed up through the night many times. Many nights."

He chuckled again, crossing from the window and taking her hand.

"I know you have. But tonight, you have a partner."

He hadn't meant it as anything more than a statement of fact. But the words hung in the air between them, and Jane's eyes turned glassy. It was just the exhaustion, he told himself. Not emotion. Not tears. Certainly not... love.

"Lie down," he urged, squeezing her hand.

She looked ready to protest, then a yawn parted her perfect mouth. Her hand flew up to cover it, but when Roland nudged her shoulder back toward the mattress, she did not protest.

"I am not going to sleep," she insisted.

"Of course not," he agreed even as her eyelids flickered.

"Tell me a story," she said softly.

Laughter bubbled out of his chest. "Are you requesting a bedtime story after weeks of insisting you are not a child?"

A smile played on those pretty pink lips. He wanted to kiss them, but doing so now would be taking advantage of her sleepy state.

"We both need to stay awake. Talking shall do for you, and listening for me. Unless you are a dreadful storyteller," she quipped, that smile now fully in place. "Learning about one another can only help us work better together. It is all quite logical," she added.

Roland coughed. "You want a story about me?"

"Mmhmm."

Her eyes were fully closed now. She looked so peaceful like that— no spectacles to look down at him over, no pert mouth chastising him. When he'd stumbled across her in Lord Remington's study, he'd never imagined so many different dimensions could fit into such a petite body. It seemed only fair, he supposed, to share another side of himself as well.

So he told her about Charlotte.

He detailed how the princess had nearly gotten them all hauled before the magistrate at Weymouth in her less-than-subtle search for illegally smuggled French silks.

His mouth stretched into a smile as he recounted her daily rides, racing down the long drive that led up to Cranbourne Lodge.

And his heart was heavy when he recounted the afternoons she spent playing the piano in the falling light, looking every bit the angel she would become just a few years later.

Roland nearly leapt out of the bed when her fingers closed around his. He'd thought she'd long gone to sleep. "She was the daughter you never had," she murmured.

His chest tightened painfully. "I suppose so."

They were silent for a long time after that. Roland thought about Charlotte, the young princess, and about her grandmother, the queen. A daughter… He'd never thought about having one of his own. It had not even been a consideration. But suddenly, with Jane warm at his side, a picture formed in his mind. Jane, in miniature, but with his wide and welcoming smile.

His chest tightened until he could hardly breathe.

It took several long minutes before he could draw air in and out without the pain of memory and the joy of hope mingling together to strangle him.

Then Jane spoke.

"The summer before I was presented at court, I traveled to visit my cousin in Cornwall. We are of an age, but she was unable to travel to London for a Season of her own. She's always been a bit delicate."

Jane paused. But by the way she held her breath, the soft rasp in her throat, he knew the next words before she spoke them.

"I met a young man."

Gently, he squeezed her hand as she had his minutes before.

"It is no great or interesting tale, really. I was enamored, and in the beginning, so was he. But his parents had already made an advantageous match for him in Town, and my parents would never have deemed him suitable. When the summer ended, I cried my tears and returned to London. He married the young woman his parents selected for him, and by my cousin Franny's report, has three young children."

"Shall I hunt him down and gut him for you?" he finally said, voice deadly soft, meaning every word.

Jane chuckled softly, eyes still closed. "No, I'd prefer that my husband was not a resident of Newgate."

"I'd make sure it wasn't traced back to me," he said, with only the slightest hint of jest. "Or I suppose we could do some investigation. I'm sure someone as heartless as that has violated the law at least once."

Jane brought their joined hands to rest on her chest, just between her breasts. "He was not heartless. We were both very young," she said.

"Must you be logical about everything?"

"I used to be emotional about it," Jane admitted, massaging the back of his hand with her thumb the way he had done to her dozens of times. Her eyes opened then, looking straight up at him. "But lately things have felt different."

More words.

Roland couldn't respond to them. If he tried, his chest would tighten again and he'd never get another thought out. He'd die, surely.

But he could kiss her.

Jane didn't protest as he covered her mouth with his. She let out a little hum of appreciation as he nudged her back onto the bed, sliding down beside her.

Her gentle hands tugged at his shirt. Roland answered the request by pulling it up over his head and discarding it once again. As he moved back over her, she was already reaching for his trousers. But he caught her hands, holding them in place on her chest. Not hard or controlling—though the notion of tying her hands to the bedposts someday was quite appealing. No, he simply needed to slow her down so he could savor every inch of her.

She made a little sound of protest in her throat, but once his tongue swept into her mouth, she quieted and gave herself over to him.

Slowly, Roland peeled away the layers of silk and muslin and linen that covered her until she was naked beneath him, and he left trails of soft kisses in their wake. Only then did he release her hands so she could urge his trousers away.

Skin to skin, he just lay there with her for several minutes. Jane arched against him sweetly, but he kept his touch light. His fingertips circled her nipples, while his tongue drew spirals along the column of her neck.

He buried one hand in her silky brown curls, rich as the molten chocolate he'd once tasted on the southern Spanish coast. When he finally, finally, slid his hand between her legs, he found her wet and waiting.

When he slid into her, it felt like coming home. More than returning to England or some neglected ducal estate had ever offered—this, her, was what he wanted. Needed.

"My love," she said softly as she raised her hips to meet his, and that undulating pressure built between them.

Love. The word skittered through the air, landing directly in the center of his chest. She'd never called him such a thing. It was just an endearment whispered in the throes of pleasure, his logical mind insisted.

But Roland had never been particularly good at listening to logic.

And the feeling bursting forth in his chest as they climaxed together defied all reason.

CHAPTER TWENTY-EIGHT

B Y THE TIME Roland returned from the village, Jane was awake again. Once he was safely ensconced back in the bedroom, as if he'd never left at all, she rang for a maid and they dressed. The poor woman was jumpy, jabbing Jane accidentally with a sharpened hairpin. She must have felt the tension in the room. Not between Jane and Roland, for once, but palpable nonetheless.

But they were both professional agents. When they descended the stairs to breakfast, their masks were back in place—Jane, the picture of cool composure, Roland, grinning easily.

The breakfast table was unusually busy. Lady Leicester and Lady Chatterley were both dining already, the latter's husband across from her and the former conspicuously absent. Jane wondered if Leicester had been found yet, or managed to drag himself upstairs. Mr. Archer sat by himself, peering over a periodical while he sipped coffee, exchanging an occasional comment with a gentleman seated at his side.

Jane poured tea for herself and Roland then went to sit near the two other women, offering morning's greetings. She watched from the corner of her eye as Roland filled his plate from the sideboard. Across the table, Chatterley stood and moved to join him, his own empty teacup in hand.

She forced her attention toward the ladies. "How lovely to see you both this morning," she said brightly, despite the bare two hours of sleep she'd managed. "The light is so lovely, I was contemplating a walk in the garden or a bit of sewing in the morning room."

Lady Leicester made no bones about glaring at her over the rim of her steaming coffee.

But Lady Chatterley offered a tight smile. "I can send for a shawl—"

Jane didn't hear her.

Something was wrong.

Roland was about to break the teacup. His knuckles were shining bright white against the blue-patterned porcelain. He kept a half-smile in place as he listened to Chatterley, but Jane could read the signs—the lines that had appeared around his eyes, the slight flicker of his throat as he forced himself to swallow.

"Excuse me," Jane said, interrupting Lady Chatterley.

The blonde woman squeaked in surprise, and Lady Leicester whispered a scathing epithet. But Jane's mind filtered it all out. She set down her teacup so that trying to balance the hot liquid would not slow her down. Even so, she forced herself to walk around the table at a reasonable pace.

It almost hurt to force the smile to her lips as she placed a hand on Roland's arm. "Are you well, husband?"

Roland exchanged a look with Chatterley, who was looking at her as if she had grown a second head. "Tell her."

Chatterley's mouth quirked, disbelief written in the motion. But Roland only raised an expectant gray eyebrow.

"Maltby is gone. He left just after dawn, headed straight for London."

Jane's grip on Roland's arm tightened. "How strange, for the earl to leave all of his guests so abruptly. I hope his family and business interests are well."

"Very good, Duchess," Chatterley said softly. "I almost believe you."

"Go, now. Report to whomever you answer to, the both of you. I will remain here to ensure things do not escalate and bolster your excuses for leaving so abruptly." Even as he spoke, Chatterley's eyes were casually assessing the other occupants of the room, monitoring them for any sort of awareness to the exchange happening over the sideboard.

Another agent.

From whom or where, Jane knew they didn't have time for now. They had to get to Maltby before he got to the queen. But Roland did not agree.

His hand fell over hers, holding her in place. "Whom do *you* answer to, Chatterley?"

Chatterley flashed them a wry smile. "Tell your superiors the Jaguar sent you. They'll vouch for me."

With that, he nodded and went to join Mr. Archer and his companion, asking after a section of the periodical. Roland guided her out into the hall, his eyes already clouded with thoughts that she knew would quickly turn to actions. Her own mind was churning.

"I will go and ask around casually in the stables, verify that Maltby truly did depart this morning. Go upstairs and start packing. We leave in an hour."

Luckily, Jane didn't need to argue with any of his instructions.

TWO HOURS LATER, they were on horseback once again. This ride could not have been more different than the one that had brought them to Maltby Manor. This time they'd abandoned their carriage willingly in the first village they passed through, which was little more than a hovel. But there was a barn to hide the carriage if any of the Roses of Union came looking, and a family hungry enough for coin to keep their secrets—at least long enough for Roland and Jane to get to

London.

Roland glanced over at his wife's horse galloping headlong beside him, and Jane's seat was as elegant and accomplished as everything else that she did. As much as he'd enjoy having her pressed against him in the saddle, they had no time for any considerations of comfort and preference.

Jane had left a note for the Countess of Maltby begging her pardon for needing to attend to a sick aunt, and they were off. Hopefully, Chatterley would do as he said and clean up the ruckus they'd surely left behind with their hasty departure.

Roland could feel it in his bones—this was the end. The mission had accelerated so rapidly, careening toward climax, and they would have little impact on how things unfurled. The cogs were already set in motion. If they made it to London in time, if they could catch Maltby, then maybe they could change the final outcome.

As THEY RODE hell for leather through the countryside, Jane felt the wind whipping away the haze of emotions she'd lived in for the past week. When they reached London, there would be no time for feeling, only cold calculation and brutal efficiency. She would not fail the Lady Knights. She would not fail her queen.

There had been no time for idle talk, only to map out the specifics of their plan. By the time she was swinging out of the saddle in front of Roland's London house, it was fully dark. The night they'd shared, tender words and even tenderer touches, seemed like from a different lifetime.

If Roland was surprised at how quickly the groom came forward to take their mounts, he didn't remark upon it. He simply led the way up the stairs. The door swung open before he could reach for the handle, and by then Jane expected the words from the butler:

"Guests await in your office, Your Grace."

Roland's thanks were nothing but a sharp, military nod. Jane offered a soft smile from behind her spectacles.

"Tea," she said, following her husband's gargantuan strides. "As well as something stronger, I think."

The butler bowed and disappeared to the rear of the house. Jane took a moment to brace herself, catching her reflection in the hallway mirror. She straightened her pelisse, looking grimly at her hair. Nothing to be done there. She paused and retrieved her spectacles from the inner pocket of her skirt, poising them on the bridge of her nose.

She looked calm and ready.

She could carry on. She always did.

CHAPTER TWENTY-NINE

"**D**O NOTHING."

The words ricocheted through him, nestling into the grooves forged by a lifetime in service to Crown and country. "I must be losing my hearing in my old age."

Jane inhaled sharply. She shouldn't be surprised by his flippant impropriety anymore. But he imagined that for someone so devoted to rules and logic, such a comment must actually set her bones ill at ease. They'd work on that—later.

"I am sure that your hearing, like the rest of your senses, remains in perfectly honed working order," the Duchess of Guilford said, her face implacable.

Cartwright, at her side, looked ready to combust.

"As I explained before, the Earl of Maltby's mother is quite ill. I saw her keel over myself during the Sheraton ball," the duchess repeated, as if she were speaking to a child who failed to understand the lesson.

Roland understood well enough. He just didn't believe it.

"Maltby would have poisoned her himself if he thought it could be used to his advantage. He is nothing like Remington. He is cunning and he is committed." As he spoke, Roland had moved forward without realizing it. As if by coming closer, just across the desk instead of leaning against the mantel across the room, he could force them to see reason.

"I slipped a maid into the dowager Countess of Maltby's household, who has verified that a doctor is indeed coming and going, and the woman is quite ill. Furthermore, she reports that Maltby himself has been dutifully at her side since he arrived in London," the duchess continued, her face and posture utterly unchanged.

"It is all wrong," Roland said, shaking his head. "He must have deduced that I was not sincere, and taken it upon himself to do the job sooner. Or perhaps he received a new report about the queen's morning carriage rides." He paused, raking a hand over his stubble-covered jaw, hoping the rough scratching would shake some other explanation loose. "It does not make sense."

"No," the duchess agreed. "It does not. The only thing that does is that Maltby's mother fell ill and he came to her side, as any dutiful son would."

Roland scoffed loudly, spinning on his heel and stalking back toward the mantel with the blazing hearth beneath.

Silence from Jane. She'd given details as they made their joint report, recounting everything that had happened while they were at Maltby Manor. But she hadn't said a single word since the duchess had explained, and Cartwright had decreed, that they were to do nothing.

He shot Jane a look, but her face was unreadable.

So he spun back for the other two. "We must set a watch up on Maltby. Or better yet, I can call upon him now that we've our own excuse for rushing back. Sick relatives, and all that. I'll fetch an expensive brandy from the cellar and—"

"That's enough, Hawkridge," Cartwright interrupted, massaging his temples.

The Duchess of Guilford was slightly more circumspect as she spoke. "We must do everything to preserve the inroads you've made with Maltby's Roses of Union. The goal of this quest is not just to protect the queen, but to bring down the society as well. You look too desperate if you go to Maltby now. We must wait, and watch. The moment he leaves his mother's house, I will send word."

Just like that, the Duchess of Guilford stood and straightened her skirts. She wasn't happy to dismiss him, her expression said, but she'd do it even so because she trusted her own judgment. Roland looked past her and fixed his imploring gaze on Cartwright instead. They'd worked together for a decade. Surely the man owed him enough to trust his instincts in this, his final mission.

"Miss Jacobson," Cartwright said, avoiding Roland's eyes. "Are you in agreement with Hawkridge?"

Jane didn't glance in his direction. There was not a hint of emotion in her voice as she began speaking. For a moment, Roland thought he had been transported backward in time by a month, when her regard for him had been so brutally cold. Mutually, if all truths were told.

But as she spoke, he realized the truth.

"Yes, sir. Everything in Maltby's actions has driven us to conclude that he is dangerous, even when away from his so-called Roses. Whatever excuse he has made to come to London, I find it difficult to believe that he will not use the opportunity to further his plot," she said in measured, judicial tones.

Jane wanted them to know the words came from the cool lady knight, not from the woman who had turned to putty in his hands the past few nights. She wanted to be regarded as the courageous, meticulous professional that she was.

Roland loved her so much in that moment, he wanted to yell it to all of London.

Instead, he watched as the duchess and Cartwright exchanged a look. The former shook her head. It was a slight motion, really just a twitch of the chin, but they were trained spies, all.

"You two will be the first to know if Maltby moves," Cartwright said as he followed the duchess out of the study. "Be ready to act."

Roland let the pair of them escort themselves out. He dropped his head to the mantel of the fireplace, closed his eyes, and let the disappointment fill his chest. His last mission, and it was going to absolute shit. Everything about this felt wrong. Even Jane's damn logic was on his side, and still he was bridled.

To hell with all of it. He'd go and watch Maltby himself. Cartwright and the duchess could not stop him, short of putting him under house arrest. This was his last mission. What was the cost of insubordination now?

The cost was standing in the doorway to the hall when he spun around, her brown eyes wide as she marked his sudden movement.

Jane's future with the Lady Knights. If he acted against orders, she'd be honor-bound to report it. If she went along with him, she'd likely never be trusted with another quest.

Hell.

The situation just kept getting worse.

Roland watched as Jane swallowed. The delicate line of her throat bobbed.

"I am going to try to sleep for a few hours," she said, ever practical. "Whatever tomorrow brings, it will be better faced with a bit of rest."

She was right, of course.

But that didn't stop him from saying, "They are wrong."

Jane bit her lip hard. "I do not have the answer," she said softly. Roland could tell how much that pained her.

But from the tight press of her lips, he could tell she did not wish to speak of it. Not now, when they'd been days without rest and the sharp orders of their superiors were still smarting.

"I will fetch our things," Roland said, his legs still burning with energy. If he went up to their suite of rooms now, he'd end up wearing a hole in the floor with his pacing. After nearly a week of being confined to one safe place—their bedroom at Maltby Manor—he was aching to walk the halls with freedom.

Jane nodded. For a second, Roland thought she would say more.

Perhaps she did want to speak, to lay down those burdens and sort through them together after all. But then it was gone, and so was she, up the stairs and away.

Roland waited for all sounds of her retreat to die away before striding out of the townhouse to the mews. Of course, their luggage had already been unloaded and brought upstairs. They'd been closeted in his study for nearly an hour.

He did several circuits of the ground floor. By the time he arrived at the first, Roland found his feet leading not toward the long hallway of the guest wing, but toward the door that opened on his and Jane's shared sitting room. He wanted his wife.

Nothing this night had gone right. But one thing still could.

He'd already kicked off his boots and tossed his jacket aside, and the sound of the boots was unfortunately loud. He hoped he hadn't woken her. If he did, he'd lull her back to sleep with a few kisses before he took her in his arms. Tonight would not be about lovemaking, but about breathing in her scent, letting her soft curves comfort the tension corded in every muscle of his body.

But the door was closed.

The door that connected the sitting room to her bedroom was shut, the panel of oak ready to jump out and hit him with all the force of a brick wall. His eyes slid across the room, to his own door, which stood open.

He crossed to it in three strides. Maybe his little mouse had climbed into his bed—

No creases marred the coverlet, no small, wife-sized bumps.

For the first few days of their marriage, that door between them had remained closed. Then slowly, over the course of their time working together, it had cracked open and allowed something beautiful to enter his life, his heart.

Now it was closed again, and he had no notion why.

Roland had never been in love before. But he could see now why so many rakes avoided it.

That ache in his heart as he went to bed alone was damned painful.

>>><<<

RELIEF WASHED THROUGH her as she recognized Roland's heavy, unguarded step. He could move in silence if he wanted; she'd seen that often enough. But here, in the safety of his own chambers in his own house, he moved with easy grace that she'd recognize anywhere.

She heard two telltale thumps—his boots being discarded. She rolled to her side, angling her face to the door, waiting. She'd closed it while she undressed, without the help of a maid, not wanting to see or talk to anyone but *him*. The fire in the sitting room was not yet banked for the night. Jane did not know if that meant that a servant would be in soon to see to it, or if Roland took on that task himself.

A door could not stand between the force of desire that burned between her and Roland. Even after a night like this—two nights, really—she still wanted him. If only for the comforting warmth of his touch as he curled around her.

But the minutes stretched out, and the door did not open.

Jane found herself questioning things—had it really been Roland entering the room? Could those thumps have been a servant knocking something over?

No, she was certain. Even if she was exhausted.

But still the door did not open.

Another minute passed, then came that familiar tread. Not toward her door, but away from it. A breath later, the sound of another door closing followed. Roland's door.

He wasn't coming.

Jane rolled to her back, trying to make sense of it even as her chest hollowed out to cold nothingness. They were both very tired. Maybe he preferred his own bed, especially after so many nights away.

Though he could have come and fetched her...

But no matter how she tried, she could not reason her way to understanding, leaving her quite alone with nothing but the ache in her chest for company.

CHAPTER THIRTY

S LAM!

The force of his door hitting the wall reverberated through the room. Roland was on his feet, a knife in his hand and eyes sweeping the room before the door swung back and then stopped, caught in Jane's hand.

"What's happened? Get behind me!" His strides ate up the space, the instinctive need to protect ruling as he put a gap between his wife and whatever dangers had chased her into his room.

Jane didn't push away his hand, but she gripped it with her own. "No, I am fine," she said.

His body, still in a defensive position, every muscle ready, could not quite comprehend what she meant. But the warm brown eyes staring up into his were clear, if a bit wide.

"Roland," she said softly but with complete authority. A command—to him, to stand down.

Slowly, he lowered the knife and relaxed his grasp. She rocked back on her heels. He hadn't even realized he'd practically lifted her off the ground to bodily shove her to safety.

"Roland," Jane repeated, still holding tight to his arm. "What if we are wrong?"

His brows knitted together. "What do you mean?"

"It all fits. Despite what Miranda and Cartwright say, it all fits," she said. "There was warmth on the breeze last night. The daffodils will bloom any day now, maybe even as we speak." She paused, darting a glance toward the windows. It was predawn, but the blackness of the night had softened. The sun would appear very soon. "The queen will be out there this morning, in her carriage with none but a footman and a driver to guard her. Maltby is here in London. Why would he wait?"

When Roland did not respond immediately, Jane rocked back on her heels, releasing him and wringing her hands. He'd never seen her like this—eyes darting, shoulders trembling. Jane wasn't anxious. She was calm and composed.

"Have you slept at all?" he asked slowly. His own sleep had been brief, perhaps four hours, judging by the sky outside the windows. But it had at least been deep.

Jane jerked her head from side to side. "We cannot afford to be wrong, Roland. If we are—the Queen of England will be murdered."

Roland worked his jaw, trying to decide what to say.

"Cartwright and the duchess have thought things through logically as well," he finally said. He didn't necessarily agree with the words. But he did want to ensure that Jane was certain, that she understood fully before they undertook what she was proposing—direct insubordination.

She nodded sharply, seeming unoffended by his apparent lack of faith in her deductions. She recognized his words for what they were—an aid to her own thinking.

"I have thought about that too," she said. "But I cannot help this…" She raised one hand to her chest. "This feeling that we are doing the wrong thing. That staying here, doing nothing, is wrong."

"An instinct," he said softly, catching her eye.

Despite the fraught moment, a small smile curled his lips. Jane gave him a grim one in return.

"Yes, an instinct," she replied.

"What do you want to do?"

Relief washed over her features, changing her completely. The transformation was incredible. Gone were the wringing hands and the slight tremor in her shoulders, replaced by that calm persona he'd come to know and respect.

"Send messengers to Jacquetta and Dominique. I shall give you the addresses. Your fastest, most reliable servants. The queen could be anywhere this morning. Send Jacquetta to St. James's and Dominique to Regent's. You and I shall go to Hyde," she said, her hands already moving to the laces to untie her nightgown.

Roland cocked a brow in surprise.

"Not now," she said, pursing her lips. "Send the messengers while I dress. Bring weapons."

As his wife disappeared and he called for the servants, he wondered if he'd ever heard sweeter words from her lips.

THEY RODE THROUGH the Cumberland Gate and straight into a wall of fog.

Dawn was upon them, by the tick of the clock. But Hyde Park was drenched in thick morning fog, making it impossible to see more than a dozen yards in any direction. London had no bright morning sun to offer on this cold April morning. They had only each other and their wits to keep them alive. More importantly, to save their queen.

Roland slid from the horse first, then reached for Jane's waist and pulled her down as well. The second her feet touched the ground, she was already checking each of her weapons. The penknife in her bodice was easy to reach. She'd shoved the dagger into her boot instead of strapped to her leg, so she could grab it without as much maneuvering of her skirt. Her twin dueling pistols were strapped to her waist.

The blasted moisture threatened to fog her spectacles, even with the application of her special mixture before she set out.

She was ready.

She was also expecting the pained expression on her husband's face as he turned to her.

"We need to split up," he said, forcing out each word.

Jane did not dwell on the knot forming in her throat. They did not have the time.

"They will be near the paths, lying in wait for the queen's carriage. You go that way," she said, nodding straight ahead, toward the middle of the three pathways that split off from the park's entrance. "Toward the Serpentine. I shall go directly south. The queen is in residence at Buckingham—that is her most likely route."

"Should I argue that I am the better shot?" Roland asked, raising one eyebrow in that way that had always annoyed her and now tugged at her heart.

They'd never discussed it, she realized. There was so little they truly knew about each other, even after the close proximity of the last month, even as man and wife. She'd never told him the extent of her skills.

But her mouth and voice were steady as she simply said, "No."

To her eternal gratitude, Roland did not argue. He inclined his head.

"Good hunting, little mouse," he said.

For once, the nickname did not rankle her.

She sucked in a breath, caressing the pistols at her waist, and made to turn away.

But strong hands caught her hips, dragged her up, up, up, until their lips were together in a crushing kiss.

Jane felt that kiss in the corners of her soul. Not a goodbye, but a promise. Roland's promise that when this was over, when they were both safe, they would sort out whatever was between them. Together.

He set her down as abruptly as he'd lifted her up, as if tearing her away was the only way he could force himself to end the embrace.

There were no words between them, not now. Only the quest. The mission.

Roland turned away to hobble the horse, and Jane moved into the cover of the trees along the southern path. It was time to save the queen.

CHAPTER THIRTY-ONE

S HE MOVED AS quickly as she dared through the trees. The grass was wet and mucky beneath her feet, sucking at the soles of her boots with every step. It was nearly impossible to move in silence. The fog made things worse still, carrying sounds and distorting them as they bounced between the trees.

By some miracle of grace, she was still able to see the carriage path from the tree line. Not for any substantial distance, but at least it was there. It was almost comical. Jacquetta might call it fateful—that her weakest point, her sight, was even further hobbled here in the final moments of her quest. She'd have to rely on her other senses, would hear the queen's carriage coming long before she saw it.

Thankfully, she'd had plenty of practice.

She counted each step, tracking her progress down the edge of the park. It was just under a mile from the Cumberland Gate to the southeast corner of the park.

She'd made it a third of the way when she heard voices. One she recognized instantly, though she had not heard it in weeks.

She drew the dagger from her boot and cocked one pistol, bracing it over her opposite arm as she slowed her steps, willing them to silence. By another miracle, the muck was not as deep here, and she was able to move softly over the dew-wet grass.

He was nothing more than a hazy form beneath the tree. She

couldn't see the Grosvenor Gate, but by the steps she'd counted and the gap in the trees, she knew it must lurk beyond. He'd been placed here to watch, to either take the shot or run and give word if the queen entered there.

Jane held her pistol tight, but did not let her fingers close around the trigger. They needed to find Maltby. The sound of a gunshot in the park would alert him to their presence. She crept closer, marking his weapons. She did not see a pistol, but he might have one tucked inside his greatcoat. The tip of a rapier poked out from the black folds. She could not see his hands.

When she was close enough that he would not doubt her shot, she stepped out of the protection of the trees.

"Remington."

He spun to face her, surprise playing across his expression. Then, slowly, a wide grin crawled up his face.

"Miss Jacobson," he said, laughing even with her weapon pointed at his chest. "I admit, I had not expected you. Your husband, perhaps, based on Maltby's description."

"It's the Duchess of Hawkridge now," she corrected him sharply. "Toss your weapons aside."

Remington didn't move.

"Would you prefer to die?" she said. She'd killed men before. A woman, once. She regretted none of it and would do it again, easily. Though for Remington, a shot to the leg would be more appropriate. She'd wager good money he was the type to talk under harsh persuasion.

Remington didn't laugh, but his smile remained in place. "I can hardly believe you're standing here at all, Duchess. I doubt very much you will pull that trigger."

How wrong he was, Jane thought. But also—for the moment, he was correct. Until they caught Maltby, she needed to avoid firing her pistols.

"A bold chance to take," she said, edging closer. She was fast. If she could conjure up a distraction, she could probably get close enough to disable him.

Perhaps if she feigned reluctance—

She felt the movement at her back a second before the swipe of the blade. She twirled to the side with the dancer-like grace she'd learned from Dominique, but felt it slice through the outer layer of her woolen pelisse. If she'd been without it, the blade might have found skin.

Years of training kept her pistol trained on Remington even as she spun, but still he stalked closer. He truly did not believe her that she'd fire, and now she was fighting off two of them. She brandished her dagger, trying to keep them both in her sights.

The man who'd snuck up on her appeared to be a footman, one of Remington's, based on the crest embroidered in his livery. She had to get them talking, buy herself time to come up with a strategy. She couldn't hold them off indefinitely on her own, not without shooting someone. She'd never thought her most reliable weapon would be a liability.

"You cannot face a tiny woman such as me by yourself?" she said, pinning her eyes to Remington. She didn't let the footman out of view, not for a second. But she let them think she was distracted.

"I was not certain whom we would encounter," Remington admitted, that oily smile still in place. The rapier was now in his hand, the pommel seated loosely against his palm.

"You expected Hawkridge," she guessed.

"He seems the type," Remington agreed. "No one really knows what he's gotten up to all of these years. He led Maltby to believe his activities were less than savory. But perhaps he was working for someone else entirely."

The mist was thickening. Jane was thankful she'd smeared the solution over her spectacles, or she would have been truly blinded. But even without the lenses, she could see the smug expression on

Remington's face.

"I suspected Hawkridge from the beginning," Remington said. "But not you."

Her gut clenched. They were stalking closer. She'd put several yards between them initially, but she had to be careful or they'd herd her until her back was against a tree. A thought occurred to her. Maybe she could...

"Although my new employee did warn me there was likely a woman involved."

Jane darted a glance at the footman, using that motion to peer over her shoulder so quickly, she hoped neither of them would notice.

"The footman who went silent," she said, looking the man over with new eyes.

He shrugged. "His lordship made me a better offer."

They were herding her back toward the trees. A tall, proud walnut tree waited less than a yard behind her.

She had to get one of them to act.

"What offer is that? To act as his blade? Are you too much a coward to do the dirty work yourself, Remington?"

Remington's smile faltered, and his glance slid to the man at his side.

"A lord does not lower himself to dealing with such petty nuisances."

Her back was at the tree trunk.

Remington's chin dipped.

The footman sprang forward, knife in hand.

Jane rolled around that tree just in time, hearing the thunk of the knife as it landed deep in the water-softened wood. She grabbed a low-hanging branch and shoved herself back in the direction she'd come, her own dagger out and ready. She sliced through the layers of his livery until she reached skin, and the force of her impact sent blood spraying.

The footman yowled, giving up on retrieving his blade and falling among the tree roots, cradling his arm. Jane didn't wait to see if he'd stay down. She was already spinning, ready to use the few maneuvers she knew when pitted against a much larger, swifter weapon.

But when the kiss of metal filled her ears, it was not her blade meeting Remington's.

Rapier met rapier in a swift, melodic song of steel and determination. And the blade that battled Remington back, so obviously his superior from only a few swipes?

That was Ethelreda McGovern.

Jane didn't waste time being thankful, not yet. Red would have Remington subdued in moments. She had to take care of the footman. But that, too, was attended to.

A man with long, dark hair, tied in a tight club at the base of his neck, had his own long sword pressed against the footman's neck. He'd even demanded the man put his hands against the tree, so that blood was flowing from the wound unattended. Jane dimly realized that if it wasn't stanched soon, the brigand would lose too much blood as well as his ability to testify against Maltby, Remington, and all the others.

Jane took a deep breath of cold air as she examined the dark-haired gentleman standing over the footman with a soldier's poise.

"Sir George Caldwell, I presume?"

Red's new husband smiled—grimly. But she could imagine how he would look with his mouth stretched in happiness. Jane could just as easily imagine Red falling for the poised soldier, despite her friend's utter lack of skill with men. One warrior soul recognizing another; that was what Red and George had found.

"Indeed. A pleasure to meet you at last, Miss Jacobson. Perhaps you have something we could fashion into restraints?" He jerked his chin at the silently sobbing man.

"Two sets, if you please," Red said, slightly breathless and full of victory as she led Remington to stand beside his accomplice by the tip of her blade nestled to the nape of his neck.

Jane produced two leather thongs from her deep pockets. She waited until both men were restrained, Sir George still standing over them, before she dragged Red several yards away and whispered, "What are you doing here?"

"The duchess has deemed my exile at an end. George and I arrived yesterday. Jacquetta has been kind enough to offer us rooms, since we have no residence here in London," Red explained as she wiped a bit of blood off the edge of her rapier using a damp leaf. "Jacquetta and Grayson went to St. James's. I thought you could use our help here, since Hyde is the biggest of the three."

"Thank you," Jane said. She didn't have time to be relieved. She had to get to Maltby.

Red seemed to read the thoughts in her head. "You're welcome. Now let's go beat some information out of those wretches."

⟫⟩⟫⟫⟪⟪⟪⟪

IT WAS THE less likely path, but damned if it wasn't the more dangerous.

A single row of trees lined each side of the path through the center of Hyde Park. Without the fog, they would have provided no cover at all. As it was, Roland was sprinting from tree to tree, taking note of his surroundings, and then sprinting to the next. He knew the park well, though he hadn't spent much time here in recent years. It was as much a part of London as Westminster Abbey or Covent Garden.

The path was beginning to curve, and the thicker groves of trees were just ahead. They were still growing their leaves for the season, not yet fully frocked out in decadent green. Not that he could see any of it. The fog was too dense. But he knew that beyond those trees was another clearing, just before one reached the edge of the Serpentine.

If Maltby had chosen this park, this pathway, that was where he would lie in wait. There, at the intersection of multiple paths beside the waterway. It was strategic and smart. He could see the queen's approach from multiple directions. Or, at least, he would have been able to if not for the fog.

He could still hear, and carriages were not known for their stealth.

But Roland should have expected that Maltby would be.

"Come to help me, Hawkridge?" The villain's voice sliced through the fog, seeming to come from every direction.

Roland pressed his back to the trunk of a tree; at least that was one less direction he had to defend himself from. He hated revealing his own position, but he needed to hear Maltby again.

"I think we both know the answer to that," Roland said.

His voice must have carried well enough, because he was met with Maltby's dark, snakelike chuckle.

"We took odds upon you, you know?" The bastard sounded amused.

But Roland didn't focus on the content of the words but their echo. Ahead—Maltby was ahead of him. How far, he couldn't tell, not with the fog.

"Tell me I fared well," Roland said into the looming white.

"It depends on perspective, I suppose." Further away. Maltby was moving away from him. That tracked with Roland's initial suspicion. He was moving toward the crossroads near the Serpentine, where the closely planted trees would provide cover to watch the queen's carriage approach from three possible directions.

"I shudder to hear what you think a success," Roland called, lifting his sword. Something told him Maltby was near, some sense he could not name.

"Half of us thought you were loyal to our cause. The other half suspected this," Maltby said, much closer now. He was trying to confuse Roland. Well, they could both use that to their advantage.

Roland gained several yards south, moving as quickly as he could while keeping his footfalls silent, before yelling over his shoulder, "That I would hunt you down?"

A sound of frustration rolled through the mist. "That you were leashed to the Crown. No more than a dog."

The fog was shifting here, the breezes coming off the waterway sweeping the white curtain back and forth. A spot that one moment was safe, hidden, would the next be exposed. Even as he listened, his blade ready, Roland was scanning the landscape, trying to decide how he would draw Maltby out.

The villainous lord was to his left now, yammering on. "What you did not realize is that I am a wolf."

Roland hardly heard Maltby's words, feeling them as little more than reverberation through the trees and mist.

Because there, on the opposite bank of the Serpentine, was Jane. He had only a glimpse of her, a moment before the fog shifted and she was obscured in haze once more. But Roland understood what he needed to do.

"No, Maltby," he called, dashing between the trees. "You are a snake."

⇛✳⇚

THEY'D LIED TO her. She'd gut them for it later.

Remington had said that Maltby waited on the King's Road, lying in ambush for the queen. He reported that they'd received word late last night that she'd requested a carriage for Hyde Park this morning.

But it had been a lie—the first part, at least.

Now Jane was on the wrong side of the Serpentine, and Roland was trapped with Maltby in that damned fog.

She'd seen him for a second, her husband, angled against a tree a stone's throw from the road. Then the fog shifted again, and she was obscured from view. But the stance, the way his chin had tipped in her direction, told her the most vital bit of information. He'd found Maltby.

"We need to get over there," Red said, sheathing her rapier once again. She'd only just pulled it free after their madcap run from the east side of the park.

But Jane shook her head. "No."

Red's bright copper eyebrows climbed her forehead. "Still hating your partner that much? I thought Jacquetta was jesting."

"I don't hate him," Jane ground out, refusing to take her eyes off the scene on the other side of the water. All she needed was a glimpse, a parting in the fog, and she could shoot. "But the fog is too thick. The extra noise will cause confusion, make it harder for Roland to draw Maltby out. We stay here."

Red did not argue, but her face was lined with questions that Jane could detect even in the periphery of her vision.

But she did not have time for it.

Someone was yelling on the other side of the water. The wind carried the sound, faint by the time it reached her. But Jane recognized it instantly.

"Maltby. He's close. I just saw Roland a minute ago," she told Red.

Her friend came to stand beside her, squinting. "Maybe I need spectacles."

Jane ignored the jest, cocking her pistol. "Take the other from my belt," she instructed Red.

Her friend did as she was told, cocking that one as well, but she did not point it over the water with Jane's. "I cannot make that shot," Red said.

"I know," Jane said. "Be ready to hand it to me if I miss this one."

She felt rather than saw her fellow lady knight's nod.

Suddenly, another sound reached them across the Serpentine. Not voices, but blades.

Jane's heart was in her throat as a breeze whipped at her skirts, rippling the water before her and pushing away the fog to reveal the clearing just on the other side. She realized in an instant what Roland had done upon seeing her. He'd led Maltby into the clearing, engaging him with blades—real ones this time—so that she might have her shot.

"No," she whispered, the word torn from her very heart.

"Jane," Red said, voice already soothing, already knowing. "You can do it."

"No. I could hit him."

"Hawkridge is a smart man. He knows what he's doing. He understands the risks," Red said, her voice low and soft. She spoke to Jane as if she were a frightened child or animal.

But Jane had no jokes to make about Red's newfound maternal instincts. All she had was fear in her heart.

"Roland is the better fighter," she said, remembering that duel at Maltby Manor. "He will subdue Maltby."

Before she could offer up a prayer for that outcome, the sound hit them.

Carriage wheels.

The queen.

Red shifted closer. Jane knew she wouldn't touch her, wouldn't risk compromising her shot. But her voice was close and steady as Jane inhaled and aimed for Maltby.

"You can do this, Jane."

She took the shot.

A heartbeat later, the other pistol was in her hand. She fired it immediately as well. She had to be certain Maltby was down.

The horses carrying the queen's carriage screamed. The sound of yelling voices filled the air. But Jane didn't run for the queen. She ran for the clearing.

Maltby was on the ground.

But so was her husband.

CHAPTER THIRTY-TWO

THE CARPET IN the sitting room was going to be ruined. The track she was walking around it, the repetitive speed, the amount of wear it had already endured... Jane calculated that if the physician remained in Roland's bedroom for another hour, the rug beneath her feet would be beyond saving.

To say nothing of her husband lying prone in the next room.

"Sit down and have a nip to steady your nerves," Jacquetta said from the armchair.

"No."

"The water is cool and fresh," Dominique suggested, leaning forward from her position on the chaise and pouring a glass without waiting for a response.

"No."

"You are his wife, you know," said Red, not bothering to offer a cup of tea from the steaming pot on the low table in front of her. "You could go in there."

Jane stopped. She stared at the closed door to Roland's bedroom, where the physician tended his wound. The wound she had given him.

If he died...

"He will not die," Dominique said firmly, setting the water aside and coming to take Jane's hands.

"Too damn stubborn," Jacquetta added from across the room.

"Jane or Hawkridge?" Red asked with a tilt of her head.

Jacquetta lifted her flask in toast. "Yes."

Dominique sighed heavily. "How can you all be so flippant?"

"They are trying to help," Jane said, her eyes still fixed on that door. She was vaguely aware of Dominique's hands tightening on hers, trying to lead her back to the sofa. But she couldn't move.

"The only thing that will help is going in there and seeing for yourself that he is well," Dominique said gently. She'd always been the gentlest and kindest among them. But not the most optimistic, not after the difficulties she'd faced in her life.

Still, she held tightly to Jane's hands until her eyes went there instead.

Jane stared at Dominique's olive skin, at her long, graceful fingers twined around her own pale ones. She tried hard not to think of the feel of Roland's enormous hands as they enveloped her, body and soul.

"What if he is not well?" Jane said softly. "I shot him."

A tear rolled down her cheek.

Before it could reach her chin, Jacquetta was there, wiping it away. Red was on her other side, her warm, solid presence a wall that Jane knew she could relax into—fall into, if she could no longer find the strength to stand.

"If he dies, it will be me that killed him."

Jacquetta grabbed her shoulder fiercely. "No, Jane. Hawkridge has been at this"—she paused to calculate, then gave up—"longer than any of us. Hell, longer than some of us have been alive. He led Maltby into that clearing. He understood the risks."

Jane opened her mouth to argue, but Dominique's solemn nod cut her off.

"He wanted you to take that shot," Dominique said. "To bring down Maltby, to protect the queen. To be a lady knight."

Jane tried to jerk away, but her friends held her close, trapped.

"Just go in and see how he is," Red urged.

"The physician could be waiting for you," Jacquetta added.

"No matter how minor his injury, he deserves to have someone who loves him at his side," Dominique said softly.

Jane's head was moving rapidly, from side to side, so fast the muscles of her neck were already protesting. "I do not—We have never spoken of—We married for duty, not for love. There have been no tender words between us—"

Red grabbed her chin and held it in place, her sea-blue eyes daring Jane to try moving her head like that again.

"We have seen you in situations so much worse than this," Red said. "More blood, more danger, more at stake."

"We've seen you kill men, for heaven's sake," Jacquetta interjected. "But we've never seen *this*."

Jane blinked behind her spectacles. "What?"

Dominique's smile was soft. "We've never seen you lose yourself, your calm composure. We've never seen you worried."

Jane started to shake her head again, remembered the threat in Red's eyes, and stilled the impulse. "I am often worried."

Jacquetta rolled her eyes. "Yes, but you do not show it. Not even that time that Red nearly lost her finger."

"Or we thought Dominique had the pox," Red pointed out.

"Be logical, Jane. You love us," Dominique said, still the gentlest among them. "But the love you feel for him… Give in to it. Go see to your husband."

Very slowly, watching Red out of the corner of her eye lest she attempt some strange, drastic measure to immobilize her, Jane nodded. Just once.

All of the lady knights' hands fell away from her.

All except Red's, who gave her a hearty push in the direction of the closed bedroom door.

THE DOOR SQUEAKED open on its hinges.

The face that poked through was the only one he'd ever need or want.

"Finally come to see your handiwork, little mouse?"

Jane froze.

Roland immediately regretted his words. He'd never seen such terror in her eyes.

"Dr. Fleming," he managed, this throat clogged. "Will you assure my wife that I am going to live to terrorize her another day?"

"Another few decades, I'd estimate," the golden-eyed doctor said, glancing back from where he was packing up his medical bag to find Jane still poised in the doorway. "He is quite well, Your Grace. He lost some blood, of course, but he only needed a handful of stitches. I expect he'll be up and hounding the staff within a day or two."

Jane closed the door softly behind her, crossing the room on silent feet. She didn't look at the doctor, and she certainly didn't meet Roland's eyes. She was so quiet and hesitant that Roland found himself inspecting her from head to toe, searching for an injury he might have missed.

But she was as perfect as ever. Someone had convinced her to change out of the gown and pelisse she'd worn. A good thing, too. She'd been covered in blood. His blood.

Now she was lovely in a spring-green dressing gown embroidered with little golden butterflies that brought out the warmth of her eyes. She'd brushed her hair, and it now fell down her back in a simple plait. From the tremor in her hands, he supposed all of that might have to do with the gaggle of female voices he'd heard in the sitting room, rather than her own attentions.

"How often does the bandage need to be changed?" Jane asked, eyeing the wound on his side.

Dr. Fleming snapped his bag closed. "Once a day. I'll come to change it tomorrow, and then after that you can see to the dressings and check for signs of infection. Lord Hawkridge tells me you've had some medical training."

Jane nodded. "I will do my best."

"I shall leave you to rest, then." With a nod to Roland, the doctor departed, leaving just the two of them.

Still, Jane would not look at his face.

"I suppose a jest about how you've already done your best work would be ill received?"

She shivered, but came closer to the bed. Her small fist uncurled, her dainty fingers reaching out as if she would touch the bandage... then fell away.

Roland would have none of it.

He gritted his teeth against the pain, leaned forward, and grabbed his wife's hand.

Jane's eyes flew open, and she started to pull her arm back reflexively.

"None of that—you'll only aggravate my injury," he said, half command, half truth. "Come and sit with me."

She didn't pull her arm away, but she didn't come to him either.

"Please."

Her chin dipped and her eyes darted up to his face for half a second before hiding once again. She circled the bed, climbing carefully onto the unoccupied side. Luckily, the opposite side of the gunshot wound beneath his left pectoral muscle.

Luckily, because he hauled her against him.

He caught her chin before she could bury it in his side. "Don't hide, little mouse," he said, finally able to look into those warm eyes. Only to find them brimming with tears.

The moment their eyes met, they spilled out of her in a torrent, until her shoulders were shaking and her lips trembling. Roland stared in shock. He'd never known how to deal with a crying woman—least of all when that crying woman was his wife, the single most self-possessed person he'd ever met.

He did not know what to do, so he kissed her.

Roland kissed away tear after tear until his lips and cheeks were wet and salty. Jane continued to tremble against him.

"You're going to injure yourself," she managed between shaky breaths.

"I cannot stand to see you cry," he admitted, kissing another tear before it could cascade down her cheek.

Finally, finally, the tears stopped coming. When her hand landed on his chest and her lips found his, Roland felt himself begin to relax. The steady warmth of her soft palm against his skin, the way she opened her mouth and welcomed him in... Soon, a whole other need was presenting itself.

Roland covered that hand on his chest, moving it lower until—

"Are you insane? Has not the physician just been attending you?" she squealed. She didn't jostle the bed—her lady knight training kept her movements steady even as her face showed her disbelief.

"He said I was 'quite well,'" Roland quoted.

Jane's nose wrinkled. "Not *that* well. How you can want—"

He pressed two fingers to her lips. When he was assured she wouldn't try to speak, he ran those fingers up her face, brushing away a few curls that had escaped from her loose plait.

"I do not think I will ever stop wanting you as long as I live," he said softly, gazing into her eyes, letting their warmth envelop him even if her body could not just then.

Jane swallowed hard. Carefully, he eased away her spectacles, setting them gently aside. He ran his thumb across her brow, pausing in the middle to smooth the creases.

"I adore you, Jane. I worship you. I—"

She pressed two fingers to his lips, the mirror of his action moments earlier.

"You love me?" she finished softly.

Heartbeats passed between them. Beats of silence, of feeling, as their two hearts started moving as one.

Roland pressed his thumb into the small hollow in her chin. "Yes, Jane. I love you."

He leaned in to kiss her, but she ducked her head, burying it against his chest. Her shoulders began to shake once more.

Roland let his head relax back against the pillow, content to stroke her silky hair as he asked, "Are you crying again?"

"Yes," she squeaked.

He chuckled, noted the pain in his side, ignored it. "Please tell me you will not make a habit of this."

She sat up, sniffling mightily. "I promise. After tonight, never again."

"Life is long. I should know," he said wryly, tugging her back down and nestling her against his shoulder. "Cry as much as you like, my darling. I will always be there to dry your tears."

But when she stretched out her legs, settling herself against his uninjured side, the tears abated. Even with his side aching, the whisky he'd gulped down to dull the pain wearing thin, Roland could not recall a happier moment in his life. When his wife began to snore softly, he stopped trying at all.

CHAPTER THIRTY-THREE

August 1818
Four months later

H E MISSED THE shot. A sweet, doting wife would press her body
against his, soothing his pride with gentle words. Perhaps she
would make a comment about all the shots he'd made before, about
how when it truly mattered, he never let her down.

But the Duchess of Hawkridge lifted her beloved dueling pistol
and shot down the ceramic plate her husband had missed a half-second
before. Then she did a few more, for good measure. Not to keep her
aim sharp—to poke at the wound. Not the wound in his side, which
had healed beautifully. But the festering one she'd landed to his pride
when she proved that she was, indeed, the better marksman.

Jane doubted that Roland would ever get over it—especially with
her reminding him every time they went out to shoot.

"I believe you owe me"—she paused to calculate—"ten pounds."

Roland glared down at her. "You are going to make a pauper out
of me."

Jane grinned, savoring the feeling of her cheeks aching. She'd never smiled in her entire life as much as she had in the last few months.
She wondered if her face would ever grow used to the expression and
stop aching. Part of her hoped that it would not, that she would always

have this constant reminder of the unexpected joy she'd been gifted.

Roland was managing semi-retirement as well as could be expected for a man of his active nature. She'd given up trying to keep her lady knight quests secret from him. With the Duchess of Guilford's blessing, he acted as her unofficial advisor, talking through her quests and her next steps. Mostly, he let her execute them on her own. Jane did not mind that he lurked in the periphery, watching and waiting. She trusted herself, and she trusted him to let her do the work that meant so much to them both.

And she certainly enjoyed challenging him in the more physical aspects of her training.

"You were the one who suggested we wager upon it," Jane reminded him.

"I hoped it would motivate me." Roland sighed, pausing to reach for the shotgun waiting on the grass beside him. "Perhaps we ought to wager something other than money."

Jane recognized the gleam in his eyes, even across the two yards separating them—even with him towering more than a foot above her.

"Favors," he suggested.

Jane lifted an eyebrow, a mocking facsimile of the skeptical challenge he often wore. His gray brows knitted together. Oh, how she did enjoy needling him.

"What sort of favors?" she asked, already suspecting the answer.

"The sort that are executed in the bedroom."

Jane lifted her own shotgun, which was freshly polished and gleaming. "I think we have proved time and time again, husband, that those sorts of favors can be given and received just about anywhere."

Roland let his weapon hang limp. "If you'd like me to take you right here in the grass, where all the servants can see, just say the word, little mouse."

She wrinkled her nose at him, deciding not to dignify that threat with a response. Even as she clamped her thighs together to keep the rushing heat and wetness of desire at bay. She raised her hand to signal the servant hunkered down at the other side of the field.

Two ceramic plates flew into the air. This time, neither of them missed.

Jane turned to Roland, frowning. "Does this mean neither of us gets to call in the favor?"

He was already halfway to her. "Quite the opposite, my love," he said, settling his wide hands on her waist.

Egads, how she loved his hands. Huge, powerful—and *so* skilled.

Before she could protest, those hands had slid down to cup her bottom and scoop her up. Jane wrapped her legs around his trim, muscular waist by instinct.

"Roland!" she squeaked, her legs now on full view.

"There is no one around," he protested as he began kissing her neck. When he did that with his mouth, sucking on her earlobe…

"There are at least a hundred servants," she managed, though the protest had gone out of her voice.

Overhead, a piercing screech rent the air. Guinevere was there, reminding them that she was their audience as well.

It was true. With summer in full swing even at their estate tucked far away in the north, there were gardeners and grooms and more servants than either of them knew what to do with. But she also knew they would all be sure to divert their attention should the duke and duchess decide to enjoy the fresh air and sunshine.

They were, after all, a love match.

EPILOGUE

March 1819

THE ROOM WAS quieter than it had ever been. Four seats occupied, one empty. Waiting. For once, Jacquetta did not offer a flask. Dominique did not complain about the stuffy maid's uniform she'd worn so many times to enter the Duchess of Guilford's home inconspicuously. Tonight, she wore a lovely amethyst gown fit for a future countess. Red fiddled with the inlaid wooden head of her parasol, at her side even inside, even in this room. Only Jane was calm and composed, as usual.

It had been four months since Queen Charlotte's death. The nation had mourned, but for the four women seated around the table, the loss had been felt doubly. Not only had they lost their queen, but the woman responsible for their charter, their very existence.

Could it be Queen Charlotte's round table with the queen now interred at Windsor?

The door opened at last. All four women exhaled—some a small, controlled puff, others a sigh heavy enough to make the Duchess of Guilford's generous mouth curve into a smile.

"I thought you all would have enjoyed your holiday, now that you have husbands and families of your own," Miranda commented, closing the door behind her and taking her seat. "But all I find are glum faces."

A few beats of silence. Waiting.

Of course, Red could not stand to wait. "What will happen now?"

The reproval that might have shown in Miranda's eyes a year or two ago was gone, replaced with something softer. Compassion. Perhaps it had always been there, but they had been unable to see it, to recognize it for what it was.

"We carry on," she said simply.

Jane didn't need to adjust her spectacles or straighten her back. She was perfectly prim and poised already as she asked the question on all of their minds.

"There is no longer a queen to provide our charter. Do we operate now outside of the quadrants of royal approval?" she asked.

Miranda reached into her reticule—they'd all noted it, of course, unusual as it was for her to carry anything of the sort, especially while hosting a soiree in her own home. She withdrew four carefully folded notes before handing one to each of the women.

Jacquetta finished reading hers first. "Is this a jest?"

Miranda's smile was deep, gratified, true. "It is not."

"Knights... not ladies?" Dominique said carefully.

"You cannot tell anyone, of course. But if you desire, Prinny is ready to perform a formal ceremony. In private, but with your husbands in attendance," Miranda continued.

"To officially make us knights of the realm," Red said, leaning back in her seat, clearly flabbergasted.

"Think about it and come to consensus on whether you are satisfied with the letters patent or if you'd prefer some pomp and pageantry," Miranda said.

Jacquetta shot a look at Jane, who was already shaking her head. Dominique's eyes were wide with emotion, eyes glistening. Ethelreda's mouth was still in danger of hitting the floor. The Duchess of Guilford waited another thirty seconds, then cleared her throat.

"I hope you have enjoyed your holiday, ladies, for there is much to be done. Since we are all here tonight, we shall make a start. It will be a busy Season for the Lady Knights."

Jacquetta and Grayson

SHE SLIPPED DOWN the same staircase she'd taken two years ago, when she had been formally charged with capturing Lord Grayson Thane. The ballroom was not quite as full as it had been on that night, as the duchess was hosting an intimate soiree tonight rather than a grand ball. As Jacquetta entered the room, she scanned the crowd by habit, taking note and assessing.

But her eyes stopped when they found him.

She considered her quest to have been successful. She'd captured Grayson Thane. Heart, body, and soul, he belonged to her.

He was talking to his brother. His brother! That itself was a small miracle, a proof of the good in the world. After all he'd suffered, Grayson had regained the thing that had always meant the most to him—his family.

His eyes found her almost immediately. He'd been watching the doorway, waiting for her return, surely. Jacquetta doubted he would ever truly relax when she was out of his sight. An unfortunate side effect of years spent in fear.

She watched as he said words of farewell to his elder brother and then skirted the twirling couples dancing to reach her. Her own sister, Marie, stood with her new husband, her stomach swelled in the later stages of pregnancy. Jacquetta sighed at the normalcy of it all.

If having a reformed piratical brigand for a husband could be deemed normal.

"You look entirely too pleased with yourself," Grayson said as he arrived in front of her, immediately claiming her hand and lifting it to his lips. "I take it your discussion went well?"

She could not tell him here, with all the guests around them. Even a year since returning to England, Grayson was still something of a thrilling oddity. The ladies found his scars and swagger swoon-worthy. The lords wanted to hear tales of his exploits aboard the ship he'd captained himself. He sometimes indulged them with highly edited versions of his exploits.

Jacquetta settled for a bright smile instead, knowing the effect it would have on her husband. She watched his own face transform to mirror the shining in hers.

"Dance with me."

Grayson groaned. "I hate—"

"Yes, yes, I know. But I love it, and you love me. So…" She tipped her head toward the dance floor behind him.

"Give me a nip from that flask," Grayson said, eyes challenging.

"What flask?" Jacquetta said innocently.

"Nice try, Jack. But I know every curve of your body intimately, and I know you've got something tucked into that not-so-secret pocket in your skirt."

She glared at him. "I should have abandoned you in that cave."

"'I will follow you to the ends of the earth' I believe is what you threatened," Grayson quoted with a rueful smile.

"Something like that," she allowed begrudgingly. "Dance first. Cognac later."

"Deal."

Before she could take her next breath, he swept her into his arms and onto the floor, stealing the very air from her lungs. Once a villain, always a villain.

Dominique and David

"CAN WE LEAVE now?" Dominique asked by way of greeting.

David stared at her, golden hair gleaming in the light from the chandeliers, eyes bright as always, looking impossibly handsome—and confused.

The confusion quickly shifted to worry.

"Are you feeling unwell?" His eyes raked over her, even though they both knew there would be no physical sign of her ailment. She was hardly showing at all.

"No, the nausea seems to confine itself to the morning these days," she said, belatedly realizing she could have used it as an excuse.

David's eyes relaxed, and his shoulders as well. The man possessed absolutely no artifice. It was almost comical, given the number of quests she'd completed for the Lady Knights in the last two years. After that first, David had stayed well out of it, and happily.

"Then what is wrong?"

Dominique shivered, gesturing to the crowd. She would never be used to it. Never.

She may be a future countess, happily wed and expecting her first child, but she would never trust the *ton*. Not after all that had happened.

David nodded, reaching for her hand and tugging her against his side. "I see," he said before pressing a kiss to the top of her head and smoothing her hair. "I shall call for the carriage. You say your goodbyes."

Appreciation and love surged through her. Never a word of reprove or doubt, no meaningless attempts to fix her. David offered only love and acceptance, always. The warmth that suffused every limb was almost enough to hold her in place.

But not quite.

A half an hour later, they were ensconced in the carriage, a blanket over their legs, Dominique's head nestled against her husband's broad shoulder.

"Asleep already?" he teased, stroking the lines of her palm.

"Mmm," she said. "These first few months have been exhausting. I feel as if I could sleep for days and still never get enough rest," she admitted. "Well timed, I supposed."

David's hand stilled. "The meeting?"

"We shall resume our work. The dossier on my next quest is probably already waiting in my desk, if I know the duchess." As she spoke, Dominique caressed the leather roll in her pocket. Only the duchess had a key to the lock on the third drawer of Dominique's desk. Dominique did not need one. She'd pick the lock.

"You do not seem entirely happy," David said softly.

"Hmmm," she said again. "I am struggling to believe it all. The Lady Knights shall continue, with the prince regent's hearty approval. I am married to the kindest, most loving man that God has ever placed upon this earth. Now I am to be a mother... It all just seems too impossibly perfect to be real."

Tears spilled out of her eyes. In an instant, David was cupping her cheeks, lifting her face to his. The feeling of comfort was immediate, his soft blue eyes calming and anchoring her when she threatened to be swallowed up.

"It is the babe making me cry like this," she insisted with a watery smile.

David lifted her chin and pressed a soft kiss to her lips. A kiss of comfort, a promise of forever. But Dominique was feeling well for the first time in months. She could not resist dipping her tongue deeper, drawing his into her mouth, arching her body against his.

David pulled himself away long enough to thump hard on the roof of their carriage. "Take the long way home around the park!" he yelled to the driver.

Then he pulled his wife into his lap and started to make good on that promise.

Ethelreda and George

HER WAYWARD HUSBAND had wandered off course at some point during the night. Not in the ballroom, not taking refreshment, not even hiding in the Duchess of Guilford's library. Red was ready to stab him with her rapier by the time she found him on the terrace, overlooking the duchess's expansive, perfectly manicured gardens.

They were nothing compared to Oxley Park.

Which was precisely where her husband's mind was, by the longing glint in his eyes.

She might sympathize. Maybe.

But she still brought her parasol down on the stone balustrade hard enough to make him jump.

Which, of course, he did not.

"You do realize that it is night. It is neither raining nor sunny," George pointed out drily, eying the parasol that had come perilously close to his arm.

"How did you hear me coming?" Red asked, ignoring his silly statements of fact. "I used to be able to sneak past you so easily."

"I did not hear you," George said. He closed his hand around the parasol, pulling hard, dragging her closer. "I felt you."

Red rolled her eyes, but allowed herself to be drawn in closer. "Whatever does that mean?"

George pulled her closer, until he could wrap an arm around her waist and press her against him. Red did not bother to resist. She loved the feeling of his lean, muscular body pressed against her voluminous curves. Already, with just those few moments of contact, her senses were crackling to life, and desire flared.

"It means that when you enter a room, my heart knows it. Even if the logical parts of my brain do not."

"You, soldier, have turned absolutely maudlin," she said, half exasperated. The other half of her loved it. When they first met, he'd hardly been able to name his feelings, let alone express them to anyone else. Especially not a prickly governess.

"Not a soldier, but a scientist," he reminded her.

She could see the light from the ballroom reflecting back in his eyes, making them shine. It was true. After endless rounds of revisions and review, his treatise on the behavior of honeybees in the English countryside had finally been published—to overwhelmingly positive response.

"That is just as well," she said. "Your new membership at the Royal Society will bring you often to London. As will my continued work for the Crown."

This time when George's eyes lit, it was for her. "You have been granted a reprieve?"

"Even better." She extricated the letters patent from her reticule, handing it over for George to read. As his eyes widened, a sudden wave of shyness swept over her.

"Red," he breathed. "This is—"

Whatever it was, she didn't get to hear. He swept her up in his arms, kissing her everywhere his lips could reach.

Oh, yes, that desire is a fully fledged flame now.

"This… this is magnificent," George exclaimed when he finally set her down, handing her back the paper and watching with awe in his eyes as she carefully refolded it and replaced it in the safety of her reticule.

"I know we cannot tell Eveline… but for her to know such things are possible," Red said. Her stepdaughter was the strongest-willed person she'd ever met—and that included each of her fellow lady knights. And herself.

George took her hand, pressing it to his lips. "Someday, you will tell her. Until then, she knows that she loves you. She and Archie both.

And I—"

Red grabbed his shoulders and pulled him down into a scorching kiss. Enough maudlin words. She'd always been a woman of action.

Jane and Roland

JANE LINGERED LONG after her friends departed the small dressing room.

Even the Duchess of Guilford did not seem inclined to stay and discuss particulars of their upcoming quests. Jane wondered if it had to do with Cartwright's attendance in the ballroom below. He'd been out of mourning for a month now, and in that time seemed to have formed a close friendship with Miranda—beyond the professional one they'd apparently maintained for years in secret.

The round table seemed smaller than it had when she first sat at it, now nearly five years ago.

It had always been nondescript, her logical mind asserted. Nothing more than a table stuffed in a dressing room in an unused corner of a widowed duchess's townhouse.

It was the women who sat around it who made it something special. Something that could change England. Perhaps even the world.

It had certainly changed Jane's world.

Miranda had doled out quest after quest, until each of their heads were full of the possibilities and requirements. Someday, it would be too much. Dominique was early in her pregnancy, but Jane had noted the way her hands kept drifting toward her stomach. She'd keep that secret until her friend was ready to reveal it. Red... Red would go to her grave with that rapier in her hand. Jane suspected she'd already begun teaching her stepdaughter how to wield it.

Perhaps that was for the best. Jane had no plans to step away from her duty. But when she was ready to retire to a life of idleness and harassing her husband, she did not intend to leave a hole for the Duchess of Guilford or her successor to fill.

Jane already had a few prospects to put forward. Her status as the Duchess of Hawkridge afforded her an even better view of the *haute ton* than that of a wallflower. She'd already discussed it with Roland. He'd love nothing more than to host new lady knights at their secluded northern estate, training them for the future. A new generation.

A new knighthood.

But all of it could wait another day. Another year. Another decade or two, if she was lucky.

Jane was smiling as she closed the door to the dressing room and stepped into the darkened bedroom, with the furniture all covered in sheets to protect it from dust and light. All but one chair.

She paused in the center of the room, waiting to see if he would speak.

Her waiting was rewarded.

"You were in there for a dreadfully long time," her husband said.

He couldn't see her face, but she wrinkled her nose anyway as she turned, drifting toward him. Roland had chosen a wingback chair tucked into the far corner of the room, opposite the door to the dressing room that contained the round table.

"Did you listen at the door?" she asked, crossing her arms beneath her breasts. A move that usually brought him to heel immediately, but was decidedly less effective in the darkness.

"No need. You shall tell me everything later," Roland said, cocky as ever.

"Not everything."

Somehow, even in the dark, he was able to snake an arm out and grab her hand. One strong tug, and she was in his lap. Not that she'd resisted. She'd found a certain amount of enjoyment in holding court over the other ladies of the *ton* as a duchess. But she found infinitely more wrapped in Roland's arms.

But holding her close, it seemed, was not his motive.

No, those large, magnificent hands of his were tugging at her skirt, caressing her leg.

"Has anyone ever made love on the round table?" Roland breathed into her ear.

Jane shivered at the delicious impropriety of it. "Someone might come looking for me."

"Then lock the door."

"Dominique has never met a lock she could not pick," Jane reminded him, even as his fingers climbed the inside of her thigh.

"Dominique and David left a few minutes ago," Roland said. He shifted his position, and the next thing she knew he was rising, bringing her with him.

"You are going to get me stripped of my knighthood," she said, even as she tightened her legs around his waist.

Roland's laugh reverberated through her as he kicked open the door and laid her right across the polished wood surface. Jane came up onto her elbows, looking down at herself and finding herself hardly able to believe the sight—rumpled dress rucked up around her knees, breasts spilling out of her bodice, and her husband, stepping up to claim her.

"Last chance," he warned, pressing closer.

But when she felt him at her entrance, she arched her hips, drawing his proud length deep into the center of her womanly core. He was so very, very wrong. This was not her last chance.

It was only the beginning.

Author's Note

To the best of my knowledge, there were no assassination attempts on Queen Charlotte, at least not that were recorded by history. While Jane and Roland's story takes place in the spring of 1818, the imaginary reprieve would have been short-lived, for Queen Charlotte died in November of that same year. Queen Charlotte's popularity did decline in the later years of her reign, but the Roses of Union and their motivations are entirely my own fabrication.

What did I get right? Queen Charlotte was an amateur botanist and a leader of high society up until her death. I cannot attest to whether she took any note of the first flowers of spring, but I do love the image of her riding through London in the wee hours of the morning in search of daffodils, just to be the one to declare spring's arrival.

The grandchild that did eventually inherit the throne—Queen Victoria—was not quite as lucky as her grandmother. She survived no less than seven assassination attempts, more than one of them featuring shots fired while she rode in her open carriage. Even though these two venerable women never met, I am honored to have been able to connect their stories by borrowing from one and giving to the other.

All other inaccuracies are either the product of a brain addled by months of research, or a conscious subversion of history in service of true love. Either way, I hope you'll forgive me.

About the Author

A lifetime reader of romance, Cara put pen to paper (or rather, fingers to keyboard) in 2019 and published her first book. She hasn't slowed down from there. Cara is an avid traveler. As she explores new places, she imagines her characters walking hand-in-hand down a cobblestone path or sharing a passionate kiss in a secluded alcove. Cara is living out her own happily ever after in Seattle, Washington, where she resides with her husband, daughter, and two cats, RoseArt and Etch-o-Sketch.

Instagram: caramaxwellromance
Facebook: caramaxwellromance

Printed in Great Britain
by Amazon

36322987R00150